FAE-TED TO THE BEAR

HARMONY RAINES

***Fae*-ted to the Bear**

The Bond of Brothers

Book Four

* * *

Sign up to the Harmony Raines Newsletter by going to:
http://www.harmonyraines.com/newsletter-sign-up/
Never miss a new release!
You'll also receive the EBOOK '*A Bond to Bear*'
Just to say thank you!

SERIES ORDER

1. The White Wolf of Wishing Moon Bay
2. The Horse Shifter's Mate
3. Her Fae-vorite Bear

4. Fae-ted to the Bear

5. The Snow Leopard's Love
6. The Dragon Shifter's Desire

US LINKS

Website and Newsletter: harmonyraines.com

Facebook: facebook.com/harmonyrainesauthor

Amazon Author Page: amazon.com/Harmony-Raines/e/B0090Q3DWM

Bond of Brothers Series Page

On Amazon: amazon.com/dp/B08T6JF1QZ

On My Website: harmonyraines.com/all-books/bond-of-brothers-series

UK LINKS

Website and Newsletter: harmonyraines.com

Facebook: facebook.com/harmonyrainesauthor

Amazon Author Page: amazon.co.uk/Harmony-Raines/e/B0090Q3DWM

Bond of Brothers Series Page

On Amazon: amazon.co.uk/dp/B08T6JF1QZ

On My Website: harmonyraines.com/all-books/bond-of-brothers-series

FAE-TED TO THE BEAR

THE BOND OF BROTHERS

Book Four
A silverback shifter romance

Caleb's mate came to Wishing Moon Bay to kickstart her career after giving up on the idea of settling down and raising a family.

Can he rekindle her desire for a family of her own? Can he help her see she can have it all? With him by her side.

Elise has worked hard in her pursuit to become a chef. Seizing the chance to work with Caleb's brother Ivan in his acclaimed restaurant, she is willing to make sacrifices to prove she has potential.

She knows she's going to have to work hard to win Ivan over since he's a dragon shifter and she's a fae. Not a good mix.

However, she has one thing going for her. Caleb. Elise soon learns these brothers are willing to do anything for each other.

As she falls for the handsome growly bear shifter, Elise

realizes she will do anything for Caleb, too. Especially when his sister is threatened.

Even if that means giving up her hopes and dreams.

1

ELISE

Elise's stomach bubbled with nerves as she stood in the reception area of the Wishing Moon Bay Hotel.

After her brother, Karros, came home last night and announced that he'd freed Flora from their arranged marriage so that she could marry her shifter mate and avoid being banished from the fae realm, Elise had decided to make her own bid for freedom.

As the milestone age of forty approached with no sign of her ever finding a man to settle down with, one of her grandmothers had become very vocal on the need for Elise's parents to step in and find a suitable husband for their daughter.

They'd been in contact with a dating agency that specialized in matching single fae men and women. Despite Elise's objections, they had filled out various questionnaires on Elise's behalf and arranged to meet with someone from the dating agency.

Emboldened by her brother's actions toward Flora, Elise had grasped the opportunity to tell them she would find her own husband or else remain single.

Her parents hadn't been impressed and an argument had ensued. Unable to get her parents to understand she didn't want to marry for the sake of marrying, Karros had eventually taken her outside for some air while everyone cooled down.

She loved her brother. Karros was loyal and true and always fought in her corner.

So when he told her Flora's mate was related to Ivan Kelts, the head chef at the Wishing Moon Bay Hotel, he'd agreed to come with her to ask for a large favor. Elise, who had always worked to fulfill her dream of owning her own restaurant, wanted to train as a chef under Ivan.

And now, here they were, against their parents' wishes, in the Wishing Moon Bay Hotel reception area.

Her heart ached for her brother, who could barely make eye contact with Flora or Aiden. However, that didn't stop him from asking them to help Elise. Perhaps he thought that getting them to help Elise fulfill her dream was the least they could do since he'd given up on his own happiness for their sake.

"Do you think there's a chance Ivan will say yes and let me learn from him?" Elise asked.

"I don't know, Elise." Flora glanced awkwardly at Aiden. "You're a fae."

"And so are you." Elise lowered her head, not really understanding Flora's meaning.

Aiden stared over her shoulder at something. However, before she turned around to see what had captured his attention, the bear shifter beckoned to Elise and Karros. "Shall we go somewhere private and discuss this?"

"Sure." Elise bobbed her head. Discussing it meant they thought there might be a chance. Didn't it? "Karros."

"Coming." Her brother hesitated for a moment, his eyes lingering on Flora for a moment longer than necessary.

"I'm sorry," she whispered as they followed Aiden and Flora through a door toward the kitchen. Not that she knew the layout of the hotel, but the smell of aromatic food wafting over them gave it away.

"For what?" Karros asked.

"I shouldn't have let you come with me. I know how you feel about Flora. Seeing her with another man must break your heart." She slipped her hand into his.

"I wanted to come." He smiled down at her, his eyes filled with barely contained sadness. "When I see Flora so happy with Aiden, it just reinforces the knowledge that I did the right thing."

"In letting her go?" Elise slowed and stood on tiptoes, kissing her brother's cheek. "She doesn't know what she's missing."

He smiled sadly. "On the contrary, she does."

"You're going to have to let her go." Elise sighed. "Now that you've seen Flora, why don't you go home?"

"Not yet." He shook his head. "I expect Mom and Dad are already trying to marry me off to someone else. I'm going to stay here for a while. I'll treat it like a vacation."

"You never know, you might find yourself a shifter mate all of your own." She arched an eyebrow. "Can you imagine how Mom and Dad would react?"

"Not well." He glanced at Flora and Aiden who were waiting for them at the end of a corridor. "But when I see how happy Flora is with her shifter mate, I'm not saying it would be a bad thing. Can you imagine having a mate? You don't have to worry if you're compatible, you just know."

"I'm not exactly looking for a husband or a mate." She patted him on the shoulder. "But I do wish you would find a mate, so I know you are going to be happy. You want a wife and children and all that goes with it."

"I would be lying if I said I don't." He sighed and ran his

hand through his hair as he glanced sideways at Flora. "Instead, I just get to see what I'm missing."

"I can do this on my own from here." Elise let go of his hand. "Why don't you go get something to eat in the restaurant. Once you taste the food, you'll know why I wanted to come here."

"Your food is good already, Elise. You have a natural flair for flavors." He glanced over his shoulder.

"Flavors, yes. But I need to learn the skills that go along with it and I won't do that in the fae realm." She took a couple of steps away from him. "Go and eat."

"I suppose you should go meet Ivan without your big brother breathing down your neck. Or his neck." Karros half-smiled. "I wanted to be there in case he said no. I was going to be very persuasive."

"I want to do this based on my own skill. I don't think threats are going to get me very far." She grinned. "But I appreciate the thought."

Karros turned around and walked away. For a moment, she stared after him then she turned and hurried toward Flora and Aiden. She'd kept them waiting long enough.

"Elise, are you sure about this?" Flora asked.

"Yes." She nodded and rolled her shoulders back. "I've wanted to train under a chef for years and I admire Ivan. I ate here a few months back, just to see what all the fuss was about. I want to show my parents that I can succeed. This might be my only chance to prove to them I don't need a husband."

"What's wrong with a husband?" Aiden asked sharply.

Flora eyed him warily. "There's nothing *wrong* with a husband, but Elise is right, no woman *needs* a husband."

"But you do need a mate." Elise arched an eyebrow at Flora.

"Okay, this is not the time to get into this." Flora's eyes fixed on Karros's retreating back. "How is he?"

"You broke his heart," Elise answered bluntly. "But he'll get over it. Honestly, he's happy you are happy. He always knew he wasn't the love of your life. But he thought he could make you happy, give you a good life."

"I know," Flora answered softly and squeezed Aiden's hand. "When fate steps in, there's nothing you can do."

Aiden inhaled deeply, his gaze resting on Elise for a long moment, his expression unreadable. "Fate has a mind of its own."

"Like Elise." Flora nodded toward the double doors leading into what looked like a kitchen beyond. "Do you think Ivan will let Elise be his student?"

"We should go ask him." Aiden spun around to look at the door to the kitchen.

He just kind of stared at it as if he could see through the door to the room beyond.

Maybe he could connect telepathically with Ivan. She'd heard that shifters had super senses. No, that was crazy.

"Okay." Elise nodded and inhaled deeply, trying to suppress her nerves. Fae were normally good at appearing aloof and hiding their emotions. Elise was the opposite, she struggled to keep her emotions in check. Why shouldn't she be open with how she felt?

Aiden turned around to face her. "Okay." He swallowed nervously, and then glanced at Flora, who cocked her head to one side while staring at him.

Shifters were kind of weird. Aiden looked as if he had a guilty secret he wanted to hide.

But a shifter wasn't supposed to hide anything from their mate.

"Shall we go in?" Elise shuffled her feet but didn't move, maybe there was something she was missing. Perhaps there was a shifter tradition she was unaware of. She glanced at Flora, looking for help, but Flora just shrugged.

"Yes. Let's go in." Aiden pushed the door open and went in first, before turning around and holding it open for the two fae.

"Wait. You look..." She stared at the man who stood in the kitchen, his expression matching her confusion.

"Caleb." Flora greeted the man who looked identical to Aiden. *Almost* identical. There was something different about him, not so much in his looks but in the way he *felt*.

If she held out her hands, she'd be able to feel a certain vibe coming off him, as if he were set to a different frequency to Aiden. Elise curled her hands into balls and dug her nails into her palms, resisting the temptation to try out her theory.

"I..." Caleb opened and closed his mouth as he looked at her.

"Is everything all right?" Flora asked. "We were just coming into the restaurant to join you and Valerie when we met Elise and Karros in the reception area."

"Elise." Caleb stared at her with a small smile on his lips.

"Yes." Elise stepped forward and held out her hand, partly because people in Wishing Moon Bay and the world beyond greeted each other this way, and partly because she really wanted to touch him. "Good to meet you. I didn't realize Aiden had a twin."

"Elise." Caleb slipped his hand into hers and warmth spread across her skin and up her arm. He certainly did resonate at a different frequency.

She leaned forward and stared into his eyes. "Are you okay?"

"Yes." He blinked rapidly as his fingers closed around hers, holding her as if he were never going to let her go.

"Oh!" Flora's shock registered in Elise's brain even through the fog that filled it.

"Oh, what?" Elise half-turned to look at her friend.

"You and Caleb are mates." Flora stated it as fact, but how could she know when Elise had only just met Caleb?

It was a redundant question. Elise knew the truth. She suspected Aiden had known even before they entered the kitchen, that would explain the faraway look on his face.

"I don't want a mate," Elise answered. "I've come here to learn to be a chef. I don't want to be the mate of a shifter." She let go of Caleb's hand, noting her own reluctance to break the connection between them. "No offense, and I'm sure you are a perfectly nice shifter, but getting married and having kids is not my thing."

"What are you all doing in my kitchen?" A tall, dark-haired man with gray flecks at his temples and eyes that bore into her entered the kitchen carrying a box of fresh vegetables.

"This is Elise," Aiden introduced her. "She wants you to teach her your ways."

"My ways." Ivan's expression darkened. "You mean train her?" His nostrils flared. "She's a fae."

"She is," Elise answered.

"I don't think that would be a good idea," Ivan replied.

"You don't want me to work for you because I'm a fae?" Elise forgot all about the shifter who was her mate. Even though he didn't take his eyes off her. She could feel the caress of his gaze as if he were actually stroking her skin. She shivered and the hairs on her arms stood on end.

"Yes. I don't think we'd be a good mix." Ivan placed the box of vegetables on the countertop and removed the contents, examining them closely before lining them up.

"Because shifters and fae don't get along?" she asked.

"That would be the start of it," Ivan confirmed.

"I am very open-minded about shifters," Elise replied. "When Karros told me that he'd ended the arrangement with

Flora's family so that she wouldn't get banished from the fae realm, I was very supportive."

"Good for you." Ivan didn't look at her, he just continued emptying the box.

"I am good. At cooking."

"Then you don't need me," Ivan retorted.

"I'm good, but you are so much better. I don't think I have ever tasted a hollandaise sauce like yours. And your desserts are so creative," she gushed but Ivan was unmoved.

"There are plenty of other chefs you could train with." He turned to face her, his eyes flashed bright, and she gasped. "Yes, now you're getting the point."

"You're a dragon shifter?" Her eyes widened, she'd never seen a dragon shifter outside of the dragon isle.

"Exactly. Fae and dragons are like oil and water. We do not mix well, so I certainly don't think it would be a good idea for you and me to work together in my kitchen."

"Please, give me a chance." She didn't care what he was, to her he was a man who knew how to turn quality ingredients into something incredible.

"I don't think so..." Ivan suddenly noticed Caleb's expression. "Are you all right?"

"Will you reconsider?" Caleb asked. "For me?"

"For you? Why would I?" Ivan moved closer to his brother and stared into his eyes before swinging around to look at Elise. "No!"

"Yes," Aiden answered. "And I think it's your brotherly duty to help Caleb's mate."

Ivan's jaw tensed and he shook his head before burying his face in his hands and groaning. "I know I'm going to regret this, but what choice do I have?"

"None," Aiden answered.

"You'll teach me?" Elise answered.

"Yes, because you are my brother's mate. But don't expect

me to go easy on you." Ivan went back to examining his vegetables.

"Welcome to the family," Aiden said drily and then slapped his brother on the arm. "Snap out of it, Caleb."

"Sorry." Caleb shook his head and ran his hand through his hair. "It's a shock."

"It sure is." Elise's excitement at Ivan accepting her was tempered by the knowledge that if she wanted to stay here and train at the hotel, she'd have to give Caleb a chance.

A shiver of apprehension passed down her spine. Everything she wanted was within her grasp, she'd always dreamed of becoming a great chef and running her own restaurant. However, her connection with Caleb might just scupper those plans.

His touch had awoken something inside of her, something she'd never experienced before. As she stole a glance at him, a vision of them together with a bunch of children running around swam through her head.

He made her dream of being a wife and a mother, and that might mean the end of her culinary career before it had even started.

2

CALEB

Caleb's brain seemed to have disengaged itself from his mouth. He couldn't think of anything to say. Instead of fighting for his mate as she tried to persuade Ivan to take her on as his trainee, he'd just stood there.

"We should all go get something to eat," Aiden suggested, placing his hand on his twin's shoulder. "You'll feel better then."

Would he? His mate was a fae.

We shouldn't be surprised, his bear said. Not when Aiden has a fae mate, too.

True, we are so similar in everything, we should have guessed fate would spring this on us.

"I should go find Karros and tell him the good news." Elise paused and glanced at Caleb. "About Ivan accepting me as a trainee chef."

"Rather than about you having a bear shifter as a mate," Ivan said drily. Caleb's brother still didn't look so happy about the situation.

"Thanks, Ivan." Caleb finally moved, going to his brother and hugging him. "I appreciate it."

"You know I would do anything for you," Ivan replied.

"There, you and Caleb do have something in common," Flora told Elise. "Karros will do anything for you and Caleb's brothers would do anything for him."

Elise stared at Flora for a moment before she sighed and turned around to face Caleb. "Thank you."

"For being your mate?" Caleb gave a wry smile.

"Something like that." Elise grinned. "My parents are going to be *so* happy."

"Do I detect sarcasm?" Caleb asked.

"Maybe a little." She held up her thumb and forefinger together. "But since Flora has a shifter mate, perhaps things will change in the fae realms and I won't be ostracized."

"Flora is changing the world." Aiden slipped his arm around his mate's shoulders and pulled her close.

"If you don't mind, I do have work to do," Ivan snapped.

"Oh, when do you want me to start?" Elise spun around to face him.

"Tomorrow morning. I expect you here before seven so you can help me with the hotel breakfasts. We'll start with you showing me exactly what you can do." Ivan eyed her critically for a moment. "You do know how to cook non-fae food?"

"Eggs, bacon, toast, pancakes, that kind of thing?" Elise nodded. "We do eat those, too, you know."

"Great. Then I'll see you in the morning." Ivan shooed them out of his kitchen. "Go, I don't need to be reminded of how many of my brothers have found mates while I'm still alone."

"Thanks again, Ivan." Caleb lifted his hand and waved at his brother then followed the others out of the kitchen.

"I should go find Karros," Elise insisted as they reached the hotel reception.

"You're sure you can't come and eat with us? I thought you loved Ivan's food," Flora replied.

"I do." She eyed the restaurant hungrily. "But I should update him on the situation."

"Do you want me to come with you?" Caleb offered.

"No!" She held her hands up to him as if she could push him away. "Thanks. But I think it'll be better if I talk to him alone."

"My mom would love to meet you." Caleb didn't want her to leave, he was scared that if she did, she might disappear as quickly as she had appeared in his life.

"How will she feel about your mate being fae?" Elise edged away from them, although her eyes flickered toward the restaurant.

"As long as her sons are happy, she's happy." Caleb forced himself not to follow Elise.

She needs space, she needs time to get her head around all of this, his bear advised.

She is not the only one, Caleb said. I never expected us to find our mate so soon after Aiden, but at least we won't feel left out.

When Aiden met Flora, Caleb knew his life would change, that his brother would naturally drift away from him. He'd worried how he would fill the gap left in his life.

Now there won't be a gap. Elise will fill it.

Hopefully, Caleb answered. She didn't look especially pleased to find out she belongs to us.

His bear chuckled. Don't say that to her. I get the feeling Elise doesn't want to belong to anyone.

You know what I mean, Caleb replied. She's ours, she's our mate.

We just have to make her fall in love with us. We need her to want to be with us. And not just because it means Ivan will let her in his kitchen.

I hope that turns out okay, Caleb said. *Ivan was right when he said fae and dragons don't mix well together.*

Perhaps this will be a new chapter for fae and dragons. His bear chuckled.

"Can I meet you later?" Caleb asked.

"I don't know." Elise shook her head. "Karros and I have to find somewhere to stay."

"Karros is staying in Wishing Moon Bay with you?" Aiden asked quickly.

"Yes, right now we are laying low. Our parents aren't happy with him for letting Flora slip through his fingers. As for me..." She held out her hands. "They've never been happy with me wanting a career. They've always wanted me to meet a man and get married. However, I don't think they will be impressed with my choice."

"Does that mean you have chosen me?" Caleb asked hopefully. Perhaps this was going to be easier than he thought.

"Oh." Her cheeks flushed pink. "I didn't mean it like that. It's too soon. I don't know you."

"Why don't you get to know each other?" Flora suggested. "Caleb could help you find somewhere to live."

"I could. I know the town well. I could ask around to see if there are any houses or apartments to rent." His offer was met by a nod from Elise.

"I'd appreciate that. We don't know the town at all." Her mouth turned down at the corners as a hotel guest walked past and stared at her. "And not everyone here likes fae, do they? My mom used to always warn us not to come here."

"It's not that people here don't like the fae. It's more that...they think you don't like us," Aiden explained.

"Then it's time we all learned more about each other and how to get along." She bowed her head, her eyes twinkling. "So, I guess, we should lead by example. I would love to meet you later."

"Like a date?" Caleb needed to know they were on the same wavelength.

"A date. Yes." She plunged her hand into her purse as her phone rang. "It's Karros. I need to go meet him."

"Here. Let me give you my cell phone number." Caleb dashed toward the reception desk and grabbed a pen and paper from a startled Jeremy. "Sorry, it's an emergency."

"Don't mind me," Jeremy said drily.

"Thanks." Caleb scribbled his number down on the piece of paper, double-checking it was legible before handing the pen back to Jeremy. "Here." He handed it to Elise, who was talking on the phone to her brother. "Call me if you need anything."

"I will," she mouthed and then turned and walked out of his life.

"I have no words." Caleb stood watching her go like a lost puppy with his tongue hanging out.

"Let's get you some food." Aiden grabbed hold of his brother's arm and turned him around. "Valerie must be wondering where we are."

"Oh, Rift is with her. He is watching Milo today, so he said he'd join us for lunch." Caleb ran his hand through his hair as he went with his brother and Flora to the restaurant. Perhaps food would help, although he doubted anything would stop his heart from aching. He longed to be with Elise, he hated that she'd walked away from him.

"There they are." Aiden raised his hand and crossed the restaurant to a table near the window where their mom and Rift were sitting, while Milo stood with his hands on the glass watching a bird on the lawn outside.

"We thought you'd gotten lost." Rift got up as they approached. "Nice to see you again, Flora."

"Rift." She bowed her head and glanced at Caleb with

concern as he pulled out a chair and nearly tripped over one of the legs.

"What happened to you?" Rift asked his brother. "You look pale." He leaned closer as Caleb sat down. "You look as if you've seen a ghost."

"I met my mate," Caleb blurted out and Rift reeled back as if he'd been struck.

"Where is she?" Rift looked around. "Don't say you lost her already."

"No." Caleb shook his head and then glanced at Flora in concern. "She isn't going to skip town, is she?"

"Is who?" Rift demanded while Valerie sat patiently waiting for more details.

"Elise. Her name is Elise," Flora replied. "And no, she isn't going to skip town."

"Why would she?" Valerie asked at last.

"She's a fae," Aiden explained.

"Oh!" Rift's eyes widened. "I bet she's not happy that she has a shifter for a mate."

"She's not unhappy. More shocked," Flora replied. "But she'll come around." She placed her hand over Aiden's. "I did."

"It took a while." Aiden kissed her cheek.

"Why is she in Wishing Moon Bay?" Valerie asked. "We don't get many fae visitors here."

"She came to ask if Ivan would train her as a chef," Flora replied.

"Wow. How did that go?" Rift glanced at Milo, he took the job of looking after the boy seriously, while also enjoying every moment of it. If any of the brothers deserved children, it was Rift.

"He wasn't too eager. But once he realized that Elise was Caleb's mate, he came around." Aiden grabbed a menu and opened it up, although he knew exactly what was being served.

"So that's why she's not going to leave town. She wants to train with Ivan." Rift chuckled. "A dragon shifter and a fae, now that is going to be an interesting combination in the kitchen."

"Don't remind me." Caleb sighed.

"That's between Ivan and Elise," Valerie said sagely. "You stay out of it."

"How can I?" Caleb asked. "If Elise and Ivan don't get along, my mate might go back to her world and leave me here. I need time for her to get to like me."

Valerie reached for her son's hand. "You listen to me. If fate threw the two of you together, it was for a reason."

"Let's hope that reason is simply for you to help Ivan and Elise learn to get along." Rift held up his finger. "One, because Ivan really does need help in the kitchen. He needs someone who can eventually run the kitchen so he can have some time off." He held up another finger. "And two, we've had enough drama surrounding mates, thank you."

"Rift is right on both counts," Valerie agreed. "If all you have to worry about is how to help a dragon shifter and a fae get along, I'll be happy."

"It's a good thing we already have a fae in the family." Caleb held his hands out to Flora. "Please help me."

She laughed and shook her head. "I will help you all I can, but Elise is a free spirit. She has never really pictured herself settling down and having a bunch of children. She's worked in several restaurants in the fae realms, but she's never been taken seriously by her parents."

"Elise doesn't want to be tied down?" Caleb's heart sank a little.

"Worse, working with someone like Ivan is the opportunity she's always wanted." Flora's expression turned to one of pity. Which made Caleb feel even gloomier.

"The very thing that's holding Elise in town is the thing that might possibly push us apart."

"Yes," Flora agreed. "However, the one thing I have learned about you, Caleb, is that you are smart, and you'll figure this out."

Caleb only hoped Flora was right.

3

ELISE

"How did the job interview go?" Karros met her in a small diner overlooking the beach.

"It sure is beautiful here." Elise slid into the seat across the table from him and picked up the menu. As she glanced at the dishes, she sure wished she'd taken Caleb up on his offer to join his family in the restaurant. Ivan's food was the best she'd ever tasted, his reputation didn't do it justice.

"That good, huh?" Karros leaned his elbows on the table and tried to ignore the two women seated at the next table who kept staring at him.

Elise studied the menu before placing it down on the table. "It had some unexpected surprises."

"Like what?" Karros chuckled. "Did he ask you to cook for him?"

"No." She ran her finger along the edge of the menu. "I met his brother."

"Ivan's brother? Or Aiden's brother?" Karros's tone sharpened.

"Well, both. Ivan's adopted brother and Aiden's twin brother. You do know Aiden was adopted by Valerie Kelts along with his twin brother and another four shifters." She lowered her voice and held up four fingers.

"And the point of this is?" Karros asked.

She sighed and looked down at the menu.

"No. Oh, no." He leaned back in his seat and studied her for a long moment. "Not you, too? What is it with those bear shifters? It's bad enough that I have to live with the knowledge that one of them is going to spend the rest of their life with the woman I love. But now my sister, too?"

"It isn't my choice."

Karros ran his hand through his hair and blew the air out of his cheeks. "Did I do something to deserve this?"

"No."

"Then why is fate torturing me?" He leaned forward and rested his elbows on the table. "Are you sure?"

"Yes."

"Do you feel it?" He placed his hand on his heart.

"Oh, Karros." She reached for his other hand and held it in his. "You want to know if Flora feels a connection with Aiden."

"Yes," he croaked hoarsely.

She nodded. "I do. It's like there's a part of me that's connected to him. It took me a moment to realize because I was so focused on Ivan and persuading him to take me on as a trainee chef. But then I felt it."

"So, it's real. Undeniable?"

"Undeniable." She brushed her hand over her eyes. "I wish I could deny it. I wish I could just walk away and forget all about him."

"We could. We could get in the car now and drive back to our world. The connection would fade."

"Can you be sure?" Elise wasn't sure she wanted to find out. She kind of liked the sense of being a part of another person.

Oh, goodness, she was doomed.

"We can try." He shuffled his feet and was about to stand up, but the server approached with coffee, expecting to take their order.

Karros settled back in his chair and gave his order, then tapped the table with his fingertips as Elise did the same.

"You're being rude," Elise hissed when the server left them alone.

"Sorry." He sighed. "Are we going to leave? After we've eaten, are we going to go back to our world and forget all about the bear shifter twins?"

Elise clasped her hands together and stared down at the table. "No."

"I didn't think so, but you can't blame me for trying."

"Karros, why don't you go back? I'll be okay here," she insisted. "I know it must be torture seeing Flora with her mate."

"No. I said I'd help you and that's what I intend to do." He picked up his coffee cup and took a sip. "I think you need me now more than ever."

"Thank you." She smiled at him, her sympathy overwhelming. "You'll find someone."

"Maybe." His mouth twitched at the corners. "Are you going to tell Mom and Dad?"

"No." She held up her hand. "Not yet."

"Normally, I'd say it was a bad idea to keep something like this from them but under the circumstances, I think you're right. Let's give them a few days at least to get over me breaking up with Flora and you wanting to carve a career for yourself before we drop this bombshell."

"They're not going to be happy, are they?"

"No." Karros winked at her. "But they'll get over it."

She giggled nervously. "No, they won't." She glanced up at

him. "Unless you find yourself the perfect fae bride. Then they'll just forget about little old me."

"If only it was that easy." Karros moved his elbows off the table as their food arrived. "Thank you."

"You're welcome." The server smiled at him, her eyes lingering on his face a little longer than was polite.

"Why do people stare?" Elise asked.

"I thought it was my good looks." Karros turned his face to the right and cupped his chin in his hand so she could see his perfect profile.

Elise giggled. "You're probably right, you are the best-looking guy in the diner."

Karros scanned the other diners. "I'm the only male in here. Unless you count the cute kid over there."

She picked up her fork and dug into her salad. "I didn't see him. That makes you the second-best-looking male in the diner."

"Hey, I'm way cuter." He chuckled as he ate.

"You used to be cute, but that was twenty years ago."

"Ouch, that hurts." He sucked in his breath.

"You know I don't mean it. Any woman, fae, shifter or witch, or any non-magical person, would be lucky to have you as their mate...husband. Significant other."

"I appreciate your effort at making me feel better." He glanced up at her as he forked spaghetti into his mouth. "Caleb is lucky, too, you know."

"I don't know about that. He's a shifter, he wants nothing more than a wife who will give him a handful of children."

"And he told you this in the few moments you spent with him this morning, while also getting yourself a job at the restaurant?"

"He didn't have to tell me. We both know that's what shifters want. All shifters are driven by a need to procreate." She waved her fork at Karros. "You would think our parents would be happy I've been chosen by a shifter. They might get their grandchildren after all."

"Does that mean that Caleb has already changed your mind?"

"No," she insisted. "I want a career. I want to be the best chef I can be, and I know that's possible if I learn from Ivan."

"Did I ever tell you how proud I am of you?" Karros asked. "I know Mom and Dad never praise you enough, so I thought I should remind you of your awesomeness."

"You're much too kind but I appreciate it. Sometimes I need to hear it and today is one of those days."

"You got the job you wanted, why aren't you celebrating?" Karros asked. "You don't exactly look as if your dreams are starting to come true."

"I suppose I'd feel better if I'd gotten the job on my own instead of having to rely on your ex-fiancée and my mate." She speared a piece of tomato and popped it in her mouth.

"Sometimes it's good to depend on other people."

"It would have been great to get the job on the merits of my cooking and not my connections." She looked down at her salad. "If Caleb wasn't my mate, Ivan wouldn't have agreed."

"Okay, here's the thing. Caleb got you this chance at your dream and you should be grateful for that. But mate or no mate, Ivan is not going to let you stay in his kitchen if you aren't any good." Karros inclined his head toward her. "The restaurant is a success, he's not going to jeopardize that, not even to keep his brother happy."

"You're right." She cracked a smile. "I knew there was a reason I brought you along."

"I wouldn't have let you come alone."

"You don't think I can look after myself?" Elise asked.

"Oh, I think you can more than look after yourself. But I

want to be here for you in case you need me. In case you want someone to talk to. You have never spent more than a few days out of the fae realm. This is going to be a huge adventure."

"Starting with finding somewhere to live." She stared out of the window at the buildings across the street. "Caleb offered to help us."

"That might be a good idea." He studied her expression. "Don't you think?"

"So I can be indebted to him even more?"

"No, so you can get to know him."

"I said I'd go on a date with him." She reached into her purse and took out the piece of paper with Caleb's phone number on it and set it down on the table. "I need to give him a chance, don't I?"

"You don't need me to answer that question." He smiled sympathetically. "You have been given this gift of love. Love with a man who knows he's yours and you are his. If Flora had fallen for any other man, who wasn't a shifter, I wouldn't have let her go so easily."

"It sounds as if you like shifters," Elise said.

"I don't dislike them. The shifter bond is unique. Don't you think it's an incredible gift to be able to know who your mate is the moment you see them for the first time? You don't have to second-guess yourself, Elise."

"I see your point. But I counter that point by reminding you that it takes away a person's free will. What if a shifter finds their mate and learns they don't want the same thing? The poor guy, or woman, is stuck. They can't walk away because fate takes their choice away."

That's what scared Elise. She didn't want to hurt Caleb, who seemed to be a really great guy. Just maybe not the great guy for her.

"I can't answer that. Meet Caleb, talk to him. Meet his

family, I'm sure they'll love you." Karros finished his spaghetti as Elise sat mulling over his advice.

"I'll call him and ask if he's free to help us find somewhere to live." She ducked her head and looked at the sky. "I don't really want to spend the night camping on the beach."

"Why not? It's a lovely day, the night is clear, we can lie on the beach and watch the stars."

"I have to start work tomorrow at seven. I'd rather not sprinkle sand all over the breakfasts." She chuckled. "Although, I could just tell Ivan it's a fae delicacy."

"You'll do just fine working at the hotel. Ivan won't be able to resist your sense of humor. Or your cooking. Just relax, be yourself and you'll do fine."

"Did I mention Ivan is a dragon shifter?" Elise coughed as she nearly choked on a lettuce leaf. "Your face." She took a sip of coffee, her eyes watering as she cleared her throat.

"A dragon shifter. Did you know before we came here?" Karros asked.

"No. I'd heard of Ivan. He's got a great reputation even in our world. Which I doubt he'd hang onto if they knew he was a dragon shifter." Elise finished her salad and set her fork down on her plate. "It's going to be hard to win him over. Ivan knows that fae and dragons don't mix well."

"What is he doing here?" Karros asked. "I've never heard of a dragon shifter being raised in Wishing Moon Bay. If he were an orphan, the dragon isle would have claimed him as their own."

"That I don't know. All I do know is he's a great chef, hugely talented and I want to learn from him." Elise picked up the piece of paper and took her phone from her purse. "Shall I go call my mate and ask him for help?"

"Yes." Karros caught the eye of the server. "I'll get the check while you make the call."

"Thanks, Karros." She placed her hand on his shoulder and kissed his cheek. "For everything."

"You owe me." He took his wallet out. "When you open your restaurant, I expect free food for life."

"Deal." Elise turned around and left the diner, her hand shaking as she looked at the piece of paper and dialed the number.

She'd expected to fight for a place in Ivan's kitchen. She never expected to find her mate on the same day.

4

CALEB

"Elise?" Aiden asked as Caleb put his phone in his pocket and sat down at the table where they were finishing their meal.

"Yes." Normally he wouldn't have answered a call while he was eating with his family. Not unless it was an emergency.

Our mate calling is an emergency, his bear replied. If she needs us, we're supposed to be there for her no matter what.

"She's not canceling your date, is she?" Valerie asked.

"No, she wants me to help her and her brother find somewhere to live." He glanced at his watch. "I'm meeting them in half an hour."

"Then why are you still sitting here?" Aiden asked.

"Trying to clear my head. It's all fuzzy. How am I supposed to help them if I can't think straight?" Caleb rested his head in his hands.

"Just breathe and relax," Aiden told him. "This part fades, soon your head will clear, and you'll be back to your normal self."

"Is that how you felt when we met?" Flora asked her mate.

"Yeah. The moment I saw you outside the candy store, I knew you were the one for me. The person I was supposed to be with for the rest of my life. It was as if that one thought just pounded in my head over and over again, like a drumbeat, pushing all other thoughts away." Aiden reached for her hand. "Then it cleared because I knew you needed me."

"I did." She caressed his cheek. "I do."

"Goodness, when I see the two of you together and hear Caleb talking about his mate, it's enough to make a man cry." Rift shook his head. "I want this. I want the head-exploding, heart-pumping knowledge that I have a mate."

"It'll happen for you, Rift," Valerie assured him.

"I sometimes wonder. I'm not getting any younger and with four brothers already mated, it feels as if my luck has run out." He glanced at Milo. "I guess I'm just hoping to be the best uncle ever instead."

"That was going to be my job." Caleb half-raised his hand.

"That's true. Caleb was feeling just like you a couple of days ago. Now, look at him." Aiden glanced at his brother. "We should get going. Elise and her brother aren't the only ones who need a place to live."

"Of course." Caleb stood up. "You're welcome to use the apartment until you get yourselves settled. I could move back in with Valerie. If she'll have me."

"Always." Valerie looked up at her son. "But I suspect it would only be for a short time. Your mate will soon realize that the two of you belong under the same roof."

"I hope so." Caleb backed away from the table. "Thanks for the food. Are you okay if I run?"

"You go." Valerie waved him away. "Help your mate get settled. If you need us, you know where we are. I want Elise to know we are here for her as a family."

"Do you want me to come with you?" Flora offered.

"No, you have your own things to sort out. I can do this alone." He smiled at her. "But thanks for the offer, it means a lot to know you're there if I need you."

"It's no trouble at all, I owe you a lot. And I want Elise to be happy. She deserves it." Flora gave a half-smile. "It might also make Karros realize that there was nothing I could do to stop the way I feel about Aiden."

"If he sees how the mating bond works for me and Elise, he'll understand it more." Caleb inclined his head. "At least I know Karros won't be trying to drive a wedge between us. If he let you go, he must have some understanding of the mating bond."

"He does, but this is different. It's one thing to set me free to be with Aiden. But Elise is his sister. Karros knows how his parents will react to the news. He might not be so willing to support your relationship with Elise." Flora's knowledge of Elise's family would come in useful if Caleb had to try to win them over.

"And I thought the hard part was finding your mate," Rift said.

"Me and you both," Caleb agreed. He rubbed his hands together and backed away from them. "Okay, challenge accepted, I am going to make some phone calls and see if I can find a really great place for them to live."

"And we're going to find Logan and ask if we can move into his cabin until we've had some time to plan our future." Aiden gazed adoringly at his mate and Caleb experienced a pang of jealousy. He couldn't wait until he had such a deep loving relationship with his mate.

Don't forget they have been through a lot together and have learned to trust each other. The past few days have been tough on them, but it's drawn them together and made their relationship stronger. *His bear's wise words helped as Caleb left the restaurant and crossed the hotel reception area.*

Jeremy was typing on the keyboard of the hotel computer, but aside from that, the reception area was empty.

"Are you busy, Jeremy?" Caleb went to the desk, aware he didn't have a lot of time to spare if he didn't want to be late for his meeting with his mate.

"Always." Jeremy raised his eyes from the screen to study Caleb for a moment. "What do you need?"

"Do you know of any apartments or houses that might be available to rent?"

"Ah, you're homeless since your brother has found his mate." His eyes narrowed. "Is this your roundabout way of asking if I need a roommate?"

"No!" Caleb answered quickly. "I have a few contacts of my own, but I figured I'd ask you since you meet so many people coming through the hotel reception. I wondered if you'd heard of anything."

"Oh." Jeremy looked relieved. "Sorry."

"I'll let you get back to work." Caleb tapped the desk and turned around, heading for the door.

"Wait, there might be something. I had a couple in earlier who have come to view a new development along the coast. It's a little outside of town, which might suit your mate." Jeremy paused. "That was your mate in here this morning?"

"Yes. It was."

"Fae. She was here with her brother, they were asking for Aiden. I saw you with the whole startled *I've just met my mate* look in your eyes." He snorted. "Shifters."

"Shifters indeed." Caleb leveled his gaze at Jeremy. "Do you have any more details?"

"Oh, yes." He tapped the keyboard, his eyes fixed on the computer screen. "Here." He printed off a sheet of paper and handed it to Caleb. "A couple of the apartments are already leased. There are still two more vacant. It's a quiet development, which might also suit your mate."

"Thanks, Jeremy. I owe you one." Caleb folded the piece of paper and hurried toward the door.

"You're welcome. And good luck. You'll need it."

"What does that mean?" Caleb paused at the door.

"A fae and a shifter. Not always the most compatible of people. But I'm sure you'll make it work." He went back to staring at the screen as Caleb left the hotel and headed across the parking lot to his truck.

It was a beautiful day. The kind of day that made people fall in love with the town. He went to his truck and got inside, inserting the key in the ignition but didn't start the engine. Before he met up with Elise and Karros, he made a couple of phone calls.

First, he lined up a viewing of the ocean view apartments. Competition for them was tough but he managed to talk the owner into letting them take a look this afternoon. It helped that the guy knew Caleb, by name and reputation if not in person.

The second call was to a client who he and Aiden had done some work for a couple of months back. He'd been converting an old barn into a stunning house and the twins had helped with the building work. Caleb had driven past the house last week and popped in to see the completed work. The owner, Wilf Jaeger, had proudly shown him around, only the final finishing touches needed completing before the house was ready to rent out.

"Hey, Wilf, it's Caleb."

"Caleb. How are you?"

"Good, I might have someone interested in renting your house." Caleb put his hand on the steering wheel and gripped it tightly.

"Okay. The front and back yards need landscaping, but aside from that, it's finished. I was going to start taking viewings next week."

"How about we swing by this afternoon and take a look?" Caleb asked. "They've just moved to Wishing Moon Bay and need somewhere as soon as possible."

"You mean right now?" Wilf asked.

"Yeah. I know it's short notice, but..." He knew Wilf well enough to ask him for a favor. "They're a brother and sister. The sister is my mate."

"Your mate? I never knew you'd met her. Congratulations. I couldn't be happier for you."

"I only met her this morning. So it's early days," Caleb confessed. "She's moving here to train with Ivan. I'm just worried if she doesn't find somewhere to rent then she'll leave town."

Wilf laughed. "You want her to move into a place she loves so that when Ivan chases her out of his kitchen she'll stay anyway."

"Something like that," Caleb admitted.

"Since it's you... I can't be there. I have a job to do on one of my other properties, but there's a key under the flagstone in the back yard. You can let yourselves in. If they like it, give me a call and we'll see what we can work out. They just need to be flexible while I finish up all the little jobs around the place."

"Thanks, Wilf. I appreciate it."

"It's the least I can do. You and Aiden did a great job on the house. And for a reasonable price." He laughed again. "Although, you may have to raise your prices now that you both have mates. I did hear it right, didn't I? Aiden met his mate and she's a fae."

"That's right. News sure does travel fast."

"I heard it from Oscar. We play pool together on a Thursday night."

"And my mate is a fae, too," Caleb admitted. If that was going to be a problem, he'd rather know now.

"Ah. Okay. A fae renting out my house is fine as long as they're good for the money. I don't want to have to go chasing them for the rent across their realm. That never ends well."

"I'll guarantee their rent," Caleb offered.

"Then we have a deal. If they like the place."

"I'll call you and let you know." Caleb ended the call and started the engine. Those were two places they would go look at today. Two that weren't being advertised by a real estate agent.

You're hoping to impress Elise and Karros. His bear had been sleeping.

I am. You know how hard it can be to get a decent place to rent in town. If Elise is working at the hotel then she's going to need to be close by. Her hours will be long, and she can't afford to be late, you know how Ivan hates tardiness.

And then there are the areas of town they need to avoid. Not everyone would welcome a fae as a neighbor. Especially if the residents are shifters.

That's why I thought Wilf's house might be the best idea. However, the apartments Jeremy told us about are very nice, with great views over the ocean.

He drove toward the beach, where he'd arranged to meet Elise and Karros. As he parked the truck, his stomach flipped with nerves. What if he blew this? What if Karros tried to persuade Elise to leave Wishing Moon Bay and her dreams behind just to spite Caleb? It would be one way to get revenge for losing the woman he loved.

Caleb parked the truck. As he switched off the engine, he was suddenly alert to the feeling he'd experienced this morning. His mate was close by.

He closed his eyes and let his shifter senses roam free until he pinpointed his mate among the dozen or so people on the beach. It was as if they were connected.

We are connected, his bear reminded him. *We're connected by the shifter bond. We're connected by fate.*

Caleb only hoped that connection was strong enough to keep his mate by his side.

5

ELISE

"He's here." Elise turned her back to the ocean as she sensed Caleb.

"How did you know?" Karros spun around and stared at the cars parked next to the beach. "You can sense him?"

She smothered a smile. "I can. It's as if we're connected."

"I know shifters experience the connection, but I always figured that was because of their unique senses. But you're saying you have them, too?" Karros looked at her with disbelief.

"I don't think I've got shifter senses." She looked from side to side and then kept her head still as she focused on her hearing. "Nope, my vision and my hearing are just the same."

"So, the only thing that's changed is that you can sense Caleb."

"Yes. I'm a little disappointed. I'd really like to have super speed." Her eyes widened. "I wonder if that's how come Ivan is so good in the kitchen. He uses his shifter speed to cook super-fast." Then her mouth turned down at the corners. "Wow. What if those same senses are the reason he's so good at cooking."

"You think his enhanced sense of smell and taste help him?" Karros slid his arm around Elise's shoulders and guided her toward Caleb. The bear shifter was waiting for them at the top of the steps leading down to the beach. Karros didn't need his shifter senses to tell him that.

"Yes. It's possible." Her shoulders sagged. "If that's the case then I have no chance of ever being as good as him."

"If that was his secret then the world would be filled with shifter chefs. And it's not. I think Ivan's talent in the kitchen is something else. Something he can teach." Karros, always the voice of reason.

"Hi there." Caleb raised his hand as they approached. "When you said you were at the beach, I wondered if you were checking out the caves in case you didn't find a place to stay tonight."

"I didn't know the man who wants to be my sister's mate was so funny." Karros shot Caleb a slightly hostile look.

"Now, now. We're on the same team." A shiver of excitement rushed through Elise as she climbed the steps to Caleb.

"We are." Caleb bowed his head to Karros. "I know you're upset about Flora and my brother, but I hope you don't take it out on us."

"Us." Karros arched an eyebrow at Elise.

"Stop it," she warned her brother. "You are trying to pick a fight."

Karros sighed. "Sorry. This has been a strange few days. My world and my future have been turned upside down."

"Karros expected to be sitting on a throne one day beside the next Lady of the Starlight Realm. Instead, he's here on a beach outside of our world with me." She held out her hands. "Not exactly a fair trade."

"None of that is my fault," Caleb reminded them.

"No, it's not," Karros agreed. "So let's start again." He held out his hand to Caleb. "Friends."

"Friends." Without hesitation, Caleb thrust his hand into Karros's and the two men shook and made up.

"Thank you. I'm nervous enough about tomorrow without worrying about you two." She gnawed on her bottom lip. "Is Ivan all right about me working in his kitchen? He was put on the spot and I know he wouldn't have accepted me if it wasn't for you."

"Ivan might have agreed for you to work in his kitchen because of me," Caleb began. "But whether you keep that position is up to you. He won't let you stay if he thinks you can't cook or can't learn to cook. That would be wasting your time and his."

"Oh, Elise can cook," Karros said with the enthusiasm of a loving brother. "She just needs to refine her talent and learn to explore new dishes."

"*She* also needs somewhere to sleep tonight." Elise blushed at her brother's compliments. He'd always been supportive but maybe he was blinded by love.

She mentally berated herself for not believing in herself. She'd had plenty of jobs in restaurants, working hard to get better until she'd hit a roadblock in her career. No one would take a chance on her running her own kitchen even though she knew she could do it. If she was ever going to realize her dream, she needed to have faith in her talents.

"We visited the two realtors in town." Karros pulled a small selection of brochures out of his jacket. While they were waiting for Caleb to arrive, they'd sat on the beach, reading through the brochures and deciding if any of the apartments were worth viewing.

They had a shortlist of two.

"Great. I also have a couple of places we can look at." He handed Elise the piece of paper Jeremy had printed. "This is a brand-new development."

"Oh, this looks wonderful." She glanced sideways at Karros. "It's more than we budgeted."

"We could go see it. I will need to get a job in town if we're staying here long-term."

Caleb jerked his head up at the word if. "Aren't your plans long-term?"

"That depends," Elise said. "But let's not focus on what will happen if things go wrong. Instead, let's try to make sure things go right."

"Okay. Well, I also have a house for you to look at. I worked on it a few months ago. I spoke to the owner and he's happy for you to go check it out. However, the front and back yards still need landscaping and there might be a few small jobs that need doing inside."

Karros tucked the brochures from the real estate agents into his jacket. "Why don't we see your properties? Hopefully one of them will be suitable. If not, we'll arrange to view these apartments."

Caleb looked at his watch. "We don't have time to view the house before our appointment at the apartments. Shall we drive to the apartments now? We can check out the area before we go in."

"Sure." Elise glanced at her brother who seemed okay with the situation. Maybe things would work out. If they could find a great place to live and she could show Ivan she was a good chef who could become a great chef, then they could settle here and be happy.

Then she could take her time and get to know Caleb, who seemed like a real sweetheart. Although he might just be trying to win them over, so she'd accept being his mate.

"Shall we leave your car here and go in my truck?" Caleb asked.

"There seems little point taking two vehicles and since you know the way to both properties..." Karros raised a questioning eyebrow at his sister. “Unless you’d rather go separately?”

“No, I think it’s a good idea.” She’s expected to be the one convincing Karros it was a good idea. Her brother truly was trying to start over with Caleb.

“Okay.” Caleb turned around and headed for a blue truck, twirling his keys in his hand as he walked.

Elise took one last look at the ocean before she followed. “Is it true the town is called Wishing Moon Bay because wishes come true if you throw a stone into the ocean?”

“Sort of. I’ll help you find a wishing stone to throw in.” He put his hand on the tailgate of his truck and turned to face her. “As long as you promise not to wish me out of your life.”

“Why would I do that?” She tilted her head to one side. “I’m willing to give us a chance.”

Caleb’s warm smile spread across his face. “I’m happy to hear it. This is a shock for me, too. We can just take things slow.”

“I like slow.” Color covered her cheeks, and she ducked her head and went around to the passenger side of the truck.

Caleb opened the driver’s door and climbed in. Elise took one last look at the ocean, inhaling the tangy air before she clambered onto the front passenger seat. Karros slid in next to her and closed the door, before casting a cursory glance around the truck.

“I use it for work.” Caleb glanced down at the collection of invoices stuffed into a folder on the dashboard and the empty coffee cup on the floor.

“I wasn’t criticizing,” Karros replied.

“Your expression was.” Caleb wagged his finger at Karros. “It’s not all about looks. My truck is reliable and able to stand up to the worst of the weather.”

“How bad does the weather get?” Elise shivered. “Do you get a lot of snow?”

"Over the mountains. We do get some in town. And some winters the river freezes over, and we ice skate on it." He chuckled. "You'll love it here, honestly."

"I don't really like the cold." She hugged herself as he drove away from the beach.

"The thing about the cold is when it's freezing outside, or raining, then you stay inside in front of a fire, drinking hot chocolate and eating brownies." His eyes lit up. "Then you get to snuggle up in bed. There's nothing like feeling safe and snug while the wind whistles outside the window."

"Does that mean you don't like the cold either?" Elise asked.

"The cold never bothers me. I'm hot-blooded." He side-eyed her, his expression telling her he would be good to keep her warm on a cold winter's night. "My bear loves rolling in the snow. He likes playing in it, too."

"Your bear." She rocked back and forth as if trying to warm herself from the cold even though it was summer, and the weather was sunny. "What's he like?"

"He's a bear," Karros said drily. "I guess he's like any other bear."

"Are you being tetchy again?" she asked.

"No, I'm just saying. A bear is a bear. Nothing special."

"My bear is a part of me. I'd argue he isn't just any bear."

"Will you show me? Tonight. If we're still on for our date?" Elise asked excitedly.

"Sure," Caleb replied. "Once we've figured out where you're going to live."

"We don't have a lot of stuff to unpack," Elise replied. "And if we don't find anywhere, we might have to book a room at the hotel."

"I think they're fully booked," Caleb replied. "You can stay at my apartment if you're really stuck."

"Oh, no," Karros replied.

"Why not?" Elise swung around to gaze at her brother.

"I thought you lived with Aiden?" Karros asked bluntly. "I'm sure Flora told her father that Aiden lived with his twin."

"Oh. Okay. Cancel that idea. Sorry," she told Karros.

"Aiden and Flora are looking for a place of their own. Until they find somewhere, they're planning on staying in Logan's cabin in the mountains," Caleb quickly explained. "Our apartment isn't very big. But if you're stuck, you can stay there for a couple of nights and I can move back into the hotel. My mom has a spare room in her apartment."

"Okay, we have a backup plan." She nudged Karros in the ribs. "That's a really kind offer, isn't it?"

"It is. Thanks, Caleb." Although Karros looked mutinous over the idea of staying in his love rival's apartment, even for a night.

Caleb drove out of town and their conversation faltered as Elise and Karros admired the view. While the bay was a haven from the ocean, as they rounded the headland, huge rocks jutted up and the waves crashed upon them, sending white plumes of water into the air.

"The story is that long ago, when the town was first settled, the witches who cast the spell to protect themselves and their supernatural secrets, also made rock monsters who would sleep until they were called upon to protect the town. These rocks are those sleeping rock monsters. If ever there's a threat from land or sea, they would rise up and fight."

"Children's stories," Karros replied. "Like the ones the people in the world beyond tell about the fae folk."

"Oh, fairies with magic wands!" Elise chuckled. "I love those stories."

"Those stories make people believe we are benevolent creatures who leave money beneath a child's pillow in exchange for their teeth." Karros rolled his eyes. "What do they think we do with all of those teeth?"

"You are such a sourpuss," Elise complained.

"Do you always fight like this?" Caleb drove the truck along the meandering road with the sun shining through the windshield.

"No, we fight much worse," Elise replied lightly. "But we also get along really well. We've learned to stick together. We might fight but no one comes between us."

"Ah, but now that you have a mate that might change." Karros was good at identifying her troubled thoughts and magnifying them. "You will soon pick Caleb over me. Over your brother who has known you all your life."

"Just like you would have chosen Flora over me if you had married her." Elise arched an eyebrow at her brother. She had learned his ways and was more than capable of pushing back.

"True," Karros agreed.

"So what about you and your brother?" Elise asked.

"You mean Aiden? Because I have four other brothers. He just happens to be the only one related by blood," Caleb reminded her.

"Let's start with Aiden. We can work our way through the rest of them." Elise would like to glean as much knowledge as possible about his family. Not only would it help her make an informed decision about Caleb but also help her learn how to handle Ivan. Hopefully.

"Aiden and I have a strong bond. We lost our parents and ended up in foster care before we were taken by a man who planned to sell us."

"What?" Elise hadn't expected this story. "Taken? You mean kidnapped?"

"Yes. Sort of. We were stolen from our foster parents and ended up in a small apartment. Luckily, the authorities found us, and we ended up here in Wishing Moon Bay. Valerie adopted us along with my other brothers."

"That's quite a story." Elise shook her head. "I might not get along with my parents all the time, but I don't know what I'd do without them." She put her hand over Karros's. "Do you?"

"No. Our parents have their faults, like most parents. But we owe them so much."

"They've obviously raised you both to be free thinkers. I spent some time with Flora since she met Aiden and I have to say she was a little more...reserved."

"Flora was raised to take over from her father and has always tried to please him even when that's next to impossible. Our parents were more liberal. I didn't plan to marry Flora for her wealth or her status, I genuinely love her. When she told me her parents were pushing her into an arranged marriage, I stepped forward because I knew I could make her happy."

"Even though she didn't love you in return?" Caleb asked.

"She did love me. Just not in the same way as I love her." He ran his hand over his chin and stared out of the window.

"My brother wanted to do the right thing. He always does." Elise's heart ached for Karros. He'd been so sure he could find a way to make Flora love him. Once they were married, he would have spent the rest of his life trying to find a way. "Flora would have been lucky to have him as a husband."

"I respect what you tried to do," Caleb said.

"But she is better off with her mate." Karros nodded. "Elise has told me she has feelings for you..."

"Karros!" She elbowed him in the ribs.

"You need to be honest with Caleb and yourself, Elise," Karros replied.

"So you have feelings for me?" Caleb raised an eyebrow as he looked at her.

"Not feelings, as such. But I can sense you. When we were

on the beach, I knew you were there." She shrugged. "It's kind of like a sixth sense. Something that's just there. It's not as if I've fallen in love at first sight," she warned him.

"It's a start." Caleb grinned.

"It certainly is," Elise replied.

6

CALEB

Caleb pointed to a small collection of houses to their right. "This is it. The houses have been transformed into luxury apartments."

"Wow, what a view." Elise leaned forward and looked past Karros to the view of the ocean.

"It is stunning," Karros agreed.

"My only issue so far is that we're a little farther out of town than I'd have liked. I'll be driving along this road in the dark when the winter comes. If I keep my job with Ivan." She pressed her lips together. "Which reminds me, I'm going to need a car."

"Yes, one car between the two of us is not going to cut it this far out of town," Karros agreed.

"Shall we go have a look around?" Caleb parked the truck in a spot in front of the apartments.

"Yes. I don't want to rule it out just because of the distance from town. I'd get up fifteen minutes earlier each day if the accommodation was worth it." Elise shuffled across the seat as Karros got out of the truck.

"Wow, it's stunning here." She walked to the edge of the

small parking area and looked out at the ocean below. "Your rock monsters will guard us against the rough ocean in a storm." She half-turned to Caleb who joined her to look at the view.

"There's nothing like the smell of the fresh ocean." He inhaled deeply, catching his mate's scent along with the smell of the ocean. "What's the ocean like in your realm?"

"Calmer. The weather is altogether more temperate, we don't have such noticeable seasons. Everything about being a fae seems to be smooth." She sliced her hand horizontally through the air.

"We've mastered our emotions," Karros explained. "At least most of us have."

"Karros once described me as an excited puppy." Elise turned on her heel and stared up at the apartments. "I'm certainly excited now."

"See," Karros began. "She *is* just like an excitable puppy."

Caleb's bear bristled. *He's teasing our mate.*

I think Elise can handle Karros, Caleb replied. And she might take offense if we stepped in.

True, she certainly doesn't seem offended, his bear replied, but he still wanted to swat Karros with his massive paw.

You're just being defensive because you see him as a potential threat to Aiden's relationship with Flora. Caleb could understand why.

When he talks about being in love with Flora...of still being in love with her, it's not right. Flora belongs to Aiden and nothing is going to change that.

It's a pity we can't find a mate for Karros. Caleb led Elise and Karros across to the front entrance leading into the apartments. The doors were freshly painted, the smell still lingering in the air.

"It's so fresh and light," Elise remarked as they entered into a small communal hallway. "I love it."

Caleb took his phone from his pocket and pressed dial to tell the developer they were here. The phone rang and rang before finally going to voicemail. "Strange, Mr. Kipper said he'd meet us here."

"Perhaps he's on his way. He might not answer a call while he's driving, particularly on the coast road." Elise smiled patiently, while Karros cast a suspicious sidelong look at Caleb.

He thinks we've messed up, his bear said. He thinks we're wasting their time.

If Mr. Kipper doesn't arrive soon, that's exactly what we'll have done. Caleb looked up, there was a car approaching. *He's here.* With some relief, Caleb went outside and met Mr. Kipper.

"Sorry I'm late. I had trouble with a warlock, he'd managed to seal himself into one of the apartments. Some kind of *transmorphic* spell gone wrong." He shook Caleb's hand. "I should have a no-magic-allowed clause written into my leases."

"How did you sort it out?" Caleb asked.

"I had to call a spell repairman out. Donald Miller. He's an expert at these kinds of things, took care of the problem in minutes. I handed the bill to the tenant, he wasn't happy, but then I pointed out to him that it's a good thing I didn't bill him for my time, too." Mr. Kipper straightened his suit jacket as he strolled toward the apartments.

"The building looks stunning," Caleb said as they mounted the steps where Elise and Karros were waiting.

"It does, doesn't it? I'm pleased with how it turned out. As you know, the apartments used to be a single row of houses." He stopped at the top of the steps and turned to look at the view. "That never gets old."

"No, it doesn't," Caleb agreed, happy Mr. Kipper was in such a good mood despite his tenant's magical mistake.

"Hello." Elise came to meet them. "I'm Elise and this is my

brother, Karros." She smiled warmly.

"And the apartment is for you?" Mr. Kipper stared at Elise, his eyes narrowing before his expression cleared. "You're a fae?"

"We are," Karros confirmed. "Is that a problem?"

"No, not at all. I've only ever had a handful of fae tenants, but they've always been reliable and keep the properties clean and tidy." He laughed good-naturedly. "They also don't tend to try experimental magic, at least not indoors. Although I did once have a fae rent an apartment from me who brewed a sweet concoction from some fruit, I can't remember the name, but I never could get rid of the smell. Very sickly."

"Parder. The fruit is used to make a very potent wine," Elise said.

"Ah, parder, that was it." He wagged his finger at them. "No parder brewing."

"I can't stand the stuff," Karros replied.

"That's good." Mr. Kipper took the keys from his pocket and jingled them on his finger as he led them up a flight of stairs. "The apartment is on the first floor."

"The view will be even better from up there." Elise's eyes lit up as she followed Mr. Kipper upstairs.

"Thank you for doing this." Karros stopped at the bottom of the stairs and half-turned to face Caleb.

"I want you to stay in Wishing Moon Bay, so I'm not exactly doing this out of kindness. I have a vested interest in the outcome," Caleb admitted.

"And that's why I like you, Caleb." Karros studied the bear shifter. "You're an honest man. My people are renowned for their trickery."

"But not their magic wands." Caleb chuckled. "We have a lot to learn from each other and I want you to know that I intend to do whatever it takes to win Elise's heart."

"I get that." Karros glanced upstairs. "All I've ever wanted was for her to be happy." He turned his attention back to Caleb. "But her happiness doesn't revolve around being a homemaker. She wants to be a chef. Children haven't fit into her idea of a perfect life for a while." He lowered his voice. "At least that's what she's convinced herself."

"So, you're saying she does want children?" Caleb's brows knitted together. After Karros's admission that his people were tricky with their words, he didn't want to get caught in a trap.

"She does. At least she did until she got scared."

"Scared of what?" Caleb asked, wanting to run past Karros and join his mate in the apartment above.

"Scared that she was too old to find the right man and settle down. It was easier to convince herself that she didn't want those things anymore." Karros held out his hands, palms up, as if he were balancing scales. "Now she believes that being a chef is all she needs for a fulfilling life. At least until she met you."

"And now?" Caleb asked hopefully.

"Now I think there's going to be a war inside her, a battle for what she truly wants." Karros placed his hand on Caleb's shoulder. "But maybe with you, her true mate, she might get to have it all."

"I'd give her everything if I could," Caleb assured Karros.

"I believe you." Karros glanced upward. "We should go join Elise, she'll wonder where we are."

"Sure." Caleb hoped his mate was wondering where he was. Or maybe she didn't care at all.

She cares, she feels the connection, his bear replied. I can see it in the way she looks at you.

Are you sure that's concern and not annoyance? Caleb asked. Meeting us sure has messed with her plans.

Without us, she wouldn't have gotten the chance to work with

Ivan. It's one of the many ways she needs us. His bear was resolute in his conviction. She also wouldn't have a chance to view this apartment.

True. He followed Karros up to the first floor and headed down a short hallway. The first door on the right stood open, the light from the apartment spilling out.

"Wow." Karros stood in the doorway and stared at the view that met them.

"Stunning, isn't it?" Mr. Kipper turned to face them.

"It sure is." Karros crossed the apartment to stare out at the ocean beyond.

"I'm not sure anything else about the apartment matters except for the view." Elise's eyes shone as if filled with tears as she turned her face to her brother. "What do you think?"

"I think you should thank Caleb for bringing us here." Karros looked over his shoulder to where the shifter was hanging back by the door.

He was afraid to intrude. The decision as to where they lived was not his to make. This was between Elise and Karros.

But we certainly wish it was our decision, his bear said. If only we were moving in with our mate.

That would be incredible, Caleb agreed. And one day it will be us. We will win Elise's heart and she'll live with us and wake up each morning beside us.

"Shall we check out the rest of the apartment?" Karros tugged at Elise's sleeve.

"Sure." She cast a beautiful smile in Caleb's direction as she followed Karros toward the bedrooms. "Thank you, Caleb."

"My pleasure," Caleb answered.

And it truly was. He loved seeing his mate so happy.

From this day onward that would be his sole goal in life.

7

ELISE

"What did you think?" Elise asked Karros as they left the apartment building. She'd have agreed to rent the place right away, but she suspected Karros had some reservations.

"I like it. I like it a lot."

"But?" They turned around and looked back at the apartment.

"I wish there was some outdoor space. A back yard or a front yard. Somewhere I could grow things." He shrugged. "But this isn't about me."

"Yes, it is," Elise insisted. "This is about us finding somewhere for us to both live."

"Why don't we go look at the house," Caleb suggested. "Mr. Kipper doesn't need an answer right now, but you're going to have to be fast if you do decide to rent this apartment, it won't be available for long."

"Are you sure you don't want to say yes now?" Karros asked.

"No." Elise shook her head. "Well, yes. But you know me, I'm impatient and it would be better to at least look at another property, so we have something to compare it to. The rooms were a little small."

"But the view is magnificent," Karros added.

"Come on, the house has a good view, too," Caleb herded them toward the truck. "Not of the ocean, but the mountains. The rooms are also bigger and once the yard has been landscaped, you'll have outdoor space, too."

"Okay. Let's go." Elise sighed and took one last look at the view as Karros opened the truck door and waited for her to get in.

"We have to go back across town." Caleb started the engine. "It'll give you a chance to get a good look at the place and I'll point out anything I think might be useful."

"Our very own tour guide." Elise grinned.

"I'm trying to make myself useful." Caleb drove along the coast road with the window rolled down.

"You've already done that." Elise glanced at her mate. Caleb must feel like the odd one out since Elise and Karros were the ones searching for a home and were so used to being around each other, it was as if they knew what the other was thinking.

"Yes, you have, Caleb." Karros chuckled. "So far, you have excelled in proving what a good mate and husband you would be for Elise."

"Karros." She dug her elbow in his ribs as Caleb shuffled uncomfortably in his seat.

"That isn't why I'm doing this," Caleb said. "I would help you even if Elise and I weren't mates."

"A good Samaritan." Karros nodded. "I believe you."

"What are your other brothers like?" Elise figured this was a good time to get an idea of Caleb's family and what she could expect from them.

"My brothers." Caleb rubbed his chin. "Aiden is a lot like me."

"Do you have a connection? Do you know what the other is thinking?" Elise asked.

"Some of the time. We've spent so long together, living together, working together, it's hard to know if it's a twin thing or just because we're so close." He gnawed on his bottom lip.

"You're worried that's going to change now that he has a mate."

"And I have a mate." He glanced sideways at Elise.

"Of course. I should have said now that you both have mates." She looked down at her hands clasped in her lap.

"Things change. Life changes." Karros stared out of the window at the road ahead.

"It does." Elise nodded. "Whether we want it to or not."

"But surely you want things to change," Karros said. "As a shifter, you want to find your mate. And you must wish for your brother to be happy, which means you wanted him to find his mate."

"Of course," Caleb quickly agreed.

"I wanted to come and work in the hotel and learn from Ivan. But it's still scary," Elise said. "So, I can understand what you mean."

"But you're both up for the challenges that lie ahead," Karros replied. "Especially since you have each other."

"And we have you, big brother," Elise said. "And Caleb's brothers, of course."

"You're not alone." Karros's expression faltered. Was he scared of being alone? With their relationship with their parents fractured, and his sister mated to a shifter, he must be scared he'd end up alone.

"Neither are you," Elise reminded him. "We are family and that will never change, in the same way that Caleb will always have his family."

"Elise is right. When a shifter meets their mate, their family simply gets bigger," Caleb replied.

"Oh, no." Karros waved his hand at Caleb.

"What's wrong with that?" Elise asked.

"That's like saying that we will now be related to Flora's parents." He chuckled. "Hey, you should lead with that fact when you tell Mom and Dad that you are mated to a shifter."

Elise laughed. "Oh, they will forgive you for ruining their plans to be socially mobile. I'm sure they'll figure out a way to tell their friends that they are related by marriage to the Lord of the Starlight Realm after all."

"Yeah, it won't matter that it's not directly through marriage." Karros leaned back in his seat and chuckled. "You've saved us, Caleb."

"You're welcome." Caleb chuckled and shook his head as if he thought they were crazy, which they probably were.

"We're on the other side of town already." Elise leaned forward and stared out of the window as they drove past houses on the edge of town.

"How much farther is it to the property we're going to view?" Karros asked.

"It's about another mile."

"There are the mountains, I see what you mean about the view." Elise's blood quickened in her veins. The ocean view had been stunning but the pull of the mountains in the distance excited her. There was so much to explore.

"It's all so green," Karros murmured.

"There's the house." Caleb pointed to a house set back from the road. It was nestled amongst a small copse of trees, and behind it was a cluster of farm buildings.

"It looks cozy," Elise said.

"Is that a bad thing?" Caleb asked.

"No, not at all. I like cozy." She smiled softly, she'd like to get cozy with her mate. Her cheeks flamed red as that thought intruded her thoughts.

Caleb turned off the road and drove down a rutted track toward the house. The front yard, if you could call it that, was just bare dirt that had been churned up by heavy vehicles during the building works.

However, she looked past that and imagined what the house could be. It was more of a home than the ocean view apartment. She could imagine raising children here, she could imagine them playing out in front of the house on a green lawn bordered by flowers.

"I like it," Karros said with the same conviction she'd felt for the apartment. "I'd love to help with the landscaping."

"Yard work is to Karros as cooking is to me," Elise informed Caleb.

"I like working with my hands and watching plants grow," Karros admitted.

"When we were younger, that's what Karros wanted to do but our parents didn't think it was suitable work. Not when they wanted him to marry for money and status," Elise explained.

"But now you're here, you are master of your own destiny," Caleb parked the truck in front of the house. "I can speak to the owner and ask him if you can do the landscaping."

Karros looked sideways at Elise. "Let's look at the house first. We might not like it."

He opened the truck door and got out. Immediately, he crossed to the dirt and leaned down, picking up a handful of the rich brown soil and let it trickle through his fingers. Standing straight, he brushed his hands clean and stared at the house. He liked this property best, she could see it in his expression.

"Shall we go inside?" Caleb asked from beside her.

She looked up at him and nodded, wanting to kiss him for being so kind. They would never have had the chance to view these properties before anyone else if Caleb hadn't made the arrangements. He'd gone out of his way to help them even though they were strangers.

"Yes, please." Elise followed him toward the house while Karros stood with his hands on his hips and stared up at the mountains in the distance.

"Your brother likes it here," Caleb said.

"He does." She waited for Caleb to find the key which was hidden.

"Are you going to argue as to where you live?" Caleb asked. "You did like the apartment better."

"I did. But this house is beautiful. We'd have more privacy. Not a bad thing when you are a fae in a foreign land." She smiled brightly.

"You belong here," Caleb assured her. "And people are very accepting of everyone else. If you are friendly to them, they will be friendly to you."

"We can be friendly." She held her breath as he opened the door. Already she wanted to be more than friends with Caleb. She wanted to explore what it meant to be his mate.

"It's not as impressive as the ocean view apartment." He stepped inside and Elise imagined what it would be like if they lived here together.

Caleb would come home after a day at work and slip off his shoes before coming into the kitchen where she'd be waiting with a wonderful meal she'd made especially for him. They would sit and talk while they ate, discussing their day, sharing intimate moments.

"It's bigger than the apartment." Karros had entered the house. Elise had been so lost in her daydream, she hadn't heard him approach.

"I like it." She cleared her throat. "It's closer to town, too."

"Is the kitchen okay?" Caleb asked. "Or will you be so tired of cooking at work that you don't like to cook at home?"

"I love to cook at home. I like watching people enjoy my food, that's what makes it all worthwhile." She imagined standing in the kitchen with her children and teaching them how to cook, sharing with them the joy she found in creating dishes.

"Although Elise's first attempts at cooking were not wholly edible," Karros chimed in, earning himself a reproving look from his sister. "You know what I'm talking about."

"Of course I do." She just didn't want to share that anecdote with Caleb right now. She didn't need him having second thoughts about asking Ivan to take her on in the kitchen.

"Elise loves the wildwood nearly as much as she loves cooking," Karros continued the story despite her warning. "When we were young, we used to go stay with our grandma who lives on the edge of the wildwood. She taught us how to forage and what was safe to eat and what was poisonous."

"You poisoned people?" Caleb asked in shock.

"No!" Elise reached out for his hand, the sudden shock of recognition silencing her explanation and allowing Karros to continue.

"The fruits and herbs found in the woods can have strange effects on people."

"Ah, like the *sycombre* fruit. Flora used it when we were searching for Imelda," Caleb said.

Karros's eyes widened at this morsel of information about his true love. "Did she? On her bear shifter mate?"

"No." Caleb tensed. "And don't get ideas, you can't use it on Aiden to make him forget her. Or to make Flora forget him."

"Firstly, the sycombre fruit isn't potent enough. Not to break the mating bond," Karros replied.

"Does that mean you have thought about using it?" Caleb's hands tightened into fists.

"No. But I remember my grandma saying she had a visit from Delphine's father. He hoped to break the mating bond so she would marry Tisserand instead of running off with a bear shifter." Karros held up his hand as Caleb opened his mouth to protest. "Not because they didn't want her to marry Mikka. It was more because they hated the idea of losing their daughter."

"They didn't want her banished," Elise explained.

"You're not promised to another man already, are you?" Caleb asked quickly.

Karros snorted. "Our parents wouldn't dare, but they did always hope she would marry a fae nobleman."

"So, no banishments?" Caleb asked Elise.

"No banishments." Elise smiled shyly at him. She was all his.

"So, back to my story," Karros said.

"We really don't have to." Elise's jaw tightened as she glared at him.

"It's not that bad," Karros insisted, "and you were young."

"Eight." Elise held up her fingers. "Please remember I was only eight when this story took place."

A smile twitched at the corners of Caleb's lips. "I'll remember."

"Anyway, we'd been foraging in the woods and then went back to our grandma's house. Elise wanted to make cookies to take home. Grandma helped, but she was tired after being out all morning and sat down for a cup of herbal tea while Elise mixed the cookie dough."

Elise's cheeks flushed pink as she recalled adding ingredients to the mixture. She'd been so happy to make the cookies and was already experimenting with different flavors and textures. Which was how come she'd added what she thought was cinnamon.

"It was a mistake, and the cookies still tasted good." Elise folded her arms across her body.

"What did you add?" Caleb asked.

"I added *lilipat*." She inhaled sharply as Karros laughed. "It's used as a laxative."

"No one tried the cookies until we got home. I have never seen so many people needing the bathroom at one time." Karros laughed until tears rolled down his cheeks. "The worst thing was Elise had already taken some over to the neighbors before we realized what was in them and what the result of eating them was."

"Oh." Caleb put his hands to his cheeks.

"It was years before they ever tried any of my cooking again," Elise recalled the moment of mortification when she realized what she'd done. "It nearly ended my career before it began."

"Don't worry, your secret is safe with me," Caleb assured her solemnly.

"It's a pity it's not safe with my loving brother," Elise said drily.

"I'm sorry." He wiped his eyes and then pointed at Caleb. "Anyway, he's your mate, he's got to learn everything about you. That's how a good marriage survives. No skeletons hidden in the closet."

"I can't wait for you to find your wife or mate. I know where you have plenty of skeletons hidden." Elise cocked her head to one side and opened her eyes wide in defiance.

"Point taken." Karros lowered his head. "Okay, let's look around the rest of the house."

"Let's. The downstairs is perfect," she told Caleb.

"Let's go upstairs." Caleb led the way and they followed,

checking out a small dining room on the way. The extra room would mean they could both have some privacy. A good thing since she didn't want to spend all her time getting to know Caleb in the presence of her brother and his stories of her past.

"These bedrooms are bigger." Elise walked across the empty room and stared out at the mountains in the distance. "And the view is just as spectacular, if not as invigorating."

"I like it," Karros announced.

"So, we're going to choose this one?" Elise asked.

"Only if you like it, too," Karros answered.

"If you could work on the yard, it would keep you out of trouble and away from the restaurant." She went through to the bathroom. "Oh, this bath is to die for." She ran her hand along the curved top. "It's so deep, perfect for a long soak after a hard day."

"Will you call the owner now?" Karros asked. "I'd like to sign the lease today, if possible, and then we can arrange for furniture to be delivered. We could always sleep on the floor tonight. We have blankets and cushions, we can treat it as a campout."

"We're really going to do this!" She covered her face with her hands. Until now, this had seemed like a dream but if they signed the lease on the house, they were committing to a life in Wishing Moon Bay. A life outside of the fae realm where they were born and raised.

"We're really doing it." Karros nodded.

As Elise met Caleb's expectant face, she nodded. This was where she was meant to be.

And Caleb was who she was meant to be with. But it started here, with Karros.

8

CALEB

"Thanks, Wilf. I'll pass the news on." Caleb ended the call and tucked his phone in his pocket before heading outside where Karros was walking around the patch of bare dirt that he hoped to turn into something beautiful and Elise was seated on a bench staring up at the mountains.

"What did Wilf say?" Elise jumped up off the seat. She was full of energy and enthusiasm for their new life in Wishing Moon Bay. Or maybe she was always this happy and excited.

Life sure will be fun with our mate, his bear said. She's smart and funny and loves life.

"Wilf said he'll meet you here in an hour or so and you can sign the lease." He ran his hand through his hair and let out a long breath. "It's all yours if you want it."

"Do you think it's a good idea?" Elise's enthusiasm ebbed as she studied his face.

"This house?" Caleb nodded. "Yes. Wilf said he'd also talk to Karros about the yard. The job is yours if you want it."

"I do." Karros glanced at his sister's troubled expression. "What's the catch?"

"Wilf wants me to be a guarantor in case you both bail

and leave town." Caleb could have tried to hide this piece of information from them, but he wanted to be honest and truthful with his mate and her brother.

"He doesn't trust us because we're fae?" Elise asked.

"No. Well, yes, in a way." Caleb inhaled deeply, Wilf's worries mirrored his own. "He's just concerned that you are both new in town and it's rare for a fae to settle here."

"He thinks this is a phase and in a couple of weeks we'll head back home and forget all about our responsibilities." Karros nodded. "Understandable. Inaccurate, but understandable."

"If we sign the lease, we're committing to our life here." Elise reached for Caleb's hand and warmth spread across his skin where their fingers touched. "Are you worried that's what's going to happen?"

"I'd be lying if I said it hadn't occurred to me." Caleb wished he could be sure Elise would stay if things didn't end well with Ivan and the restaurant.

"I like that you're honest," Elise replied. "We plan to stay here."

"Caleb is worried your life might implode if things go wrong with the dragon shifter." Karros certainly was good at reading people.

And I always thought the fae lacked empathy, Caleb's bear said. I can see why Flora agreed to marry him. Even though she didn't love him in the same way he loved her, he would have made a good husband.

Do you want to marry him? Caleb joked.

Funny. His bear grumbled as he walked away.

"I have a feeling it's all going to work out just fine," Elise's smile returned. "This house, the restaurant. It's all falling into place."

"You're right." So why did he still feel apprehensive?

Because he didn't know where he fit into Elise's world.

She would live with her brother and work with Caleb's brother. Caleb was on the peripheral of her life. Somehow, he had to find a way to connect with her.

Aiden might have had a rough time with his mate to start with as they searched for Imelda, but at least they had been forced to spend time together.

When would Caleb get to spend time with his mate?

"An hour?" Karros looked at his watch. "We could go back to the beach and pick up my car."

"And Caleb could take me into town and show me around. We need some groceries if we're going to stay here tonight. Even if we camp out, I'm still going to need coffee in the morning." Elise spun around and looked at the house. "We'll need furniture, too."

"I can help you out there," Caleb replied. "My mom has a stack of old furniture at the hotel. When we extended the restaurant a couple of years ago, she sacrificed a couple of rooms in the hotel and her apartment. She hates throwing anything out, so it all got stored away."

"Would she mind letting us borrow some?" Elise asked.

"It would really help us out," Karros confessed. "At least until we have time to buy something else."

"She'd like to help," Caleb insisted. "Why don't we go back there now? We have enough time to pick out what you need. I can load some in my truck and then I could ask Logan to drive over with whatever won't fit."

"Excellent." Elise clapped her hands together.

"Let's go." Caleb jogged back to the house, locked the front door, and replaced the key. Then they hurried to his truck and climbed inside. After a quick phone call to Mr. Kipper to thank him for showing them around the apartment but it was too far out of town, due to Elise's job at the restaurant, he drove away from the house. Ten minutes later, they were back at the beach where Karros got out and picked up his car, leaving Caleb alone with his mate.

"I want to thank you." Elise's eyes shone with excitement. "And I want to ask if we can postpone our date."

He swallowed hard. "Of course, you have so much to do today."

"I thought that I could cook something for us. Tomorrow evening. I'd like you to be our first houseguest." She shuffled closer to him. "Don't worry, I'll figure out how to get rid of Karros so that it's just you and me."

"I'd like that. Although, since you'll have been working all day, I could take you out to dinner," he offered.

"No, honestly, I'd like to cook for you." She shrugged. "It's the least I can do."

"You don't owe me anything," he assured her.

"I appreciate you saying that. But it would be good to get to know you a little better. Since we are mates." Her cheeks turned pink. "Maybe if I cook, you could explain to me exactly what being your mate entails."

"Entails, you make it sound as though it's a job. Being my mate is just you being you and me trying my hardest to make sure you are happy."

"Oh, that has to work both ways," she replied. "I am not interested in being in a one-sided relationship. We're equals." She fixed him with a hard stare. "In everything."

"Don't worry, I spent a few days with Flora, remember? I know that you and I are equal. And that's great. I want you to be my life partner. Everything we do should be a joint decision. Not the small day-to-day stuff, of course. But where we live, whether we have children..." He paused briefly, as if trying to gauge her response. "Those are joint decisions."

"I agree." She watched as Karros started his car and pulled out of his parking spot. With a glance in the mirror, Caleb drove onto the road and headed toward the hotel. "As for children, I need you to know how important this job with Ivan is. It's what I've been dreaming of for the last few years. Someone to give me a chance."

"I know." He gave her a sidelong glance. "Does that mean you don't want children?"

"I...I always dreamed of a family. I love children. But as you get older and the chance to have your own family passes you by, you have to move on or go insane." She leaned her elbow on the door and cupped her chin in her hand. "Meeting you feels as if someone threw the pieces of my life in the air and they've landed scattered all over the ground."

"And together we have to see how they fit together." Caleb could understand her worries and fears. "I don't want to end your dreams, Elise. I want to support them. I want to make them a reality."

"So, you know where the fairy godmother keeps her magic wand," she said lightly.

"I wish I did." They were nearly back at the hotel. He'd enjoyed this time alone with his mate and didn't want it to end. However, they needed to sort out what furniture Elise and Karros needed and get back to the house before Wilf arrived with the papers. If they were late, they might risk losing the house his mate had fallen in love with.

The house Karros has fallen in love with, his bear reminded him. I think if this was Elise's decision, she would have taken the apartment with the ocean view.

Possibly. But it's good that she is willing to compromise for her brother. Caleb parked the truck in front of the hotel.

"I didn't expect to be back here today," she admitted. "Maybe I should avoid the kitchen in case Ivan has changed his mind about me working here."

"He won't," Caleb assured her. This chance to work with Ivan meant so much to her.

"I don't want to mess up before I have the chance to

show him I'm worthy of the chance." She opened the door and slid out of the truck as Karros parked his car next to the truck.

"Ivan has agreed to the job, he doesn't change his mind on a whim." Caleb strode around the back of the hotel. "This way, we need to hurry."

"Coming." Elise and Karros jogged to catch up with him.

When he reached the door leading to Valerie's apartment, he knocked before opening the door and stepping inside. "Mom!"

"Caleb, how did it go with..." Valerie came out of the living room and stopped dead. "Sorry, I didn't know you brought company. Shall I put a fresh pot of coffee on?"

"No, we don't have time...but thank you." Caleb went to his mom. "This is Elise and her brother, Karros."

"Hello." Elise waved and smiled brightly while Karros nodded.

"What do you need?" Valerie looked at her son with concern.

"It's okay, there's nothing wrong." He kissed her cheek. "Elise and Karros are going to move into Wilf's house. The one he's just finished."

"Oh, the one you and Aiden worked on. Ivan brought me to see you for a visit just before I had my operation." She placed her hand on her knee.

"That's the one." Caleb nodded. "They're moving in today and they don't have any furniture."

"Oh, furniture, that I can help you with," Valerie clapped her hands together. "I'll grab the key to the garage. We also have linens if you need them."

"We don't want to put you to any trouble," Elise said quickly.

"It's no trouble and even if it were, you're family now." Valerie's cheeks flushed with happiness. "Caleb, go show

Elise and Karros what furniture there is while I round up a couple of your brothers to help."

"Thanks, Mom. I wondered if Logan was around with his truck." Caleb took the key Valerie handed to him and headed back out of the apartment.

"He's at the candy store. But I'm sure he can spare you some time. I'd call Aiden but he and Flora have taken off to Logan's cabin. They're going to stay there for a few days. Get to know each other a little." Valerie puffed out her cheeks and followed Caleb out of the apartment. "It sure has been a crazy few days."

"Tell me about it," Caleb agreed.

"A good strong man like you can take it." Valerie patted her son on his back. "Life has changed for good now that you have a mate."

"I am not complaining." Caleb grinned and headed for the garage filled with furniture, with Elise and Karros following.

"You sometimes sound as if you're complaining," Karros accused.

Elise chuckled. "Ignore my brother, he's trying to wind you up. Which isn't fair when you've been so helpful."

"It's okay, I have enough brothers to know when someone is trying to poke me with a stick." He swung his head around and looked over his shoulder at Karros. "I'll get my revenge."

"Oh, so you're challenging me?" Karros's eyes sparkled with humor.

"Oh, no, not a challenge. My revenge will come swift and when you least expect it." They reached the garage and he leaned down, inserted the key into the lock, and then pulled the doors open.

"Oh my goodness. It's like a furniture treasure trove." Elise put her hands on her hips. "I don't know where to start."

"There's a table here. This would go in the dining room.

And we need to get it out of the way so that we can get a good look at the rest of the furniture." He nodded to Karros. "Lend me a hand."

"I can do it!" Elise dashed forward and grasped the edge of the tabletop. "Equals. Remember?"

"I do." Caleb lifted the table and Elise did the same, her fingers curled around the wood as they shuffled it out of the garage to reveal six chairs and a couple of beds leaning against the wall of the garage.

As they placed the table carefully down on the ground, Caleb's head filled with plenty of ideas of what he and Elise could do with those beds.

9

ELISE

"Are you sure this isn't too much?" Elise asked for the tenth time as she surveyed the pile of furniture outside the garage.

"No, it's good to see it being used. We have no need for it in the hotel." Valerie ran her hand over a sideboard. "This used to be in my living room before we chopped it in half for the restaurant expansion."

"You're making me feel guilty." Ivan had come out to help load the furniture onto the back of Caleb's truck. He'd been friendly enough to Elise, as if he'd accepted her as his brother's mate, but he made no mention of her working in the kitchen with him.

She suspected Ivan could compartmentalize his work life and private life. It would make sense since he worked with his family. If there was trouble in the kitchen or restaurant and he fell out with his brothers or Valerie, it would be tough if those arguments continued outside of work.

Elise studied Caleb's family for a long moment. Valerie was loved and respected by all her sons, it was obvious by the way they spoke to her. Perhaps Valerie had taught them how to keep things separate, raising six boys would be hard if they were constantly fighting.

"Are you daydreaming?" A small child looked up at her.

"Where did you come from?" Elise looked around.

"I came with Logan. We're here to help move furniture." He squinted at her. "You're a fairy, like Flora, aren't you?"

A small smile hovered on her lips. "Yes, I am."

"I like Flora, even though she doesn't have a wand. She's going to take me into the wildwood and teach me all about the plants and animals there. Then we're going to make some new candies for the store." He twisted his lips as he surveyed her. "You're Caleb's mate?"

"I am."

"Do you want to help me make candies, too?" Milo had the cutest smile as he looked up at her hopefully.

"I'd really like that."

"I would, too." He paused for a moment. "You're going to be my aunt, too, aren't you?" The same hope shone in his eyes. "I like having lots of aunts."

"I suppose one day I will be your aunt, but I've only just met Caleb," she explained.

"My mom didn't know Logan very long and they got married really quick." He leaned closer and whispered, "They're having a baby. I'm going to have a brother or sister."

"That's my brother over there. He's also my best friend." She pointed to Karros. "So, I think you're very lucky that your mom is having a baby."

"Logan is my dad." Milo pointed to the man who was approaching. "He's a white wolf."

"Wow, that's not something you see very often."

"He's the best." Milo left her side and ran over to Logan, flinging his arms around the man's neck as he leaned down and scooped him into his arms.

A lump caught in her throat as she watched the boy with

his new father. There, right in front of her, was all the proof she needed that shifters were loyal and loving. Logan's expression and the adoration mirrored back at him from Milo was enough to melt even the hardest fae heart.

Not that Elise's heart was hard. It was soft and gooey and open to love.

"Okay, we've got the first load of furniture on my truck." Caleb came over to her and checked the time on his watch. "We should get going or we might be late for Wilf."

"Okay." She nodded. "I can't thank your family enough."

"They like helping. And my mom likes seeing the furniture go to a good home. She hates parting with stuff. Particularly pieces of furniture that have sentimental value."

"I'll take good care of it all," Elise assured him.

"I know you will." He slipped his hand into hers. "Come on, Karros is going to follow us back to the house. He's managed to cram a couple of lamps and some other smaller items into his car."

She closed her fingers around his and held on to him. Like a couple of teenagers, they ran toward the truck and got inside. Laughter bubbled up inside of her along with a sense of freedom as if she were the master of her own destiny.

Although, she wasn't. The man sitting next to her who called her mate had been chosen for her by some mystical power. Fate.

"This is all too good to be true." Elise watched through the window as they drove through the new town that was her home.

"No, it's not. It is true," Caleb assured her.

"I guess I'm just not that good at believing that things just fall into place. I've been struggling for so long to get to where I want to be that it's hard to believe it's true." She clasped her hands together in her lap. "I keep thinking something is going to come along and upset this perfect life that's unfolding before me."

"Why not just accept each day, each moment, for what it is?" Caleb asked. "You don't have to worry about tomorrow. Enjoy this moment with the smell of the ocean and the sound of the gulls, and the rattle of your furniture in the back of the truck. That's what's real, what's tangible."

"I've never lived in the moment. I've always worried about the future. Whether it was looking for the perfect man or trying to find the next stepping stone in my career." She tapped the side of her head. "I live in here. Not out there." She waved her hand at the view.

"Well, for now, for today, live in the now." He grinned at her.

"Okay." She closed her eyes for a moment. "I can smell the ocean." She stuck her tongue out. "I can taste the salt on my tongue."

"Go on."

"I feel the warmth of the sun on my face." She cupped her cheek in her palm. "And I can sense you beside me."

"Right where I'll always be."

"Are you thinking about the future instead of living in the now?" she accused.

"You got me." Caleb steered the truck onto the trail that led to the house. Her house, her home.

At least until she and Caleb figured out what they were going to do. Milo's words came back to her. She would marry Caleb. She was ready to accept that.

Live in the now, she reminded herself as her head filled with a hundred and one questions that needed answering. Her future was fluid, she couldn't know the answers to those questions now. Not yet, so she let them go.

"Wilf should be here anytime now." Caleb backed the truck up to the house and switched off the engine.

"It would be presumptuous to unload the furniture before we sign the lease, wouldn't it?" She itched to pull down the tailgate of the truck and carry the furniture into the house.

"It would." He nodded as Karros parked his car next to the truck.

"Now I'm nervous he isn't going to come, and we won't be able to move in." She chewed the inside of her cheek. "Or what if he's had a better offer and has decided to lease the house to someone else? He was worried about us being fae."

She clamped her mouth shut and looked at him sheepishly, but he just grinned, opened the truck door, and got out. Elise inhaled deeply and then climbed out of the truck. A light breeze ruffled her hair, it carried a sweet scent of pine resin and her eyes were drawn to the mountains in the distance.

"Here he is." Caleb turned around and watched as a new car drove toward the house. The guy behind the wheel was in his late sixties, with a warm smile and eyes that assessed people on the spot.

It seemed they'd passed his test since he got out of the car and stretched before he leaned down and grabbed a briefcase from the front seat. "Hi there."

"Wilf, this is Elise and Karros."

He held out his hand. "It's good to meet you." He glanced at Caleb. "I can see why you were willing to vouch for them. Mates." He chuckled.

"Mates," Caleb repeated.

Elise sniffed the air, the guy was a shifter, she was certain of it. The more time she spent around shifters, the easier it was to tell one at first sight. Or first sniff.

"I'm a wolf, in case you were wondering." Wilf ducked his head at Elise. "I can shift if you want."

"No, it's okay." She held up her hands. "Everything in Wishing Mon Bay is new to me. I didn't mean to stare."

"You weren't staring." He pointed to his nose. "It was more a flaring of the nostrils."

"Oh." She covered her nose with her hand, but Wilf just laughed.

"I'm not offended. It takes more than flared nostrils to offend me." He nodded toward the house. "Right, let's get on with this. I only have half an hour to spare, I have a date tonight."

"A date?" Karros asked then clamped his mouth shut. "Not that there's anything wrong with dating."

"You're never too old to date." Wilf chuckled as he took a keyring out of his pocket and opened the front door leading into the small hallway. "Here's a set of keys. Caleb showed you where the spare key is hidden."

"He did," Elise answered since Karros had gone unusually quiet.

"Do you have any questions before we get the paperwork signed?" Wilf went to the kitchen and put his briefcase down on the counter.

"Karros?" Elise urged. "The yard work?"

"Oh, yes. I'd like to do the yard work if that's all right with you. It's a passion of mine that I've never had time for. But until I find a job here, time is the one thing I am not going to be short of." Karros ran his hand through his hair. "That doesn't mean we're going to be short of money."

"As long as you don't expect me to cut the rent and you run all your plans past me first, then you can do the landscaping." Wilf nodded as he assessed, or reassessed, Karros. "I might like having fae as tenants."

"Shall we sign the lease?" Elise asked eagerly.

"Sure." Wilf opened the briefcase and took out the forms.

"We want to get the furniture moved in before dark so Elise and Karros can enjoy their first night here," Caleb explained.

"Ah, I saw the furniture piled into the truck." Wilf set the contracts down on the countertop. "Did you bring all that from the fae realm?"

"No, Valerie was kind enough to let us have it." Elise accepted a contract from Wilf and scanned it.

"How is your mom?" Wilf leaned back against the counter.

"She's good, her operation was a success and she's slowly gaining her strength." Caleb looked up at the sound of a truck approaching. "That'll be Logan with the rest of the furniture."

"You've landed on your feet," Wilf told Elise and Karros. "You're part of a good family." His eyes narrowed again. "What does your family think of you moving here?"

"They're okay with it," Elise said quickly and signed the lease before handing the pen and paper to Karros. "I am working at the restaurant, it's always been my dream."

"I don't expect it's your fae folks' dream." Wilf tilted his head to one side. "I would think they'd prefer it if you two were settled down and married in your own world. Or do you have brothers and sisters?"

"No, no other brothers and sisters." Elise shuffled her feet uncomfortably, Wilf was reminding them of all the reasons why they shouldn't be here when Caleb reminded her of all the reasons they should.

"Well, it's none of my business." Wilf watched while Caleb signed the lease, too. "Just pay the rent, keep the place clean and tidy and let me know what you plan to do with the yard, and we'll get along just fine."

Wilf checked his watch and quickly countersigned the lease before handing a copy to Caleb.

"Thanks, have a good date." Caleb winked at Elise and escorted Wilf out of the house.

"It's ours," she hissed to Karros, unsure if Wilf and his shifter hearing could hear her.

"It is." Karros slipped his arm around her shoulders. "Although, I don't know how long you'll be living here before that mate of yours tempts you away."

"Hey." She dug him in the ribs. "I'm not leaving."

"And I am not living with the two of you here," Karros replied firmly.

Elise cupped her face in her hands as heat flared across her cheeks. "I'm not thinking about the future. I want to enjoy us moving in here together."

"You're right. We'll figure everything out as we go." He hooked his thumbs into his belt. "After losing Flora, I have decided it's less heartache and worry if you just take things as they come."

"Says the man who's been planning his wedding to Flora for how many years now?" She arched an eyebrow and instantly regretted it. "I didn't mean to be so flippant. I know how cut up you are about the whole thing."

"Do you know what's worse?" Karros asked.

"No."

"This afternoon, spending time with Caleb's family, I realized Flora is much better off being part of that family than ours. They're kind, supportive, and loyal to each other. And Valerie... She just wants the best for them all."

"Our parents want the best for us. It's just unfortunate they've never really listened to us enough to know what we want." She leaned her head on his shoulder. "Maybe one day they'll see."

"Will they?" Karros asked. "The longer we stay in Wishing Moon Bay, the less I feel inclined to go back home. Not to live. Not with the pressure on us to marry well."

"Maybe one day you'll feel different." She took hold of his hand and pulled him toward the front door. "You have only been in this town for less than a day. I'm sure you'll get homesick once the excitement has worn off. This is all shiny and new, remember."

But as she watched Caleb lifting a chair down from the truck, her heart rate quickened, and she knew she'd never grow tired of the town and her mate.

If only there was a way to make their parents see that all that really mattered was that their children were happy.

Perhaps things might change once they had their first grandchild.

Elise froze on the spot. She wanted a career, not children. But Caleb would make a wonderful father.

Was she selfish to want everything? Was it possible that in Wishing Moon Bay she could find love and have a family and a career?

Or would she have to make sacrifices?

10

CALEB

"That's all the furniture unloaded." He brushed his hands down his thighs and straightened up. He'd gone back to the hotel for one more truckload after they had signed the lease. Valerie had sorted out a stack of linens for Elise and Karros, and Ivan had given him some kitchen utensils to pass on to Elise as a moving-in gift.

The house was starting to look like a home.

It's a pity it's not our home, his bear complained.

Caleb agreed. He sorely wished he was moving in here with Elise instead of Karros.

But at least they are settled and happy, his bear sighed.

Caleb smiled as he watched Elise's face, her eyes bright with excitement as she held onto the corners of a sheet and flapped it in the air. "I'll help."

He caught the other corners of the sheet and helped her smooth it over the bed. If only this was their bed. He shook his head, those kinds of thoughts weren't helpful when there was so much to do.

"Thanks." She smoothed the sheet down and tucked it

under the mattress. "Your family has been amazing." She held up her hand. "I know, I know, they're my family too now."

"You're finally getting the idea," Caleb replied. "But I'm hoping I get the chance to meet your parents and the rest of your family and win them around."

"I'd like you to meet them. And I'm sure they'll come around to the idea of me being with a shifter. Sooner or later. Maybe if we give them a grandchild, they'll get over it sooner." She put her hands to her cheeks and stared at him, her mouth open. "That just slipped out."

Caleb chuckled. "There's nothing to be embarrassed about. You know I want children. But they take a while to arrive, even if we did start practicing now." His eyes rested on the newly made bed. "And," he continued, "I'd rather not wait nine months to meet them."

"Can we just get to know each other first? With no pressure." She smoothed her hand over the bed and then headed for the door. "Are you going to help me make Karros's bed, too?"

"I guess, although he's old enough to make it himself." Caleb followed her out of the room.

"He's unpacking everything we brought with us from home." Her eyes lingered on the staircase as they walked past. "It's not a lot."

"Well, we could make a trip back to your world to pick up the rest of your stuff. I could drive my truck, and while we are there, I could say hello to your family." He couldn't help it. Even though Elise wanted to put off introducing him to her family, he didn't.

Elise is unhappy about her family situation, his bear said.

I know. I thought that if they met us, though, if I could win them over, it would be one less thing on her mind. Caleb's only desire was to help his mate.

Give Elise some time and space. We could also talk to Karros about it. He might be able to give us some more insight into our mate. His bear liked Karros and Caleb had to admit, for a fae, he was okay.

"Let me think about it." Elise handed him a sheet. "What happened to focus on the present and don't dwell on the future?"

"Ah, but this is a future we could change. If you agreed, we could go meet them in the next couple of days." Caleb threw the sheet toward her while hanging onto the corners.

"I need to focus on Ivan." She spread the sheet over the bed.

"Under normal circumstances, I'd be concerned that you want to focus on one of my brothers. But since it's Ivan, I'll let it go." He tucked the sheet under the mattress. "Honestly, he's a good guy. He loves his cooking pans a little too much. But aside from that, he's always patient and courteous with those he works with."

"So, avoid touching his pans?" She blew a strand of hair out of her face as she grabbed the bedspread and threw it over the bed. "Could you grab those pillows, please?"

"Yes. Don't touch his pots and pans. You'll know which ones I mean since he guards them like a dragon guards his treasure." Caleb's eyes opened wide. "So that's why he's so attached to them. He doesn't have any real dragon treasure and so he has to make do with his pots and pans."

"He doesn't have any treasure?" Elise plumped up the pillow he passed her and placed it down on the bed.

"Should he have?" Caleb asked. "As far as I'm aware, he never had any treasure when he came to live with Valerie. And he's over forty, so it's not as if he's waiting to come of age, is it?"

"Most dragons have treasure. All the ones I've heard of anyway." She rolled her eyes. "My father knows all about dragons. Partly because the fae are notoriously afraid of them and also because he'd love to find some treasure. It would solve all of our issues."

"Wait, back up a little. Your people are afraid of dragons?"

This is news, his bear sat up on his haunches and listened intently.

"Yes." She wagged her finger at Caleb. "Although you never heard it from me."

"I always thought they just didn't like them. In the same way they don't like any shifters." Caleb handed over the second pillow to Elise, unaware he'd been screwing the corners up in his hands.

"Okay." She plopped down on the bed and patted the mattress next to her. "Since we're mates, and you're going to promise not to repeat this to anyone..." She opened her eyes wide and inclined her head toward him. "Aren't you?"

"Oh." He nodded. "I promise. Although, I usually tell Aiden everything."

"This is between you and me." She pointed at him and then at herself.

"Okay." It felt weird promising to keep a secret to himself and not tell Aiden. But he wanted to know the fae secret since it concerned Ivan.

And possibly Ivan's treasure, his bear reminded him.

"So, my people dislike shifters because they are a little jealous of them." She held up her thumb and forefinger.

"Jealous?"

"You are part man, part bear. Two halves of a whole." She threaded her fingers together and made a fist. "The fae feel their connections to the land, to the forest, and all that dwell there. It's why the wildwood is so sacred to us."

"I get that. Flora was always going on about how the wildwood was her most favorite place in the world."

"In any world." Elise put her hands on her knees and inhaled deeply. "Fae see themselves as having that connection and yet it is the shifters who have a real connection to..." She held out her hands. "Everything."

"I don't understand," Caleb said. "You have magic."

"We do. We have learned to tap into magic and to forage in the wildwood for fruits and plants that amplify that magic. But shifters... You have enhanced senses. You have a deep magic that dwells within you. A way to connect with a primal place where another part of you lives."

"I never thought of it like that." Caleb put his hand on his stomach, as if he could feel his bear as a part of him. "I didn't know that's what the fae thought."

"Most of them don't." Her lips twitched at his confusion. "Not anymore. My Grandma Hannah told me all this. She said that the prejudice is so old that most fae don't even remember why they don't like shifters. In place of the real reasons, they've made up new excuses."

"They think we're beneath you because we shift into an animal. But really they are jealous that we have the ability." Caleb's brows furrowed together. "That's crazy."

"I know. The other crazy thing is that shifters seem to sense this mix-up in the fae which is why they distrust them." She tilted her head to one side as his eyes widened.

"That's messed up but probably true." He flopped down on the bed and stared up at the ceiling. "I would like to meet your grandma."

"Okay." Elise lay down next to him.

Caleb shifted his weight and leaned on his elbow to stare down at her. "You mean I can actually meet her?"

"Yes. If you want to meet my family, let's start with my Grandma Hannah. She lives on the edge of the wildwood. In a little cabin. Most people call her a witch since she has mastered more magic than most other fae ever do."

"When?" Caleb asked.

"Soon." She lowered herself up to a sitting position. "As soon as we have the house straight and I'm settled at work."

"What else do we need to do with the house?" Caleb asked.

"You are eager." She left the bedroom and went downstairs. "Karros."

"In here." Karros seemed filled with sorrow as she entered the living room where he was going through family photographs.

"Are you okay?" She sat down next to him on the sofa that had once belonged to Valerie. It was faded but clean and still comfortable.

Caleb touched his fingertips to the fabric. He and his brothers used to sit on the sofa and watch TV on the few days when they couldn't go outside and play. Usually when it rained, and Valerie banned them from going outside and getting wet. She hadn't wanted them to catch a chill and come home dripping like a pack of wet dogs.

"I'm fine." He ran his fingers over a photograph. "Do you remember this?"

"It's you and me and Mom and Dad. It's the first time Dad took us hunting in the wildwood. He gave us each a bow and quiver of arrows." She passed the photograph to Caleb.

He took it and stared at the happy faces of the two children in the picture before he studied the proud expression of their father, who stood with his arm around their mother. It was the perfect family photograph.

"You look so happy."

"It was before my father..." Karros didn't continue but Caleb glanced at Elise for an explanation.

"It was before our father invested in a friend's company that lost all of its money. That's when our fortunes changed, and he became obsessed with Karros and me marrying into money." She wiped a tear from her cheek. "Have we let him down?"

"No." Karros slipped his arm around her shoulders. "You have a mate and that proves you were right to come here. As for me... I've been sitting here staring at that photo and the one thing I realized was that fate sent me a message when Flora met Aiden. That wasn't my path."

"What is your path?" Elise asked.

"I have no idea." He gave a hollow laugh. "But I'm hoping I'll know it when I see it, just like you knew Caleb was your mate when you saw him."

"I think you'll do all right, Karros." Caleb handed the photograph back to him. "I'm glad you're a part of my family now. And if you need any help with the yard, just give me a shout. I'll help all I can."

"Thanks." Karros stood up and crossed the room, placing the photograph down on the sideboard they had positioned along the wall in the living room. "I might take you up on your offer. I have no idea where to buy plants from, let alone all the tools I'll need."

"Aiden and I probably have the tools you need. Tomorrow, while Elise is at the hotel, you could come and take a look. We have a small warehouse on the edge of town where we keep our tools. You're welcome to use anything as long as we don't need it." He stood up. "I should get going and let you two get settled. I have an early start tomorrow, but I'll try to pop by the hotel and check up on you, Elise."

"Don't worry if you're busy. I'll be fine. And I don't want Ivan to feel pressure from you being there. I can look after myself." Elise got up and followed him to the front door.

"Call me if you need me." He opened the door and stepped outside. Elise followed, walking him to his truck.

"What an incredible night." She stared up at the huge moon that hung over the bay.

"A wishing moon." He looked down at her, the moon reflected in her eyes as she stared at it. "Perhaps tomorrow we could go make a wish."

She switched her attention to him and stood on tiptoes as she leaned forward and pressed her lips against his. "I already have."

Before he could answer, she spun around and ran lightly back to the house. With one last look at him, she waved then closed the door, leaving him moonstruck.

11

ELISE

"Are you sure you don't mind me taking the car?" Elise gulped down the cup of coffee Karros had poured her and bit into the piece of toast he'd insisted she ate before she left for the hotel.

"I'm sure. I have plenty to do around here until you get back later." He came closer, leaning against the counter next to her. "You're doing it, Elise. You're going out there and making your dreams come true."

"I wish it didn't feel so horrible." She placed her hand on her stomach as it gurgled loudly. "I'm going to put people off their breakfast."

"You'll be fine once you get into it. It's always nerve-racking when you start something new." He sighed and folded his arms across his body. "Or end something old."

"You mean your love for Flora?" She took another bite of toast and ignored her stomach as it rolled over.

"I don't think my love for Flora has ended. Only my hope that we'll one day be together." His mouth turned down at the corners. "I lay awake last night going over it all. I couldn't sleep thinking of how she's better off with Aiden. He'll make her happier than I ever could because they are meant to be together."

"And you're going to be okay with that?"

"Yes." He shrugged. "I have no choice, do I?"

"No, I don't suppose you do. A mate is for life. Barring some kind of tragic accident, and I know you wouldn't ever wish that on anyone, Flora is going to marry Aiden and raise a family with him." She forced the last of the toast into her mouth, and then washed it down with the remains of her coffee. "And now you've realized that you're ready to move on and find the love of your life."

She jabbed her finger into his shoulder as she placed her cup on the counter. It was time to leave. She didn't want to be late for her first shift at the hotel and even though the journey to town was straightforward, last night she'd dreamt she'd gotten lost on the way and ended up back in the fae realm.

"Maybe. But I've decided to take a leaf out of your book."

"You have?" Elise asked suspiciously as she gathered up her purse and the keys to her brother's car.

"Yes. I need to figure out what I'm going to do with my life. Your passion is cooking, mine is yardwork. So, I'm thinking, once I have finished the yard here, I'm going to start a business."

"Wow." She blew out a long breath. "Here in Wishing Moon Bay?"

"Yeah." He nodded slowly. "If this is where you are and hopefully, my nieces and nephews are, then this is where I want to be."

"No pressure on me to have kids then?" She smoothed her hands over her hair which she'd pulled back in a tight ponytail.

"You have a mate, you have always wanted children, unless there's some reason you can't have children, why would you deny yourself?" Karros paused. "And deny Caleb."

"I am not getting into this right now." Elise headed for the door. "I need to focus on my job."

"I'm sorry." Karros followed her to the door. "I shouldn't have brought it up this morning. I just want you to be happy."

"I know." She turned around to face him, her eyes misted with tears. "And I want the same for you."

"We're quite the dysfunctional pair, aren't we?" He brushed a stray strand of hair back from her face. "Good luck."

"Have a good morning, Karros. I'll see you later." She backed away from him before swinging around and hurrying to the car.

As she drove to town, she focused on letting go of all the tension in her body. She could do this, she had the experience and the expertise. Sure, she might make mistakes, but nothing too serious. It was breakfast.

"Only breakfast."

Wishing Moon Bay was quiet as she drove along the beachfront and then turned toward the hotel. She could have taken a quicker route and avoided the ocean front but the view of the early morning rays sparkling off the waves as the sun rose above the mountains was worth it.

She loved the fae realm, but this town was just as beautiful in so many ways.

Perhaps her love for the town was enhanced by her feelings for a certain bear shifter. Caleb had touched her life and her heart. Even though they'd only met yesterday, she hated the idea of losing him, of him not being a part of her life.

Parking the car outside the hotel, she checked her reflection in the rearview mirror and smoothed her hair back over her head before pulling her ponytail tighter. Time to go inside.

She opened the car door and got out, breathing in the cold morning air as she turned her face to the sun. Its weak rays held the promise of a beautiful day. By the time the breakfast shift was over, the air would be warm and the light bright.

Elise loved this time of day when there was so much promise in the air.

She leaned into the car and grabbed her purse before heading around the side of the hotel to the door leading into the kitchen. Or maybe she was expected to go through the reception area. Straightening her back, she kept her composure, her ponytail swinging as she reached the kitchen door, which stood open.

"Ah, you're here." Ivan was mixing a big bowl of batter. "I wondered if you might have changed your mind."

"Why would I?" Elise asked.

"I thought you might have had second thoughts about working with a dragon shifter." His eyes glinted as he went back to stirring the batter.

"I'm here to prove that dragon shifters and fae can get along." She looked around. "Is there somewhere I can put my purse?"

"Sure, if you go through that door there, there are a bunch of lockers. Pick one and put your stuff in there." He watched her as she obeyed his instructions, while also whisking the batter smooth.

Elise put her belongings in a locker and closed the door. Before she went back into the kitchen, she washed her hands thoroughly. Good hygiene was as important as good food, one of her cooking teachers had told her.

"I'm ready. What do you want me to do?" Elise noted there were a couple of servers who were drifting in and out of the kitchen through the door that connected to the dining area of the restaurant. They were busy preparing the tables for breakfast, placing pitchers of orange juice on a long buffet table, along with butter and various jams and honey.

They were also taking a good deal of notice of Elise.

"Can you make a fresh pot of coffee?" Ivan asked.

"Coffee?" She nodded as she spotted the coffee pot on the counter. "Sure."

Coffee wasn't exactly what she'd expected to make on her first day. However, one of the other rules she'd learned was that if you wanted to make a good impression, you did as the chef told you. No arguments.

Chefs could be temperamental at times, their kitchen was their domain.

A dragon's domain. At least it beat being in a dragon's lair.

"Coffee." She held up the refilled coffee pot. "Do you want a cup?"

"Yes, please." Ivan put a ladle into the batter mixture and lifted it, letting the liquid pour off with a grunt of satisfaction. "Can you cook the pancakes?"

"Sure." She handed him a cup of coffee, which he sniffed before taking a sip.

"This is good." Ivan eyed her over the rim of the cup. "You know I only hired you because of Caleb."

She nodded. "I do. That doesn't mean I'm not going to work really hard. I'll prove to you I'm worthy."

"You'd better. This is my kitchen and I have a reputation I treasure." Ivan was deadly serious.

"I understand that. It's the reason I wanted to come and work here with you. Even in the fae realm, your skills are admired. And my people are not good at admiring anyone outside of the realm."

"Especially not a dragon shifter." He arched an eyebrow.

"Here's the thing, I don't think they know you're a dragon shifter. I didn't until yesterday." Elise set her coffee cup down on the counter. "But even if I did, I don't share their views on dragon shifters."

"What view is that?" Ivan asked coolly.

Damn it, had she fallen into a trap? Was there any right way to answer this without upsetting her new boss?

"Why don't I get started on those pancakes?" She went to the stove and heated the griddle.

"You avoided the question." Ivan carried the bowl of batter over and placed it down next to her.

"I believe that it's better to avoid a question if it also avoids disruption at work. We have guests to feed." She half-turned to meet his eye.

Ivan held her gaze for a long moment, but she didn't flinch or look away. "I think we're going to get along just fine, Elise."

She let out a long breath. "I really hope so, chef. It really does mean a lot to me that I've been given this chance."

"I believe you." His eyes glinted as he watched her ladle just the right amount of batter onto the griddle. "Although, I would like to know more about what your people think about dragon shifters."

"Outside of work hours." She pressed her lips together. "I'll happily tell you everything I know about your people."

"My people." Ivan sucked in a long breath.

"I mean... I know that Valerie's adopted you and that she's your mom." Her cheeks turned pink and not just from the heat of the sizzling pancakes. "But the dragons that live across the water are your people the same as the fae are my people even though I don't live there."

"I suppose I've never really thought about it like that." He stared down at the stove as she flipped a pancake.

"I hope I haven't upset you." Great, she'd sidestepped one conversational landmine only to jump into another one with both feet.

"No." He frowned. "I've never really been interested in the dragons on dragon isle. My life is here. My family is here. But they are part of me, and I'd like to know more about them and their interaction with the world."

"You should talk to my grandmother. She lives on the edge of the wildwood and she knows everything." Elise chuckled. "Nothing passes her by. She talks to everyone she meets and then stores little snippets of information in her head that she adds to other pieces of information she learns from books."

"I'd like to meet her. But if she lives on the edge of the wildwood, unless she visits Wishing Moon Bay, it's impossible." Ivan backed away from Elise.

"You could visit her." She put the cooked pancake on a plate, adjusted the temperature of the griddle, and then began batch cooking the pancakes.

"I can't risk it. If your people found out I was there..."

"I can help you. There are ways of disguising a person's true identity that most fae would never see through." She smiled a secret smile. "My grandma is a wise woman and she's taught me a thing or two. Or three."

"Don't let the pancakes burn," Ivan warned as he turned away, leaving her unsure if she'd offended him.

As the kitchen got busy, she forgot about their conversation as she focused on keeping up with the cooking of pancakes, which Ivan mixed the batter for. She was also expected to scramble the eggs and watch the bacon.

Not exactly a test for her culinary skills, but certainly for her time management and ability to multitask.

At the end of breakfast, her cheeks were flaming hot, and her stomach grumbled with the need for food.

"Someone has been working hard." Caleb stood in the doorway as Elise washed up the pots and pans. Not Ivan's special pans, they were stacked on the counter and she had strict instructions not to wash them.

"It's been busy. I don't think I've ever worked in such a busy kitchen." She rubbed her forehead with her elbow.

"It's not just guests who come in for breakfast," Ivan told her as he entered the kitchen from the restaurant. "Plenty of people from town come here."

"Ivan's food is addictive." He made a sprinkling action with his thumb and fingers. "He puts something irresistible into each of his dishes."

Ivan wagged his finger at his brother. "Don't go giving anyone ideas. That's the kind of rumor that spreads."

"I was joking, everyone knows the only added ingredient that goes into your food is love and care. And dragon breath." Caleb winked at Elise who smothered a smile.

"You're so funny." Ivan went to the counter and indicated a picnic basket. "I suppose that means you don't want this."

Caleb inhaled deeply, his eyes widening as he crossed the kitchen. "What is that? It smells delicious."

"If you can guess, you can have it. I thought you and Elise might like to go have breakfast on the beach since it's a nice day."

"How did you even know I'd be coming?" Caleb asked.

"Are you joking? You have come to check up on me." Ivan placed his hand on the basket handle. "Just to make sure that I haven't made your mate cry."

"He does do that," Caleb told Elise.

"Not to me. At least not today." She finished washing the pans and dried her hands on a towel. "Are you going to guess?"

"Oh. Right." He inched closer to the basket and leaned down, inhaling deeply. "Pancakes with maple syrup. And eggs. Some fruit. And bacon."

"Not exactly difficult." Ivan lifted the basket and handed it to his brother. "Go. Enjoy your breakfast."

"Thanks, Ivan." Caleb swung the basket in his hand. "Are you ready to leave? I have about half an hour before I have to get back to work. Aiden has gone to pick up some lumber."

"I have Karros's car. Shall I meet you at the beach?" She hurried to the locker room and grabbed her purse.

"Sure. We can go in separate cars." Caleb sounded a little disappointed.

"He wants to sit close to you," Ivan teased and pretended to shuffle closer to Caleb and make kissing sounds.

"Forgive my immature brother." Caleb shook his head but grinned as he went to the back door with the basket in his hand. "It's a good thing he makes such good food."

"Oh, that reminds me." Ivan followed them to the doorway. "I have some homework for you, Elise."

"Homework?" Her heart hammered in her chest. She always hated homework when she was at school. But this wasn't school. Ivan wasn't going to test her knowledge of algebra. "Okay."

"It's simple. I want you to cook me something." Ivan held out his hands. "Pick a favorite dish of yours, preferably one that isn't copied from a recipe book."

"Okay." She swallowed hard as her mind emptied of everything she'd ever cooked, all the recipes she'd ever experimented with, and all the flavors she'd tested.

"I just want to get an idea of what level you're working at."

"So you want me to cook something difficult?" Her stomach churned, not from hunger but nerves.

"No. Some of the best recipes are simple. It's all about the flavors." He chuckled. "You've gone pale."

"I have?" She put her hands to her cheeks which only moments ago were flaming hot from the kitchen.

"You have," Caleb whispered in her ear.

"I'm just nervous. I never was good at exams."

"This isn't an exam, it's not even a test. Just imagine you are cooking something for Caleb," Ivan advised.

"You were going to cook for me this evening," he told her.

"I suppose." She nodded and backed away.

"Come on." Caleb hooked his hand under her elbow. "You'll feel better once you've eaten something."

"No, I won't," she replied miserably. "After I've tasted Ivan's wonderful pancakes, I won't ever cook again."

"Yes. You will." Caleb patted his toned stomach. "This bear loves to eat."

"Oh, so that's your idea? You think I'm just here to cook for you!"

"Well, if you're not going to work in the restaurant, it would be a pity to put your hard work to waste. You can cook for me and our kids," he replied. "We'll appreciate you."

"Oh, no!" She waved her finger at him.

"That sounds like fighting talk." He opened the truck door and placed the picnic basket on the front passenger seat.

Her eyes narrowed as she unlocked the car. "You're teasing me."

"I'm trying to make you see that you can do this. You just need to dig deep and have confidence in yourself. The same confidence I have in you." He slammed the truck door shut and sauntered toward her.

"I do have confidence in myself," she replied. "I just...lose sight of it sometimes."

"And that's why I'm here, to remind you of it." He leaned down and brushed his lips across hers.

Elise reached out and grabbed hold of his shirt as her knees threatened to give way under her.

She blamed her need for food, but her heart told her it was her need for her mate that made her want to collapse into his strong arms.

12

CALEB

"This is the life." Caleb leaned back and tilted his face to the sun. His stomach was full, and his mate was by his side. What could be better?

"I could stay here all day." Elise leaned her head on his shoulder, her eyes closed against the glare of the sun.

"Which reminds me..." Caleb glanced at his watch. "I have to go. Aiden will be waiting for me."

"How is he?" Elise asked as she moved away from him and began packing away their breakfast picnic.

"You mean how are he and Flora?" Caleb asked.

"Yes, have they settled into Logan's cabin?" She placed everything back inside the basket. Everything that was left, which wasn't a lot.

"I think so. Aiden said they're going to invite us to dinner in the next couple of days. Once they have the place cleaned up. Logan hasn't used it for a while, and it got messed up pretty bad when a witch attacked Penny and Milo."

"A witch attacked them?" Elise's eyes went wide.

"Don't worry, that kind of thing doesn't happen around here very often," he assured her.

"Do you think I'd leave town if it did?" Elise sat back on her haunches and placed her hands on her thighs.

"You might not, but Karros would probably bundle you back in the car and drive you straight back to the fae realm." He inhaled deeply. "And if he does that, I will have to follow."

"You'd follow me?" she asked sweetly.

"To the end of the world." He leaned down and kissed her lips.

Elise grabbed hold of his arms and yanked them until he overbalanced and sat down heavily by her side. "Better." She curled her arms around him and kissed his lips.

Caleb cupped her face in his right hand, his left hand wrapped around her waist, holding her close, never wanting to let her go. As his lips moved against hers, heat stirred within him, and tendrils of desire unfurled. He wanted her, he needed to claim her.

His phone vibrated in his pocket and they both jumped as it started to ring.

"Hey, Zara." He covered the mouthpiece with his hand. "It's my sister."

"You have a sister?" Elise asked.

Caleb nodded and continued to help clear the food away while he spoke to Zara. "How are you?"

Elise closed the basket and stooped down to pick up the blanket.

"I'm good," Zara replied. "I miss you. I was thinking of coming to visit Wishing Moon Bay this weekend if that's okay."

"Sure it is."

"Are you sure?" Zara asked. "You don't sound it, is everything all right?"

"Yes." Caleb glanced at Elise. "I met my mate."

"You what?" Zara asked.

We should have told her, his bear said.

"Yesterday. I met her yesterday. I was going to call you later to tell you. Things have been hectic." He winced as he realized he'd completely forgotten he had a sister who should be kept in the loop where family stuff was concerned.

"Oh, I know you must be busy." Zara couldn't hide her disappointment, which made him feel ten times worse.

"It all happened so fast. Elise came to town with her brother, Karros..."

"Oh, the fae who was engaged to Flora?" Zara asked.

"That's the one. Karros came to ask Flora if she would help his sister, Elise, get a job with Ivan."

"Who is the chef. I think I'm getting the hang of this."

"You are. Ivan is the chef and it turned out Karros's sister is my mate."

"Oh. Wow, that's quite a coincidence. Just think, if Karros hadn't been so great over the whole arranged marriage thing, you and your mate wouldn't have met." Zara laughed, she'd forgiven Caleb for not calling.

"So, anyway, we spent all day yesterday trying to find somewhere for them to live. Then we had to sort out furniture and all that stuff," Caleb explained away.

"I'd love to meet her," Zara said.

"You will when you come visit this weekend. In fact, I have room in my apartment for you to stay."

"Where is Aiden?" Zara asked as if this was something else she hadn't been told.

"He's staying in Logan's cabin for now. We can go visit him." He glanced at his watch. "Oh, damn, I have to go. I took time off work to have breakfast with Elise. I am supposed to be back at the job by now."

"Oh, you go, I should have called this evening instead. Sorry."

"Never be sorry you called," Caleb replied frankly. "I always love hearing from you. We're family."

"I'll give you a call in a couple of days when I know when I'll be arriving. I'm thinking Friday evening, but I have a floor to lay that day and I can't leave until it's finished."

"Let me know. It's good to hear your voice. I hope Aunt Harriet and Uncle Peter are okay."

"They are. I wanted to talk to you about them actually."

"Are they okay?" Thoughts of being late back to work vanished.

"Yes, they are. They want us to all get together. Once they can figure out a date and time when all my cousins...our cousins can make it back home." She gave a short laugh. "We can talk about it on the weekend. There's someone at the door. I have to go. Congratulations, Caleb."

"I'll see you soon, Zara." Caleb ended the call and shook his head as he put his phone in his pocket.

"Is everything okay?" Elise carried the basket as they walked along the sand to the steps leading from the beach.

"I should have called her and told her that I met you." He slipped his arm around her shoulder. "We only found out we had a sister a couple of days ago. Aiden and I kind of forgot."

"You forgot you had a sister?" Elise's forehead wrinkled. "How could you forget?"

"Our parents died when we were young," he explained. "My aunt and uncle tried to care for the three of us, but they have four children of their own. Eventually, they were persuaded we would be better off in foster care. Aiden and I were taken from our foster parents. The police found us a few days later."

"I had no idea." Elise covered her mouth with her hands, her face pale.

"Whatever happened..." He shrugged. "We don't remember any of it. Which is probably a good thing."

"I'm so sorry. But you found your sister now." She placed

her hand on his upper arm, wanting to comfort him. She couldn't imagine not knowing Karros, or her parents.

"Yes, when we helped Flora find Imelda. We met someone who found our file, which led us to Zara."

"You had no idea she existed?" Elise's eyes shone bright with tears.

"None. And with everything that's happened, it's like it slipped my mind again." He took the basket from her as he walked her to her car.

"Don't be too hard on yourself." She took hold of his hand as she swung around to face him. "You've had a lot on your mind." Elise stroked his temples with her fingertips.

"When I'm around you, everything else melts away." He lowered his head and kissed her lips.

"Just like everything I ever learned left my head when Ivan asked me to cook something for him."

"I see, we're sharing an intimate moment and you are thinking of my brother." He pecked her lips. "It's a good thing I am confident in myself and our relationship."

"I'm very confident in you, too." Elise pulled his head toward her as she kissed him again. "I'm looking forward to us spending some time together this evening and I promise I'll give you my full attention."

"No, you won't." He held her in his arms. "You'll be trying to figure out how to impress Ivan. And I'm okay with that. This is important to you so it's important to me."

"Thanks." She pushed away from him. "Now, you should go, or I'll be in trouble with Aiden for keeping you too long."

"He understands." Caleb glanced at his watch. "We've both gone through so much together. It's surreal that we met our mates at almost the exact same time so we can empathize with each other."

"Sympathize with each other?" Elise asked in shock. "Because you both have fae mates."

"You know I said empathize, don't twist my words." He laughed as she backed away from him.

"Ah, I'm going to tell Flora what you said. I expect you and Aiden have been complaining all morning about how unlucky you are to have fae as mates." She giggled as he rushed toward her and picked her up in his arms, tickling her until she laughed and begged for mercy.

"I love that we can laugh together," Caleb told her.

"I love that, too." She caught her breath after laughing so hard. As their eyes locked together, something passed between them. Something unsaid. Laughing wasn't the only thing they shared a love of.

We love each other, his bear announced. We know it and she knows it but who will be brave enough to say it first?

I don't want to frighten her away, Caleb replied. She has so much on her mind right now, and I know she's worried about impressing Ivan. If I say the words now, I might freak her out.

"I'll see you later." He lifted his hand and waved at her, not taking his eyes off his mate as she got into the car and drove away.

Only when she was gone from his sight did he get in his truck with the remains of the breakfast picnic. If Aiden had been waiting around for Caleb to get back, he'd smooth things over by offering him some food.

No better way to a bear's heart, his bear chuckled.

Especially our brother's heart. He sure does like his food. Caleb drove away from the beach, resisting the temptation to follow his mate home.

The need to be around her was still incredibly strong, if he could stay by her side every minute of every day, he would.

I'm certain Ivan would have something to say about that, his bear replied.

I'm sure he'd understand. Caleb turned into the driveway of the house they were working on. The roof had leaked, and the two brothers were replacing some rotted-out lumber.

He'd understand more if he had a mate of his own. His bear wished they could find a mate for both Ivan and Rift.

"I thought you'd abandoned me." Aiden came around the side of his truck and pulled out a long length of lumber from the back of it. Hoisting it onto his shoulder, he strode back toward the house.

"Never." Caleb hopped out of the truck and went to help Aiden. "Ivan gave us some food, so I took Elise down to the beach. It was nice to have some time alone with her."

"It's been a hectic couple of days for sure." Aiden headed back to the truck after setting the lumber down next to the other items he'd gotten for the job. "How did she get along this morning with Ivan?"

"Good, I think. Ivan asked her to make something special for him to try. You know, her favorite dish, something that highlights her culinary skills." Caleb carried a beam on his shoulder as Aiden grabbed the last of the lumber from the truck.

"And she's nervous about it?" Aiden could always pick up on Caleb's thoughts.

"Yeah, she's worried she's going to screw it up." He dropped the beam on the ground. "It's tough not being able to help." He shrugged. "I know good food when I taste it, but I am not good at cooking."

"You're supposed to be there for moral support, that's all. Elise needs to do this herself." Aiden thumbed toward the truck. "You're making me hungry with all this talk of food."

"I'll go grab the basket." Caleb jogged over to the truck and opened the door. "I also got a call from Zara. She is planning to visit this weekend." He reached in for the basket and pulled it toward him. "I forgot to tell her I found my mate."

"Oh. How did she take it?" Aiden hovered over his brother's shoulder as he turned around.

"Here, help yourself." Caleb handed the basket to Aiden, who instantly opened it up and looked inside. "She was okay after I explained we had a hectic day. It's going to take some getting used to, though."

"Having a sister?" Aiden pulled out a breakfast roll stuffed with bacon and eggs.

"Yes. And an aunt and uncle. Until now the only family we've had is Valerie and our brothers. Now we have blood relatives." Caleb leaned against the truck while Aiden ate.

"They're going to take time to get used to it, too. So don't be too hard on yourself." Aiden bit into his sandwich. "I envy you."

"You do?" Caleb asked.

"Yes, you have a mate who is learning from Ivan. You won't have to go to the restaurant for a good meal, your mate will cook for you. Everyday." Aiden rolled his eyes in bliss. "This is so darn good."

"My attraction to Elise is more than food," he told his brother.

"Oh, I know. But it sure is a bonus." Aiden finished his roll and looked in the basket for more.

"You eat your way through the leftovers, and I'll get started on work. We both need to focus more on work now that we have mates." Caleb grabbed a toolbox from the back of the truck.

"That's true. No more slacking off to roam the mountains on a warm summer's day." Aiden leaned back on the hood of the truck and stared at the mountain range in the distance. "But I'm not complaining."

"Neither am I." Caleb grabbed a hammer and set to work. "Things are going to work out."

"They are." Aiden sighed in contentment. "Who would have thought two orphans could be so lucky."

Caleb recalled the photograph of his parents looking so happy with their three children. What would their lives be like if they were still alive, if they hadn't been murdered and the family split up?

We'll never know, his bear said. And maybe that's for the best. We have a wonderful future ahead of us with our mate. That's all that matters.

Yet ever since they found out their parents had been murdered, Caleb had an overwhelming need to find the person responsible and bring them to justice.

13

ELISE

"Is there anything I can do to help?" Karros hovered behind her as she stared at her recipe books, looking for inspiration.

"No. I'm doomed." She blew her hair off her face and closed the recipe book before pulling another one toward her and flipping it open.

"Why don't I get you a glass of wine?" Karros offered.

"We don't have any wine." She tilted her head back and stared at the ceiling. "This is a mistake. Caleb's going to be here anytime, and I haven't even started cooking."

"Just calm down. Caleb won't mind if you feed him chips and cookies, he's coming to see you." Karros was trying to help, but she wasn't in the mood to hear his words of comfort.

"He's a bear shifter. I'm pretty sure he's going to be disappointed if I serve him cookies and potato chips for dinner after he's been working all day." She gripped the edge of the counter and closed her eyes, trying to fight the tears that threatened. "And I can just imagine how Ivan will react if I don't take him something wonderful to eat tomorrow."

Karros turned around and stared at the front door. "I think Caleb is here." With obvious relief, he hurried to the door and opened it, letting in a rush of warm air.

The smell of the mountains soothed her, she could smell the warm pine resin carried down from the lower slopes, but then a cooler blast of air which carried the tang of the ocean countered it. She loved this house, she loved living in Wishing Moon Bay and she also loved working in Ivan's busy kitchen.

She didn't want to blow this opportunity at a new life.

"Hi." Caleb stood in the doorway, there was no sign of Karros. He'd probably taken the opportunity to go outside to get away from her. "Karros let me in." Caleb held up a bottle of wine. "He said you might need this."

"Karros is right, although wine won't solve my problems."

"He said you were struggling to come up with a recipe for Ivan." Caleb placed the bottle down on the counter. "Glasses?"

"We don't have any wine glasses, but there are some coffee mugs in that cupboard." She snapped the recipe book closed as Caleb went to the cupboard.

"We could always go get takeout."

"I said I'd cook for you. And I have to come up with a dish for Ivan." She hugged herself as he opened the bottle of wine and poured it into two glasses. "But I don't have a lot of the ingredients I need."

"Do you want to go to the store?" Caleb offered. "We could pick up some food on the way back."

"The local stores won't have what I need. I'm trying to figure out what I can add instead."

"Instead of what?" Caleb asked.

"The ingredients I need to pick from the wildwood. I usually go gather the ingredients when they're in season." She went to the kitchen window and looked out at Karros as he hunkered down and picked up a handful of dirt. Crumbling it in his palm, he let it fall back to the ground. "Perhaps I could ask Karros to make space for me to have a garden where I can grow some of the main ingredients I use. Not that it'd make any difference right now."

"Why don't we go there?" Caleb sipped his wine.

"Go where?" Elise asked. "The wildwood? We don't have time."

"We could go tomorrow. I could pick you up from work in the afternoon and we could go. From what Flora said, it's beautiful, her favorite place in all the world." He studied her for a moment. "Unless you don't want to go with me. I know your mom and dad don't know about us. But we could keep a low profile. We don't have to see or speak to anyone else."

"I do have the evening off. Ivan asked me to work the breakfast and lunch shift tomorrow." She sipped her wine. It was good wine, chilled to just the right temperature and full of flavor.

"Is that a date?" Caleb asked.

"Yes. I think it is." She couldn't hide her smile. "The wildwood always inspires me."

"Ah, but you have a mate now. I'll be your new inspiration." He struck a pose, sticking his chin in the air and showing off his profile.

"You might be right. But I can't decide what you would taste like if you were a food." She licked her lips, certain he would taste just right.

"I am sweet, but also spicy. And I would leave an everlasting taste on your tongue." He grinned. "The kind of taste you would never forget."

"I like the sound of that." She snapped her fingers. "Which gives me an idea."

"I've helped?" He came closer, looking relieved.

"You have. And you're right, we should go to the wildwood. Tomorrow. If Ivan can wait to try my cooking."

"I'm sure he will, because it'll be worth the wait." He drank the rest of his wine and inclined his head toward the door. "Come on, let's go grab something from town. My treat." He put his hand in his pocket. "I also have this for you."

"You bought me wine and a gift? You are the perfect man." She finished her wine and put the cup in the sink.

"Perfect for you." He cocked his head to one side and a sexy smile spread over his face. "And perfectly cheesy."

"I like cheesy." Elise couldn't see what he held in his hand as she moved closer to him.

"Hold out your hand." He clutched the gift in his fist and waited for Elise to hold out her palm before he opened his hand.

"It's a wishing stone?" She stared at the smooth golden stone in her hand. It was still warm from where he'd held it and she closed her hand around the stone, absorbing his warmth.

"It is. I was early. Too eager to see you tonight. Since you were cooking, I didn't want to impose. So I stopped by the beach to clear my head. And there it was, just lying on the sand as if it was waiting for me to pick it up."

"And you weren't tempted to make the wish yourself?" She could only imagine how he wished their relationship was different, how he wished she was the perfect woman for him. He would prefer a woman who was ready to settle down and have children with him right away instead of a woman who wanted to chase her career.

"If you make a wish and it comes true then that's good enough for me." He closed his hand around hers. "I just want you to be happy, Elise."

"I am happy. Despite this." She cast her hand toward the

pile of cookbooks on the counter. "I'm just anxious to get it right."

"Well, it couldn't hurt to make a wish. Although, I know you're going to impress Ivan anyway." Caleb stepped backward. "Shall we go?"

"Yes." She glanced toward the window. "Are you okay if we make a wish and then come back here with the food? Karros hasn't eaten yet either."

"No problem." He nodded toward her brother. "I like Karros. I think we're on the same wavelength where your happiness is concerned, we both want the best for you."

"He likes you, too." She grabbed her jacket from the back of the chair. "I think he was worried when we first met. It didn't help that you are the brother of the man who stole away the love of his life. But he appreciates what you've done for us."

"I want him to be part of my family, too. He's given up so much for everyone else's happiness." Caleb strode toward the door. "He's a shifter at heart."

"You should tell him that, I'm sure he'll appreciate it." She chuckled as he looked at her over his shoulder. "I'm kidding, I'd keep that to yourself. Karros would love to be a member of your family, but I don't think he's ready to let go of who he really is."

"Do you think he'll go back to his old life, or will he stay here?" Caleb asked as they stepped outside.

"It's too early for him to make that decision. But he's set on making a life here and starting a landscape business. He's always loved watching things grow and he has an eye for design. He's good at matching colors and textures."

"Like you are with food?" Caleb asked.

"Yes. I supposed so." She raised her hand and waved to her brother. "We're going into town for takeout. Shall we bring you something back?"

"Yes, please." Karros brushed the soil from his hands as he approached them.

"I'm not sure what we're getting," Caleb said. "Do you want to come, too?"

It was a kind offer since he wanted them to go to the beach and make a wish. Karros seemed to sense this and shook his head. "No, you can surprise me. I need to get used to your food and customs, so I'm going to try everything."

"Oh, brave man," Caleb joked. "I could bring you back something exotic."

"I trust my sister to rein you in." He cocked an eyebrow. "I can trust you, can't I, Elise?"

"Always." She kissed his cheek. "Go back to your dirt. We'll be back in an hour."

"Thanks." He locked eyes with Caleb and nodded. "I appreciate it."

"You're welcome." Caleb slipped his arm around Elise's shoulder and pulled her toward him. "Let's go make a wish."

She tightened her hand around the smooth stone still nestled in her palm. "See you soon, Karros."

"What do you want to eat?" Caleb asked as they got into the truck.

"I don't know. Do you have any recommendations?" Elise asked.

"Yes, we swing by the hotel and beg Ivan to give us some food." Caleb chuckled. "That's what Aiden and I would do."

"Do you miss him? Aiden, I mean." Elise buckled her seat-belt and leaned back as Caleb drove away from the house.

"I do." His simple, honest answer caused a lump in her throat.

"It must be a big change for you both."

"We've always done everything together. We're like two halves of a whole. But now we're split." He inhaled a shaky breath. "On the flip side of that, we both have mates. I'm sure it would have been a lot harder if I was simply going home alone night after night."

"Does that mean you're expecting to stay over?"

"No!" His shocked expression brought a smile to her lips.

"I was joking." She hesitated before she said, "I am here for you. We're both in the middle of a change of life. Things are upside down and it's hard to figure everything out. I know we're supposed to be together forever and I'm slowly coming around to the idea."

"You've had reservations?" His forehead creased.

"Of course. I've fought my parents my entire adult life when it comes to having the freedom to do what I want. And I finally made it, I finally went after what I really want, and then fate steps in and..." She held out her hand. "I got you. I got a shifter."

"And that's bad because shifters believe in fated mates, so it's like someone is trying to control you and make choices for you." He nodded his understanding. "I'd say I was sorry, but I'm not."

"Aren't you? Just a little bit sorry that I'm not the same as you?" she asked.

"The same, you mean a shifter?"

"Yes, surely that would make life easier. If I was a shifter, I'd be all over you, we'd already be planning where we were going to raise our ten children."

Caleb chuckled. "That is true. But it doesn't mean I wish you were different."

"Really?" She opened her palm and showed him the wishing stone. "If I gave this back to you and told you to make a wish, you wouldn't be tempted to wish for a mate who was ready to settle down and have kids right now?"

"No, Elise. I wouldn't." He parked the truck in the parking lot next to the beach. "The thing about being a shifter is that I believe in fate, which means I believe we are perfect for each other." He switched off the engine and reached for her hand holding the wishing stone. Closing her fingers over it, he said, "You are exactly what I need. I wouldn't change a thing about you."

"I needed to hear that," she admitted.

"See, we're perfectly attuned to each other." He cracked the door open. "Now, let's go make this wish."

Elise got out of the truck and hurried around to Caleb, grabbing hold of his hand she ran toward the beach giggling like a child. She certainly wouldn't have to wish for happiness, she'd already gotten that.

Thanks to Caleb.

14

CALEB

"Are you ready to go?" Caleb waited in the doorway of the hotel kitchen as Elise dried her hands. He'd gotten up early and put in a full day's work before leaving Aiden to continue work on the leaking roof.

Now they were ready to take their mate to the wildwood.

It'll be good to spend time alone with Elise, his bear said.

It will. Last night, after Elise had made her wish on the beach, they'd grabbed a pizza and driven back to the house. Even though Karros had offered to eat alone, they had ended up sitting outside discussing his plans for the yard. Not that Caleb was complaining, he'd enjoyed being in his mate's company and she seemed more relaxed when her brother was around.

That will soon change, his bear said. The more time we spend together, the easier it'll be.

His bear was right. Relationships took time to bloom and grow. Just because they were mates didn't mean it was easy to find plenty to talk about.

However, they were learning more about each other, little things like how much Elise loved mushrooms. She'd promised to forage for some today so that he could truly appreciate why she was so passionate about them.

She'd also promised to find some honey from the bees that lived in the wildwood. They gathered pollen from the plants that grew there, giving the honey a truly distinctive flavor.

His bear licked his lips, he couldn't wait to taste the honey and savor every drop.

"I just have to put those ingredients away in the fridge and then we can go." She went to the counter and gathered up the ingredients.

Caleb watched her as she scooped the containers up in her arms and carried them to the fridge. He loved the way she moved, the sway of her curvy hips, the way her bottom lip stuck out as she balanced the containers in her right arm while opening the fridge with her left.

"Caleb." Ivan entered the kitchen unnoticed. Normally Caleb would have sensed his brother, but he was too focused on his mate.

"Ivan." Caleb stood up straight and dragged his attention away from his mate. "How are you?"

"I'm good." Ivan's eyes flicked from his brother to Elise. "Not as good as you, though."

"Oh." Caleb's cheeks flushed pink, unsure of what his brother meant.

"Your trip to the wildwood, after talking to Aiden, I'm jealous."

"I told you, I can take you there." Elise closed the fridge door. "I'll gather what I need today to make a potion that will make you seem...different."

"I appreciate it," Ivan said. "But I like myself just the way I am."

"And Valerie has always wanted Ivan never to cross into your realm." Caleb locked eyes with his brother. "I don't think she would have told you not to go so emphatically if she didn't have a good reason."

Ivan nodded. "You're right. Although maybe it's time I asked her why."

Caleb nodded. "Perhaps it is time you talked with Valerie."

We're not supposed to repeat what Aiden told us about Fiona and what she did for Ivan, his bear said firmly.

We aren't telling him. But I do think he needs to know. Caleb's eyes lingered on Elise as she went to the small room where the staff lockers were. But think how we felt finding out the truth about our parents. Isn't it better to know?

That our parents were murdered? His bear shook his head. I'm not sure. The truth made me want to go out and rip someone's head off.

Caleb knew exactly whose head his bear wanted to rip off. But after talking it over with Aiden, they had decided to focus on the future rather than tracking down the person responsible for the death of their parents.

"Maybe I will." He glanced at the clock on the wall. "But not today. I need to get home, I have a few chores to do before I get back here for the evening."

"Are you sure you don't need me?" Elise asked.

Ivan opened his mouth as if he were going to say a smart retort but instead, he shook his head and said, "No, you and Caleb go have fun."

Caleb nodded his thanks to Ivan who could easily have pointed out to Elise that he had run this restaurant for years without her and he could continue to do so. "I'll talk to you tomorrow."

"Have fun, Caleb. Bring me back something tasty to eat." He aimed his comment at Elise who looked flustered for a moment before she let out a long breath and nodded.

"I will. I have something in mind, but it depends on whether I can find some. It's a little late in the season."

"Don't put too much pressure on yourself," Ivan replied. "I like what I've seen so far. Your trial is going well."

A big smile spread across Elise's face. "Thanks." She clutched her purse tightly as she hurried toward the door. "Have a good evening, Ivan."

"You, too." He winked at Caleb before he turned his back on them, sweeping the kitchen with his critical gaze to check if everything was ready for the evening. Ivan was very particular about leaving anything out of place in his kitchen.

It's a habit from when we all lived here and he first started cooking, Caleb's bear said. You do remember how you and our brothers used to come in and grab food for a midnight snack after going for a run in the mountains.

Caleb chuckled to himself. We used to raid the fridge and then Ivan would get up in the morning and find the food he'd prepared for breakfast was gone.

Exactly. His bear chuckled.

He should be grateful, Caleb answered. We helped make him into the chef he is today.

His bear guffawed. You mean because he had to get creative with his menu to make up for the fact that he never knew what ingredients he'd find missing?

Yes, we taught him everything he knows, Caleb said smugly as he followed Elise out to the parking lot.

"Karros dropped me at work, so I don't have to take the car home before we leave." Elise glanced at the sky. "We don't have a lot of time to spare. Not if we want to make the most of the daylight."

"Then let's go. I think I remember the way, although the last time I went to the fae realm, Ivan was carrying the car in his talons."

"You're joking?" Elise stopped walking, her mouth open in surprise.

"We were in a hurry." Caleb shrugged. "You can always depend on Ivan if you have a need for speed."

"I'm beginning to see he is a man of many talents." Elise glanced back toward the hotel.

"I'm a man of many talents, too," Caleb insisted, ignoring the pang of jealousy he experienced. At work this morning, he'd had a frank talk with Aiden about what it was like to have a mate.

Unreasonable jealousy seemed to be one of the major changes Aiden had experienced, even toward Caleb. The merest hint that his mate was showing someone else attention would send Aiden spiraling into a fit of jealousy if he didn't regain control quickly.

It's a primal urge, his bear said.

Aiden said he spoke to Logan about it and it soon passes. Mostly. Caleb chuckled. Unfortunately for Aiden, his primal urge might last longer since Karros is in town. The constant reminder that Flora was supposed to marry another man grated on his nerves.

Caleb's bear chuckled. At least we don't have that to contend with.

"So, what are your many talents?" Elise asked, pulling his attention back to her.

"I'm good with my hands. I'm good at repairing things. I'm an okay mechanic, for the basic stuff at least. I'm also a good woodsman." He started the engine. "I'm good at tracking and hunting. Although we rarely make a kill."

"I suspect that might get messy when you live in a town filled with shifters." Elise chuckled. "Just think if you caught a rabbit and it turned out to be a person."

"I can sense whether the creature I'm tracking is a shifter or a non-shifter," he assured her. "There have been no unfortunate shifter-on-shifter killings for as long as anyone can remember."

"Wow. That's a handy sense to have. You guys are full of surprises."

"I like to think so." Caleb drove toward the place where the town of Wishing Moon Bay linked to the fae realm. He only had to check for directions once. He remembered the route fairly well since he had driven back here from the fae realm only a couple of days ago. However, he had been tired and focused on getting home rather than the route they were taking.

"Have you only been to the fae realm once?" Elise asked as they reached the place where the two worlds intersected.

"Yes. When we were younger, we'd come here. But we'd take a more direct route. Straight across country rather than following the road."

"You used to come to the crossing but never enter the fae world?" She sounded surprised.

"Valerie really did impress on us the need to stay away. Not just for Ivan's sake. She thought your people wouldn't like six shifters charging through your lands."

"Valerie is very wise. One or two shifters are tolerated, but six, especially if one is a dragon..." She sat up straight as they approached the crossing point.

Caleb put his foot down on the gas. He had no idea why, but he always experienced the need to go faster as they approached, as if the vehicle needed more momentum to burst through from one world to the next. He always pictured the crossing point as like the surface of a bubble and by going faster, he would pop the bubble and arrive in the fae world.

But if he failed to pop the bubble then he would be stuck between worlds like a fly trapped in a spider's web.

His bear chuckled. You still believe that?

No, Caleb answered. I know it was a story Rift made up when we were kids. I know it's not true, but my foot has a mind of its own. He eased up on the gas as they reached the fae world.

"Well, that was interesting," Elise said. "I thought you were trying to run a red light or escape the police."

"You can thank my brother Rift for that. He used to say that you'd get stuck between worlds." Caleb chuckled. "Thinking about it, Rift used to make up all kinds of stories. I should warn Logan since Rift takes care of Milo a lot."

"You don't think he's grown out of it?" Elise asked.

"Rift?" Caleb shook his head. "I doubt it. He likes making up stories. He has a very vivid imagination. I think that's why he likes taking care of Milo so much, he can pretend to be a kid again."

"We don't make up stories. Not like you do in Wishing Moon Bay and certainly not like the people in the world beyond." Elise rolled down the window and rested her elbow on the door. "When we have children, we should tell them stories. Maybe not the ones about benevolent fairies with wings, but other stories."

"It'd be weird for me not to tell our children stories," Caleb confessed, glad that Elise was at least talking about them having children together.

"My Grandma Hannah had a big book of stories. Short ones, the ones you call fairy tales. Red Riding Hood and Cinderella. Do you know them?" Her eyes sparkled as she half turned to face him.

"I know them."

"She used to read them to us when we were small. Even Karros used to sit and listen." She smiled wistfully. "We used to love staying with my grandma in the wildwood."

"I've never had grandparents," Caleb confessed. "There was only ever Valerie."

"And she raised the six of you alone." Elise stared out of the window before quietly asking, "What is she?"

"What is she? You mean what is Valerie?" Caleb checked that he'd heard her right.

"Yes. She lived in Wishing Moon Bay and ran the hotel while raising six boys. Surely she must be a sorceress who kept you all under her spell so you would behave." Elise's lips twitched.

"She's...nothing. Valerie has no real magic. At least not the kind that the witches use to cast spells. And she's not a shifter." He thought for a minute. "Yet she has this way of...communicating with people. She can empathize with most people she meets."

"That is truly a gift," Elise said. "To be attuned to another person's thoughts and feelings."

"When we first went to live with her, we found it hard to trust anyone. Even when we misbehaved, she was always there for us. She explained the situation in a way we could understand and soon we knew we could trust her and most importantly count on her to be there for us."

"She taught you trust. And loyalty. I don't need shifter senses to know that you and your brothers are incredibly loyal to each other."

"We are. We always have been." He gave her a sidelong glance. "But that's changing. Four of us have found our mates now."

"That doesn't mean your loyalty wanes. And I doubt any of your brothers' mates would ever make you choose between them or your brothers." Elise shook her head. "You would never make me choose between you and Karros."

"No. But sometimes these choices are out of our control," he said quietly.

Elise shuddered. "We need to turn left here. The wildwood is about ten miles away."

They drove on in silence, each of them lost in thought.

"We're close," Caleb said.

"How do you know?" Elise whispered.

"I can sense your excitement." He grinned at her. "You look like Aiden when he scents a fresh hive of honey."

She chuckled and rubbed her hands over her thighs. "It's been a while since I've visited the wildwood for more than an hour or two." She glanced up at the sky. "We have hours before we have to return to Wishing Moon Bay."

"We have all night if that's what you want."

Elise swung her head around to study him. "You want to stay the night? What about work?"

"What about work? Aiden told me that a night in the wildwood is like no other night." He glanced over his shoulder. "So, I packed a tent and some sleeping bags. And some pots and pans. I figured we could spend a couple of hours foraging for food and then you could cook something over a campfire."

"Oh, you did, did you?" Elise's eyes sparkled with excitement.

"I've made all the arrangements. Karros is not expecting you home."

"You have been busy behind my back." She clasped her hands together.

"You looked as if you needed cheering up last night." He grinned. "Did I make your wish come true?"

"Wish?" Her eyes went wide. "You're asking if that was the wish I made?"

"Yes."

"No, I wished for something more." Elise ducked her head, leaving Caleb guessing as to what exactly "more" meant to her.

And if it included him.

She could have wished for more of me, his bear said lightly.

Elise can't want more of you, Caleb told him. Not when she hasn't had any of you yet.

Ah, but she will when we get to the wildwood, and when she does, she'll want more and more of me. How can she not when she sees my sleek fur, my massive paws, and my sharp claws? Not to mention my teeth. He bared his teeth to show off the whiteness.

Caleb chuckled. I'm sure she'll find you adorable.

His bear gnashed his teeth. That's not exactly the look I'm going for.

Why don't we let your mate be the judge? Caleb snickered to himself, but when he saw the tall, ancient trees ahead, he quickly sobered.

"I told you it was magnificent," Elise said.

"You did. I just never thought it would be this magnificent." Caleb slowed the truck, taking in the scene before him, while also fighting for control of his bear who desperately wanted to break free and run beneath the dense trees with their overlapping branches.

"So you like it?" Elise asked with relief.

Tell her I love it, his bear prompted.

"I like it a lot, my bear says he loves it."

"You can hear his voice in your head?" She jerked her head around, taking her eyes off the forest before them.

"Yes, we share some thoughts and can communicate whenever we want. But only one of us can ever be here in this world." Caleb's bear mentally nudged him. "He wants to meet you in person. Or person to bear."

"Yes." She shuffled forward in her seat. "If we're going to camp, we need to follow this road for a couple of miles and then follow a rutted track deeper into the forest. It's dry and your truck will handle it. The place I want to camp is about another mile into the forest. There we should have plenty of privacy."

"Great." Caleb drove on, impatient to begin this new adventure with his mate.

15

ELISE

"So, this bear of yours." Excitement pulsed through her veins, they had left Caleb's truck and were hiking through the forest to the place they would camp.

The scent of the forest filled her senses, from the pungent damp earth to the sharp pine resin, to the subtle smell of herbs and shrubs that grew in among the trees. These smells always reminded her of her childhood, of blissful days spent at her grandma's house.

"This bear of mine..." Caleb hitched the pack containing the camping gear onto his shoulder. "Do you want to meet him now or when we get to the camp?"

"If you shift now, will I have to carry all the gear?" There was no way she would be able to add Caleb's pack to the weight of the pack already on her back.

"No, if I shift, the pack kind of stays with me." He stopped walking, his eyes unfocused for a long moment before he said, "It's hard to contain my bear. He's been fighting to get free and meet you in person since we left the truck."

"Oh." Her brow furrowed. "Does that mean that once he's

free, you won't be able to come back? I mean the human you."

"No. If you want him to shift so that this part of me comes back, he will. My bear is connected to you in the same way the human me is. Which means he will never hurt you. Not ever." Caleb locked eyes with her. "You are the most important thing in our lives."

"I'm beginning to realize that." She nodded, her mouth dry as her nerves got the better of her. Despite what Caleb said, she was about to come face to face with a bear.

The only bears she'd ever met before were those that lived in the wildwood. They were fierce and territorial but rarely appeared around humans, preferring to keep to the shadows. The fae, on the whole, respected them and left them alone.

However, when she was a girl, staying at her grandma's house, she had been out foraging for mushrooms when a snuffling alerted her to the presence of a massive old bear who was following her trail.

For a second she'd frozen, unable to move. If the bear decided she was his next meal, there was nothing she could do to fend him off.

But she was a fae, and fighting wasn't her only option to escape. Tiptoeing forward, her eyes fixed on the branches above her head rather than the huge beast of a bear following her, she located a branch which she could reach.

Strapping her pack across her back, she'd run forward, arms outstretched as she leaped for the branch. Her hands curled around the rough bark and she'd levered herself up a little awkwardly. Hooking her leg over the branch, she'd hoisted herself up out of danger.

The moment of relief lasted for barely a minute as the bear reached the spot where she'd jumped up. He snorted and snuffled in the dirt, before raising his huge head and staring at her.

Huffing and puffing, he went to the trunk of the tree that supported the branch and placed his huge paws on it. The tree swayed as he pushed it hard, his claws scraping at the bark, shredding it like paper.

Clutching onto the branch, she'd fought the panic rising inside of her as she tried to figure out her next move. Going down wasn't an option and so she searched the branches above her head, looking for one stout enough to bear her weight.

With perfect timing, she waited for the bear to stop pushing the tree trunk, pulled her feet under her so her toes rested on the tree limb, then leaped for the next branch. Using her momentum, she swung forward, grabbing hold of another branch and then another until she reached another tree.

The bear didn't realize at first, giving Elise a chance to put some distance between her and her pursuer. Only when she was sure she could outrun him and reach the safety of her grandma's house did she drop down to the ground and set off at a sprint.

"Are you okay?" Caleb asked. "Your heart rate has quickened and you're breathing heavily. My bear wants to think it's because you are so excited to see him, but you seem...scared."

"Oh, I was recalling a bear attack."

"You got attacked by a bear?" Caleb's shock showed on his face. "I had no idea."

"I didn't get hurt, I outran him. And I don't ever really think about it, it didn't scare me for life or anything. But the thought of actually meeting your bear, it's brought it back to me."

"A wild bear?" Caleb asked.

"I guess so, unlike you, I can't tell the difference between a shifter bear and a real bear. But there are not many shifters in the forest." She lifted her head and inhaled deeply. "Mushrooms."

"Mushrooms?" Caleb sniffed the air. "I can smell them, too. Very sweet."

"I was collecting them the day the bear attacked me." She beckoned to him and he followed her as she left the trail and ducked under a low-hanging branch. "There."

"Maybe that's why the bear attacked you." Caleb tensed his jaw. "They are irresistible to my bear."

"Is he going to... Are you going to lose control?" Elise's face paled as she turned to face Caleb, her eyes on the branches above his head.

"No, I'm in control and even if my bear did come forth, he still wouldn't hurt you. But the mushrooms smell like heaven to him. If heaven had a smell." He tried to lighten the mood.

"You're saying that the bear wasn't after me that day, he wanted the mushrooms I'd collected." She leaned down and sniffed at the mushrooms. "Then maybe I won't pick these today. But if your bear wants them..."

"Are they safe for him to eat?" Caleb asked.

She chuckled. "That depends on if your bear likes getting drunk."

"Those mushrooms make you drunk?" Caleb hunkered down next to them. "That's weird."

"The sweet smell is caused by something similar to fermentation," she explained. "My grandma used to use them to make a kind of mushroom bread."

"Mushroom bread, that sounds...delicious." He screwed up his face.

"It is. When we go visit her, I'll ask her to make some for you." She nudged him in the ribs. "Don't knock it until you've tried it."

"Sorry, it just sounds kind of weird." He inhaled again. "Although my bear disagrees, he thinks these mushrooms smell wonderful."

"Come on, let's go. If your bear gets free and eats too many of them, he'll be drunk." She stood up. "They ferment more in your stomach." She moved her hand around and around over her belly. "So you don't feel the effects for a couple of hours."

"That sounds fun." He chuckled. "But a drunken bear would not help win you over. My bear has to prove to you that bears aren't scary."

"Oh, and please don't mention the bear episode to anyone. I never told anyone, not even Karros."

"You didn't?" Caleb was shocked. "When you got back to your grandma's house, you never told her?"

"No." Elise stood up and turned to face him. "If I had, I doubt I'd have been allowed out into the forest on my own. And I wasn't ready to give up my independence."

"Ah, now I understand." Caleb slipped his arms around her and pulled her close. "You don't have to worry about bears or anything else while I'm here. I can sense any living creature for a mile or more."

"I envy you." She tilted her head back and cupped his face in her right hand. "It must be incredible to sense so much around you. I'm good at reading nature, I can tell if it's going to rain and what direction is north. I can forage for food and I know how to find water. But you see so much more."

"When I'm with you, I see only one thing." His nervous smile took her breath away. "Too much?"

"No, not at all." She stood on tiptoes and pressed her lips to his, running her tongue along his lower lip. He shuddered and tightened his arms around her as their kiss deepened. With Caleb, nothing could ever be too much.

He groaned and pulled away from her. "We should

continue on. We need to set up camp and find something to eat."

"You're more interested in your stomach than kissing me?" Elise's hands slid to her sides as she let him go.

"No, I'd stay here and kiss you all day and all night, but in the morning, you'll have regrets and I'll feel to blame."

"Regrets?" she asked.

"Yes, we came here to gather ingredients so that you can impress Ivan. That's not going to happen if our lips are locked together for hours." He touched his lips as if savoring their kiss.

"You're right," she replied huskily. With a small self-conscious cough, Elise headed back to the trail and continued on in the direction of the place she planned to set up camp. "So, are we far enough away from the mushrooms for you to shift?"

Caleb chuckled, they had been walking for ten minutes and she suspected his bear would easily find his way back to the mushroom patch if he wanted to. "If you keep walking, my bear will choose you over a few fermented mushrooms."

"Glad to hear it." She half-turned to look at him. "Well?"

"You want to meet him now?" Caleb looked around.

"Is there anyone else around?" she asked.

"No. We're alone. There's no one else around for as far as my senses stretch. Unless you count the squirrels in that tree." He pointed at a large sycombre tree.

Elise turned around and stared into the tree. "I can't see or hear them."

"They're in their nest. It's up there." He placed his hand on her shoulder and squeezed it lightly as he guided her attention to the higher branches where two squirrels were nibbling nuts.

"I'd never have known they were there," she whispered. "You are a man of hidden talents."

"I'm willing to let you see all of my talents." He kissed her cheek, his breath caressing her skin. "Let's start with my most impressive talent."

"Okay." She smiled shyly. "I promise not to freak out."

"I'm not the same as the bear that chased you," Caleb reminded her. "I'm still me."

Elise nodded slowly. "You inside a bear skin."

He tapped the side of his head. "Just like my bear is in here right now."

"One and the same." She inhaled deeply and took a step back. "Okay, I'm ready."

Caleb closed the space between them, his lips brushing hers before he stepped back, his eyes fixed on her. "He's just like me, we share the same bond with you."

She nodded and swallowed hard as tears pricked her eyes. As the trees swayed in the breeze, she was reminded of that day so many years ago when the bear had scared her. This was not the same bear, she reminded herself as the air shimmered around Caleb.

He faded from view and the hair on the back of her arms stood on end as the air popped and fizzed. For a moment he was gone, and she felt his loss deep down inside of her. But the link between them was still there. If she reached out for him, she would be able to follow him out of this world.

"Oh!" She put her hands over her mouth as a large shape loomed before her. Slowly the edges of the shape become more defined, and the bear's features filled in as if someone was painting him on a canvas. With each brushstroke, he came to life. Each hair that made up his thick luxurious coat glistened in the dappled sunshine filtering through the trees. Tinged with silver, she longed to run her hands through it and bury her face in the soft fur.

Her nerves were gone. As she locked eyes with the bear,

she read the message he silently sent her. He wouldn't hurt her. He could never hurt her.

The loss she'd felt as Caleb disappeared was gone. Her mate was here right in front of her.

"Hi there." She lifted her hand and waved self-consciously. How exactly were you supposed to say hello to a bear?

The bear shuffled forward, his head low, then he stopped, his eyes on her as if waiting for Elise to make the next move. He didn't want to scare her away.

"It's okay. I'm not going to run." She held out her hand and stepped forward.

The bear responded by sticking his head out as far as possible and sniffing her hand. His whiskers tickled her, and she smiled. The smile was replaced by a giggle, and then laughter erupted from inside her.

"I like you a lot." She stroked his short muzzle, trailing her fingers over his broad head before stroking his back.

The bear made a face and shook his head as if to agree with her.

"Shall we go?" She cocked her head in the direction they were heading.

The bear turned around and then stepped forward, his massive paws making barely an imprint on the ground as he padded after her. He was light on his feet, perhaps he'd learned to hide his tracks when he explored the mountains above Wishing Moon Bay. Although, she doubted anyone hunted bears or any animals in the mountains when there were so many shifters around.

It was one of the many questions she had for Caleb as they walked side by side along the forest trail. Perhaps when they were seated around the campfire tonight, he'd answer them all.

She smiled softly. But if not, they had the whole of the rest of their lives to find out all about each other.

Not that she had a lot to tell. She might be a fae, but she was boring compared to the bear shifter beside her. Perhaps that was another reason why her people didn't like shifters. They resented their ability to shift, to become something else.

Where did that something else live when it wasn't in this world? Where was Caleb's human form now, stuck in some kind of limbo between worlds?

So many questions.

She wound her fingers through the bear's fur almost subconsciously. The bear turned his large head and looked at her unblinkingly. As she stared back at him, she finally understood the connection between them. A connection that was deep and unbreakable. And eternal.

16

CALEB

His bear accompanied Elise as she gathered various herbs and picked leaves from shrubs as they walked through the forest. When she stopped and knelt down to sniff the ground, he'd watched in amusement before digging in the ground with his large paws to uncover some truffles.

"I know what I'm going to cook for Ivan." She patted him on the head before leaning forward and kissing him. "Thank you."

His bear stared at her for a long moment, she was perfect in every way. And she was theirs to love and protect. *Maybe I should sleep next to her tonight,* his bear announced. *I can keep her warm and safe from anything that might try to harm her.*

We'll keep a fire burning, but if there is any hint of danger, I agree, you should sleep by her side. Caleb wanted to be the one to protect her, but he realized his bear could do a much better job. They had to think about what was best for their mate.

"Okay, here we are." Elise placed the woven bag she'd used to store the items she'd foraged carefully on the ground. "I'm going to need Caleb, the human Caleb, to come back now." She hunkered down next to the bear and cupped his head in her hands. "Thank you. I've loved spending time with you." She kissed him on top of the head, and he shivered at her touch.

He loved her. She was their mate. He rubbed his cheek against her thigh before huffing and walking backward, his eyes never leaving her face.

When he was five feet away, he stopped and stared at her for one long moment before he let go of the world around him. The air popped and fizzed and then he was gone.

Elise didn't move as she watched Caleb rematerialize. "That's the most incredible thing I've ever seen."

"My bear? Or the shift itself?" Caleb stepped toward her.

"Both, I guess. How exactly does it work?" Elise's eyes shone brightly as she placed her hand on his arm and squeezed it as if checking that he was real and not a mirage.

"I don't know exactly. It's something that just happens when a shifter reaches puberty. Then we must try to control it. It gets easier as we begin to understand the two halves that make us whole." He took the pack off his back and placed it on the ground. "We should build a fire, it's getting late."

"It is." She looked up at the sky. "Your bear and I lost track of time."

"It's a good thing I don't get jealous of him," Caleb joked.

"Why would you when you are part of each other?" Elise asked.

"I was joking. Although we're going to fight each other to spend more time with you. My bear wants to sleep next to you tonight and keep you safe," Caleb confessed.

"He doesn't think I can look after myself?" she retorted as they began setting up camp.

"No one can protect you like my bear can," he replied.

Her shoulders sagged forward a little and she looked

around the clearing where they'd stopped. "I just hate feeling like I did all those years ago. I hate feeling scared, as though I'm not in control."

"You were in control," he told her. "You didn't panic, and you figured out how to get yourself out of danger."

She stood up straight and put her hands on her hips. "I suppose you're right. I did escape. I always thought I was lucky."

"And now?"

"I came up with a plan and I executed it." She nodded firmly.

"In the same way, you came up with a plan and executed it when you wanted a job with Ivan."

"That was more luck. If Flora hadn't met Aiden, I wouldn't have had a chance. I used her as leverage." She hung her head for a moment.

Caleb came closer and slipped his hand around her shoulders. "No, you saw an opportunity and you used it to your advantage. You used it to help execute your plan." He massaged her shoulder. "I believe that you would have found some other way to set your plan in motion even if Flora hadn't met Aiden."

"I like the way you believe in me." She nestled into him. "I really do."

"That's what I'm here for, to believe in you and make your dreams come true." He wrapped his arms around her, and they stood still, caught in a moment as the late afternoon sun shone down on them.

He turned his face to the sun and felt its warmth, but the heat spreading through his body was not taken from the sun. Even the bright disk in the sky couldn't warm him in the same way his mate did.

"We really need to get a fire going." She shivered and

wrapped her arms around him, her movements in opposition to her words.

"Shall I go gather the firewood while you unpack everything else?" he murmured against her hair.

"That sounds like a good idea." She didn't loosen her hold on him.

"I like this, just the two of us." He breathed in her scent.

"I like it, too." She clung to him as if she never wanted to let go, and he tightened his arms around her. A growl from his stomach ended the mood and she laughed and pulled away. "Go get the firewood so I can cook for you."

"My stomach apologizes for ruining the moment." He bowed his head and she giggled, pushing him away.

"We can share plenty of moments once we've set up camp and eaten." She turned her back on him and crouched down next to the pack.

Caleb watched her, his eyes lingering on her face as he pushed his senses out, ensuring there was nothing close by that might threaten her safety.

Happy there was nothing but a few birds in the immediate area, he left the clearing and gathered wood. He also gathered some dried leaves and moss blown into a hole in the foot of a tree, it would make good kindling.

"This should be enough for now. I'll go get more once we've started the fire." He put the pile down on the ground next to a ring of stones Elise had gathered and arranged to contain the fire.

"Perfect." She placed a large flat stone on the ground inside the ring of smaller stones. "The fire will heat the larger rock. I can use it to keep the food warm once it's cooked."

"Okay, do you want me to light the fire?" he asked.

"I can do it." She picked up the small pile of kindling and set it down on the ground before glancing up at him. "You don't need to watch me. I can do it."

"I know I don't need to watch you, but I like watching you." He smiled softly as she blushed. "But I can go sort out the sleeping bags and set up the tent." He looked up at the sky. "I wasn't sure if it was going to rain. But if it stays dry, we can just sleep under the stars."

"You didn't check the weather forecast before we left?" Elise asked.

"I could check the Wishing Moon Bay weather, but I figured the weather here would be different since we're in another world. You did see that we crossed worlds?"

"Is that attitude I hear?" Elise teased.

"I suppose that as much as you have questions about shifting, I have a lot of questions about your world. And you." He came to her, kneeling beside her and stroking the tip of her ear. "We're so much the same and yet so different."

"But fate has chosen to bring us together." She looked down at the ground before raising her eyes to meet his. "You make me want to sacrifice everything I've worked for. Being with you makes me realize how much I want a family. Children to love and care for."

"Why does that mean you have to sacrifice everything you've worked for?" Caleb asked.

"Because there's no way I can work in a restaurant and care for our children. The hours are long..." He put his fingers to her lips, and she swallowed down her emotions.

"You're not in this alone." He placed his hand on his heart. "I promise I'll be there by your side every step of the way. Your career, your hopes, and your dreams are important to me. Somehow, we'll work it out."

She arched an eyebrow and his heart ached for her. "You're saying I can have it all?"

"I'm saying we will find a way together." He took her hand and raised it to his lips. "We're a team, a partnership. In everything. And in case you didn't notice, I have a big family and there are going to be a lot of babies soon." He smiled softly at the thought of the next generation they would soon raise. The boys adopted by Valerie would know what it was to be fathers. "We have always helped each other out and I don't see that changing anytime soon."

Elise leaned her head on his chest and took a shuddering breath. "Thank you."

"For what?" He slipped his finger under her chin and tilted her head up.

"For coming into my life. For being you."

He chuckled. "Luckily, I'm good at being me."

"Don't ever change." She kissed him, her lips hot against his as the late afternoon rays bathed them in sunlight.

"I don't plan on changing," he assured her. "Now, we really need to get this fire going. If we don't eat soon, the forest will be filled with the sound of my stomach growling rather than bird song."

"I thought when you were in love, you lost your appetite?" Her cheeks flushed pink, and she covered her face with her hands. "I didn't mean to imply..."

"That I'm in love with you?" He let her go and held out his arms. "Do you want me to shout it out loud?"

"No." She waved her hands at him and looked around with wide eyes.

"Okay, good, I never was the kind of person who liked to show off." He let his arms drop to his sides. "I love you, Elise. I am in love with you. And I will love you until the end of days."

"I don't know what to say." She shook her head and fell silent.

"You don't have to say anything. I don't expect you to love me. Of course, I hope you will one day, but I understand that my feelings are stronger because I'm a shifter and I know you are the one for me."

"I do love you," she whispered. "I've just never told anyone before. Except for my family." She came closer and placed her hand on his heart. "But this love is different."

"I'm honored to be your first and only love." His eyes darkened, in this moment he wanted nothing more than to claim his mate as his own.

"My only love," she repeated.

"Together forever," he added.

Perhaps Elise wishes she'd experienced the love of other men, *his bear was worried. She might feel as if she's missed out if we are her only love.*

"I had gotten used to the idea that love was going to pass me by. But here you are."

"Here I am." He held out his arms as if offering himself to her.

"Let's make this fire before the temperature drops or you waste away due to lack of food." She rushed toward him, kissed him on the cheek, and then went back to preparing the fire.

She loved him. The words echoed around his head as he turned his attention to organizing the camp.

She loves us, his bear reminded him.

That's what I meant. Caleb smiled as he worked. This was one of the best days of his life.

17

ELISE

"Domestic bliss." She passed him a plate of food and sat down next to Caleb who had dragged a large fallen tree trunk over to their small camping area and placed their sleeping bags on the ground in front of it. The sleeping bags cushioned them from the hard ground while the tree trunk acted as a backrest.

"I could get used to watching you cook." He leaned forward and inhaled deeply. "The smell is incredible."

"In a good way?" she asked as she shuffled around to get comfortable.

"Of course, in a good way." He picked up his fork.

"Because lots of things smell incredible. Some incredibly good and some incredibly bad."

"Don't put yourself down," Caleb told her firmly. "So far, from what I've seen, smelled and now am about to taste, your cooking is wonderful."

"But not as good as Ivan's." She pressed her lips together, her fork hovering above her plate.

"Let's see." He stuck his fork into the dish she'd prepared with the truffles his bear had dug out of the ground. After sniffing it, he opened his mouth and ate. "Oh, wow. No, your cooking isn't like Ivan's."

"You don't have to eat it," she told him quickly, her mouth turned down at the corners as she watched his face.

"I didn't say it was bad. I just said it wasn't like Ivan's. It's different." He forked up another mouthful. "The flavors burst on your tongue but then there's a subtle aftertaste. It's incredible."

"You're not just saying that?" she asked.

"Shifter here." He pointed at his chest. "Mate there." He pointed at her. "That means I can't lie to you."

"Ah, or are you telling me that because you don't want to hurt me? What would be worse, hurting my feelings with the truth, that the dish is terrible, or lying to me that you like it?"

"You're not good at receiving compliments, are you?"

"Not especially," she admitted. "You could call me modest."

"This food deserves more than modesty."

"Do you think Ivan will like it?" she asked. "I trust your judgment since he is your brother. You must know what food he likes."

"He'll be blown away." Caleb cracked a smile. "In a good way."

"Good." She ducked her head and ate her food, trying not to smile.

"It really is good." Caleb took another bite. "Are these all ingredients you found today?"

"Yes, with a little help from your bear." She ate for a moment, glancing up at him as she chewed. "I like him. I like him a lot."

"He likes you a lot." His brow creased. "If I told you he loved you, would that freak you out?"

"No, not at all. I can see he's a part of you. I can see you in his eyes. Or are they the same eyes?" she asked. "I have so many questions."

"I want to answer them all." He waggled an eyebrow. "But I also want to keep some mystery. I'd hate for you to get bored of me."

"There's no hope of that. I don't think I could ever get bored of watching you shift." She placed her fork on her plate and ran her hand over her forearm. "It gave me goosebumps. Like if you hear a beautiful piece of music, it makes your hairs stand on end."

Caleb nodded and ate the rest of his food. "So you're no longer scared of bears?"

"No, your bear has won me over." She chuckled. "When we leave, we can head to that patch of sweet-smelling mushrooms and we can pick some and save them until tomorrow night."

"Tomorrow night?" he asked.

"Yes, I figured you could come over to the house and your bear can eat the mushrooms. I've never seen a drunken bear before." She finished her food and leaned back, enjoying the warmth of the fire as twilight settled around them and the temperature dipped.

"My bear has never been drunk so it should be fun for both of us, as long as he doesn't pass out."

"What happens if he does?" Elise asked.

"I might be stuck in bear mode for a while." Caleb chuckled and shook his head. "Logan's wolf once knocked himself out."

"How?" Elise leaned closer to him, mesmerized by the warm low tone of his voice.

"I suppose he didn't exactly knock himself out. We were playing in the mountains, stalking each other. It wasn't long after we all learned to shift. Logan tried this new idea of delaying his shift. We'd all done it before, but he tried to push it too far. As a wolf, he's a lot lighter and more agile than a bear, and he miscalculated where he'd land, and his wolf smacked into a boulder."

"And he was stuck as a wolf?" Elise sat up and looked at Caleb with her hands over her mouth. "Was he okay? I mean he's alive and doesn't seem brain damaged so I guess he didn't seriously hurt himself."

"He was out for a few minutes, and we panicked. It's not something that you're ever really prepared for. We were trying to figure out how to get him back down the mountain. Dario or Ivan had carried us on their backs in their human forms before but neither of them had ever attempted to carry any of us in our shifter form."

"That must have been a long five minutes." Elise shook her head. "When we have children, they're going to be shifters, right?"

He smothered a smile, as if he could read the direction of her thoughts. "They are."

"And we're going to go through this? I mean our kids experimenting with shifting." She swallowed hard. "I don't know if I'm ever going to be ready for that."

"We'll worry about them shifting, in the same way we'll worry about them coming here." He held out his arm toward the canopy above their heads.

"What's wrong with the wildwood?" Elise's brows knitted together. "The bears? I shouldn't have told you."

"No, it's not the bears. We will worry about our children wherever they are and whatever they do. As a parent, it's only natural. But they have to be allowed to explore the world around them and figure out where they fit into it."

"So, we need to teach them common sense?" Elise nodded. "Maybe we'll survive parenting after all."

"Valerie taught us to think for ourselves and how to take care of each other. At least when Logan knocked himself out, the rest of us were there for him." He lifted his arm and then casually draped it over her shoulders. "Our children will have their cousins to play with and we'll teach them all how to look after each other. Just like me and my brothers and you and Karros."

She leaned into him as he tightened his grip around her shoulders. "Karros has always been there for me and I hope I've always been there for him."

"He's your older brother. Protecting you comes naturally." He dropped a light kiss on her head. "And even though we're mates and it's my job to protect you now, I know he isn't going to stop being your brother or watching out for you."

"A big bear shifter doesn't get jealous of that?" Elise asked.

"No, he's your brother. Just like my brothers will always look out for me and protect me." He squeezed her shoulders. "Even if I have a mate now who will also take care of me."

"And protect you." She tilted her head back and looked up at him. "I mean it. I might not be as strong as you, but strength isn't everything."

"You have an inner strength." Caleb sighed and she pressed her lips along his jawline, tendrils of desire unfurling inside her stomach. Heat flared across her cheeks as he lowered his head and kissed her lips.

Turning into him, she threaded her hand under his sweater, her fingertips brushing his bare skin. He tensed, a shiver passing through him as he cupped her cheek in the palm of his warm hand and rubbed his thumb across her cheek.

"Shall we clear the camp and get ready for bed?" She didn't want to move from his side, but she also didn't want to attract wild animals into their camp by leaving the food out. There was only one bear she wanted in the camp tonight and he was the person sitting next to her.

"Sure." He cleared his throat and loosened his arm from

her shoulders before pulling her close once more. He kissed her, and she clung to him while the forest seemed to spin around them.

When he finally let her go, she placed her hand on the fallen tree trunk to steady herself. She'd never gone weak at the knees for any man. But Caleb wasn't any man.

"I'll put the food away." She inhaled, forcing the air into her lungs.

While she packed the food into their packs, Caleb busied himself collecting the sleeping bags and laying them out in the tent before making sure the fire was out. As he moved around the camp, she was acutely aware of him.

With trembling fingers, she focused on packing the food carefully so it wouldn't spoil before they got back home. They'd come here to gather the ingredients she needed for her recipe, however, being next to Caleb in the tent was all she could think about.

The warmth of his body as they slept side by side in the small, confined space. The sound of his breathing, the touch of his fingers on her skin.

She closed her eyes and sucked in a deep breath. They were just going to sleep.

"Are you okay?" He was close, his soft voice sent shivers down her spine.

"Yeah, I'm nearly done." She dug her hand in the pack and pulled out a flashlight. The sun was setting but the moon hadn't risen yet. Soon their camp would be pitched into darkness.

"Your hand is shaking. Are you scared?" He closed his hand around hers. "There are no bears around here."

"Yes, there is," she replied hoarsely and turned to face him, her head tilted back as she faced him. "There's a bear right here."

"Who intends to protect you with his life." Caleb smiled

down at her as he flicked on the flashlight, the bright beam illuminating his face.

She swallowed hard. His eyes burned with desire, a desire matched by her. She wanted him. He wanted her. It was the simplest of recipes.

One they couldn't mess up unless they didn't act on their desires.

Elise slipped her arms around his neck and pressed her body against his. "Shall we go to bed?"

"Yes," he growled in response and lowered his head, capturing her lips with his. She sighed and nestled against him as he leaned down and picked her up.

Carrying her in his strong arms, he turned around and headed for the tent. When he reached it, he gently let her down, his arms closing around her waist as he waited for her to steady herself before letting her go.

Elise ducked down into the tent and kicked off her shoes. Caleb lingered outside, he seemed unsure as she peeled off her jacket and threw it to the end of the tent. Reaching out, she grabbed his hand and pulled him toward her, leaving him with no doubt she wanted him by her side.

Caleb knelt down and shuffled forward on his knees until he was inside the tent, facing her, his soft eyes fixed on her face. Elise leaned forward, slipped her hands around his neck and licked her lips, inviting him in.

With a deep groan, he wrapped his right arm around her waist and pulled her toward him. She gasped as he kissed her, his lips warm and insistent, and as their kiss broke, he held her gaze, his eyes asking the question—how far was she willing to go?

"Make love to me." Elise had never been a woman who liked to play games. She was not about to start now.

He slipped his hands under her sweater and pulled it up over her head. She wriggled and pulled her arms out of the sleeves before curling her fingers around the hem of her T-shirt and yanking it over her head, too.

Caleb stroked the swell of her breasts, tracing the lace of her bra with his fingertips. Damn, had the temperature just rocketed in the wildwood, or only in the tent?

Her body was on fire as he lowered his head and placed soft butterfly kisses over her sensitive skin, working his way over her breasts, along her collarbone and then up her neck. She ached for him, a deep need emanating from her core.

While he teased her with his kisses, his hands quickly unzipped her slacks and pulled them down over her hips. He let her go and she rocked back and forth before sitting down on her bottom, while he pulled her slacks off her feet.

Caleb leaned back and sat down on his heels, simply staring at her. Heat flared across her skin and she swallowed hard. This wasn't the time to fall apart, she wanted him naked beside her.

Pushing herself to a sitting position, she pulled at the hem of his T-shirt. Caleb took the hint and yanked the fabric up over his head, throwing it to one side as she unbuckled his belt.

The confines of the tent made things a little difficult, but they worked together to push his jeans down over his toned thighs. Caleb hooked his thumbs around his boxers and pulled them off, too.

He was naked.

It has her turn to stare.

Like a lioness on the prowl, she pushed herself up onto all fours and padded toward him. Caleb lay down and she lifted her right leg and placed her knees down on either side of him.

His hands encircled her waist and he guided her to sit on him, his thumb brushing her mound as she moved. Elise closed her eyes as she throbbed in need. She'd never wanted a man so desperately. She'd never wanted anything so desperately.

Caleb reached for the clasp holding her bra in place, with a sigh he freed her breasts, his hands cupping them, his thumb brushing her hard nipples. Elise closed her eyes as sensations flooded her body.

Outside in the woods, an owl hooted, and a cool breeze buffeted the tent, reminding her of where she was.

She opened her eyes, reached down between their bodies and curled her hand around Caleb's hardness. Rising onto her knees, she pushed her panties aside and guided him into her. Lowering herself down slowly, she gasped as he stretched her inner walls, the friction between their bodies intense.

Elise bit her lower lip, as she inched down slowly, enjoying the moment as they finally joined together as one.

Caleb placed his hand on the small of her back and sat up, cradling her in his arms as he lowered his head and sucked her nipple into his mouth. She gasped and her inner muscles tensed as her arousal kicked up a notch.

Placing her hands against his chest to steady herself, she moved her hips, circling them around and around. Kissing, stroking, touching, they explored each other's bodies. Each intimate moment deepening their connection.

Rocking back and forth in his lap, she guided them toward new heights. As the night sounds of the wildwood surrounded them, she imagined them as two primal creatures who had found each other against all odds. Two people from different worlds destined to be together.

As her orgasm hovered in front of her, Caleb placed his hand on the small of her back and lifted her, turning her over so she lay on her back. Nestling between her thighs, he hovered over her body, before thrusting into her hard and deep.

She cried out as he drew back and then lunged into her again, over and over, pushing her higher until she finally came. Her inner muscles gripped him, pulsing around him, setting off a chain reaction.

Caleb jerked into her, filling her with his seed, calling out her name as if to tell the world around them that she was his.

As they lay spent in each other's arms, Elise accepted that knowledge. As she accepted utterly and completely that she was a shifter's mate.

And no one would ever change that.

18

CALEB

"Good morning." He kissed her lips as her eyes fluttered open.

"Is it morning?" She blinked rapidly and rubbed her hand across her eyes.

"It's early. I thought we could enjoy the sunrise together over a cup of coffee before we head back home." He tucked the sleeping bag around her as he slipped away and went to light the fire.

"You brought coffee?" she asked.

"I did." He went to his pack and opened one of the side pockets. "Instant. But coffee is coffee."

"It sure is." She yawned and stretched her arms above her head before quickly putting them back inside the sleeping bag. "Aren't you cold?"

He glanced down at his bare arms. He'd pulled on his jeans and a T-shirt, but he hadn't retrieved his sweater yet. "I have hot shifter blood. I don't get cold."

Her teeth chattered as a light breeze ruffled her hair. "Once you have the fire lit, can you come back to bed?"

"Try and stop me." He grinned, his teeth flashing in the

half-light. He wanted nothing more than to slide back into the sleeping bag and hold her in his arms.

Caleb switched his attention to the small amount of kindling leftover from last night and quickly lit it, adding a few dry twigs to the fire. Cupping his hands around it to protect it from the breeze, he nurtured it, placing larger twigs on the small pile until the flames crackled and sparked.

Caleb sat back on his haunches, aware of Elise's eyes on him as he prepared a pan of water. When the fire was hot enough, he placed the pan on the fire, waited to ensure it wasn't going to tip over, and then got up and padded back to his mate.

"I think I could get used to seeing you in the morning." She ruffled his hair as he climbed inside the sleeping bag. "Oh, your feet are cold! I thought you said you were hot-blooded."

"They don't feel cold to me." He ran his foot down her calf and chuckled as she jumped away from him.

"They're cold!" She placed her hands on his chest. "This part is warm."

"Then let me hold you close." He wrapped his arms around her, and she nestled against him. "I want to wake up like this every morning."

"I know." Elise leaned on his shoulder. "We came here to pick up the items I needed for the recipe I wanted to prepare for Ivan. I thought it would make things simpler, but it's made things more complicated."

"In what way?" Caleb asked.

"You've woken something inside me. A deep longing I'd buried." She looked up at him, her eyes locked with his. "I want this to work. For us to work. But I don't see how that's going to happen."

"We'll figure out a way." He kissed her shoulder.

"We've just agreed to rent the house. Karros can't afford it on his own but there's no way the three of us could share the house together." She sighed and stared at the fire.

"He could take my apartment and I could move in with you there," Caleb suggested. He could barely breathe at the thought of living with his mate. He'd figured it would take her a while to come around to the idea.

"He's committed to creating a beautiful yard at the house and then making a new business in town. I can't ask him to leave. I think he's planning on working on the yard every hour of the day and some of the night." She chuckled. "Yesterday morning, he was drawing his plans while we ate breakfast. I think he was looking forward to having the day to himself so that he could make a real start."

"We'll figure it out. I could stay with you some nights and you could stay with me. Split the time between our homes. And I suppose I could live without you a couple of evenings a week if you want to spend time with Karros."

"And I thought you couldn't bear to spend one single night away from me. Since I'm your mate," she teased.

"I don't want to. But if it's what you need to do..." He nuzzled her neck. "I could survive as long as it wasn't for long."

"Life was much simpler before we met each other."

"We can't turn back time," Caleb told her.

"I wouldn't want to even if I could." Her words gave him some relief.

"I know I've complicated your life. But we'll figure it out."

"And live a simple life?" She inched away from him.

"Simple in some ways. But you want your own restaurant, so there are going to be complications, too." He wriggled out of the sleeping bag as the water began to boil.

"I should get dressed." Elise grabbed her clothes. "I have a sock missing, do you see it?"

Caleb chuckled as he hunted around the campsite for her sock. "Here it is."

"How did it get over there?" Elise held out her hand for the sock as she wriggled around in the sleeping bag. "This is not easy."

"You could get out of the sleeping bag," he suggested. "There's no one around but us and I'll look the other way if you want me to."

"I'm not shy," she replied. "It's just too cold." She ducked her head into the sleeping bag. "It's warm in here." She came up for air. "There, all dressed."

"Why don't you put my sweater on, too?" he asked. "And my jacket is here." He got up from the fireside and fetched his jacket for her.

"Thanks." She pushed her arms into the sweater and pulled it over her head. "This is warm. Are you sure you don't want the jacket?"

"Hot shifter blood," he reminded her as he went back to the fire.

"Aside from your feet." She smiled softly at him and then joined him next to the fire. "The sun is coming up."

"Here's the coffee. We can sit down and watch the sunrise through the trees and then we should make our way back to the truck. I don't want you to be late for work." Caleb quickly put the coffee in the cups and poured on the hot water. "Here. It's not the best coffee but it'll help wake you up."

"I am awake," she insisted as she accepted the cup and headed back to the sleeping bags.

Caleb pushed himself to his feet and followed her, not wanting to waste a single moment of their morning alone. Soon they would be back in Wishing Moon Bay where they would be surrounded by other people.

We need to figure this out, his bear told him.

You mean figure out how we're going to live with Elise. Alone.

His bear mulled that over. It's going to be tough. Elise is loyal to Karros and he left his life here to offer her support. There's no way she'll just ditch him.

And we wouldn't want her to. He's her family. They understood Elise's position completely, they would feel the same way about their brothers.

However, they were determined to figure out a way to make it work out for everyone.

Perhaps fate will lend a hand, his bear suggested.

We can hope. If Karros got called back to the fae realm by his family, he might leave if he knew Elise would be all right without him.

And she would be all right without him because she has us. His bear nodded sagely. I think you might have come up with a solution.

Wait, that all depends on their family needing Karros. So at the moment, it's just a dream, Caleb said.

Maybe we should find ourselves a wishing stone of our own and make a wish. His bear settled down at the edges of Caleb's mind, ready to take a nap as the sun finally rose overhead.

"This is amazing." Elise reached for his hand. "I have only ever seen the sunrise in the wildwood once. It was a long time ago."

"I've watched the sunrise from the top of a mountain many times. When we weren't helping Valerie at the hotel, Aiden and I would often spend the weekend in the mountains. We'd shift and climb to a high peak near town and set up camp." He arched his arm above his head. "The stars are so bright. It's as if you could reach up and pluck one out of the sky."

"I'd like you to show me them." Elise snuggled closer as the pale light around them changed the muted colors brought alive by the touch of the sun's rays just as he'd come to life from the touch of his mate.

Not that he hadn't been alive before. He'd been happy. He'd been content but now he'd been shown something else, something bigger and brighter than he could ever have imagined.

"When you have a couple of days off, we'll go," he promised. "The weather is still warm enough. We can hike up to the peak and camp. Or I could ask Ivan to take us."

She stiffened beside him. "Ride on the back of a dragon?"

"Yes. He might take us up there and then we can camp and hike back down the next day. It's a long way for my bear and he has four paws. On two legs, it might be exhausting." He glanced sideways at her. "I lost you at ride on the back of a dragon, didn't I?"

"Yes. You did." She turned her face toward the sun as the warmth washed over them. "That would be incredible. I mean, I've seen them across the water. When I was young, Karros and I used to go down to the beach with his telescope and we would look out across the ocean and see them flying. They would play, winding around each other before flying away at impossible speeds. I never dreamed I'd ever get to ride on the back of one. I heard they were very proud and only their mate ever rode on their backs."

"Ivan is incredible. Unique. But above all else, he's my brother. We've ridden on his back before. He brought Penny and Milo down from the mountains after they were kidnapped by a witch. He even let Jeremy ride on his back."

"Jeremy, oh, he's the guy on reception at the hotel. I like him." She smiled softly.

"Do you?" Caleb growled.

"Don't worry, you have nothing to be jealous of." She poked him in the ribs. "Although come to think of it, you do sound sexy when you get jealous."

"I'm only joking around, I know you would never hurt me or even look at another man again."

"I'm not even allowed to look?" she asked in mock horror.

"No, you only have eyes for me." He arched an eyebrow at her. "I know you feel it, too."

"I do," she admitted. "And since I've had my whole life to look and I never found anyone, then you're safe. I am not going anywhere." She snuggled closer to him.

"Except home." He sighed, the sun was rising steadily in the sky. They needed to get back to the truck and drive back to Wishing Moon Bay.

"Thank you for bringing me here," she told him. "It's just what I needed. It's reminded me of who I am at heart."

"You're welcome. Although, I'll admit I was also a little selfish in bringing you here. I wanted to spend some time alone with you." He looked down at her and she cupped his face in her hand.

"I wanted that, too." She leaned forward and kissed his lips. "We will make this work. I know we will because it's what we both want."

Those words were exactly what Caleb needed to hear.

19

ELISE

"Back to the real world," Elise said as they crossed out of the fae realm and into Wishing Moon Bay.

"Your world is just as real." Caleb glanced sideways at her. "And it's there whenever you want to visit. Don't shut yourself off from everything you love. It's a short journey from this world to yours."

"I know, but I want to spend time getting to know this world. Since this is where we'd raise our children." She smiled and ducked her head. After last night, her future seemed to have widened. It was no longer narrow with darkness crowding in, making it seem smaller and smaller as each year passed by. She had choices now that she had a mate.

"Children." Caleb chuckled and rubbed his chin. "I can't wait. Especially since Aiden and Flora will have children, too. We'll be able to raise our half-fae, half-shifter children together."

"That sounds perfect, since you and Aiden are so close, and I love Flora like a sister." Elise's cheeks turned pink as she placed her hand over her stomach and imagined her belly swollen with a child growing inside her. A child that would bring such joy into their lives.

"Oh, that's my phone. Can you reach into my pocket and get it?" Caleb asked.

"Sure." Elise still wore his sweater and jacket and so she shoved her hand in his pocket and pulled out his phone. "It's Aiden." An image of a face that looked almost exactly like Caleb showed on the screen. She could easily tell them apart in person but in photos, they looked eerily similar.

"Can you answer it?" Caleb asked. "Just ask him what he wants. It's probably work-related."

"Okay." She nervously pressed accept and answered the call. Putting the phone to her ear, she said, "Hello, Aiden, it's Elise."

"Elise." Aiden paused. "Is Caleb with you?"

"He is. He's driving and he asked me to take a message."

"Where are you?" Aiden sounded off, she didn't know him well enough to put her finger on the reason why. But her pulse pounded as tension grew in her body, as if she were preparing to fight. And she would fight for her mate.

Elise inhaled deeply and let it go. There was no one to fight. Her reaction must be some primal connection to Caleb. So it wasn't just a shifter thing.

"We're nearly in town. We're heading back to my house."

"Can you swing by the hotel first? I need to talk to Caleb. It can't wait."

Elise glanced at Caleb. "We'll be right there." Her mouth went dry as Caleb cast her a questioning look. "Is everything okay?"

"I'll tell you when you get here," Aiden answered.

"Okay." She swallowed hard as she ended the call. "We have to go straight to the hotel."

"Did Aiden say why?" Caleb asked.

"No. He said he'll tell us when we get there." She reached

across to him and placed her hand on his thigh. "Whatever it is, I'm here for you."

Caleb nodded. "It's probably nothing. A problem with a job." He was trying to reassure himself, but he chewed his bottom lip and eased his foot down on the gas.

"It didn't sound like nothing," she said quietly. Perhaps she should just leave it until they were back at the hotel. Caleb knew his brother better than anyone. Aiden might get worried about the small stuff.

"What if it's Valerie?" Caleb whispered. "What if something happened to her while we were away?"

"We'll be there soon." She breathed in deeply and let go of her own fear. She needed to be strong for her mate.

Yet she couldn't ignore the nagging worry in the back of her head that if something bad had happened while they were away, Caleb would somehow blame her. No, he wouldn't. This wasn't her fault.

But people react in strange ways. Her parents had proved that over and over again.

They drove the short distance to the hotel in silence. There was nothing else to say until they spoke to Aiden.

Caleb slowed as they reached the hotel parking lot. Once he'd parked the truck, he got out and stood still for a moment, his body rigid and his eyes unfocused. "I can sense Valerie. And Aiden and Flora."

"You were worried something might have happened to Flora?" Elise got out of the truck and went to join him.

"Yes." He glanced at Elise, his expression clearer. "I'm not sure what else it could be. Our other brothers are here. We might be twins, but we know we can count on the others for whatever we need." His eyes widened. "Unless..."

"What?" Elise grabbed his hand as he strode toward the hotel.

"Unless there's a problem elsewhere."

"You mean in the world beyond?"

"Yes. Our family lives out there. Our blood relatives. My aunt and uncle, cousins...and my sister."

Aiden appeared on the hotel steps before Caleb reached them. "You're here."

"What's wrong?" Caleb asked hoarsely as he noted his brother's worried expression.

"It might be nothing..." Aiden glanced up and down the street and Elise shivered and hugged Caleb's jacket closer around her.

"Tell me." Caleb went to his brother and slid his arm around his shoulders, but he didn't let go of Elise, as if he needed to feel her touch, to know she was there when Aiden broke the bad news.

And it was bad news, she could sense Aiden's worry, even if he tried to hide it from Caleb.

"Zara called me." Aiden locked eyes with Caleb.

"Did something happen to her, is she all right? Or is it..."

"They're all fine," Aiden replied quickly. "But Zara is certain someone is following her."

"Someone is following her?" Caleb repeated.

"Yes. She's supposed to come here in a couple of days and she's afraid she'll lead whoever is following her here." Aiden chewed his bottom lip. "We need to find out who it is."

Caleb nodded and glanced at Elise. "We'll leave today."

Aiden nodded. "We should go inside. Flora is insisting she's coming with us, but I don't want her to."

Elise followed the twins inside. Of course Flora would want to go. Just as Elise wanted to go. She'd sworn in the forest that she would protect Caleb in the same way he would always protect her. There was no way she could let him down.

"I'm going to check in on Ivan." She pointed toward the kitchen where the smell of breakfast cooking escaped through the door. Her stomach growled as she let go of Caleb's hand and headed to the kitchen. But there were more important things than food.

"Elise." Ivan glanced up at her as he plated up some eggs and bacon. "You're not due in until later."

"About that..." She clasped her hands together in front of her and bowed her head. "I'm not going to be able to make my shift."

"Oh." Ivan placed the pan down on the stovetop and came around the counter to stand in front of her. "You realize that's going to leave me shorthanded?"

"I do." She nodded and lifted her head to look him in the eyes. "But Aiden and Caleb are leaving to check on their sister and I need to go with them."

"You think they can't take care of themselves?" Ivan mocked. "You do know they are two big bear shifters who can practically read each other's thoughts. They are a force in themselves."

"Physically, yes. But this is about their sister. And family can sometimes mean you don't think straight." She inhaled deeply. "And there are some monsters you can't fight with your fists or your paws."

"You're going because you think your mate might need your protection." A smile crept across his face.

"I do." She shrugged. "I understand if this means I lose my place here."

Ivan chuckled. "You still don't know us too well." He backed away and picked up the pan once more. "Take as much time as you need. I'm happy that you'll be there for Caleb. He might need you."

"So, we're okay?" Her shoulders slumped forward, and she brushed her hand across her eyes.

"We're okay. More than if you'd chosen to stay behind," he admitted. "Your mate is more important than anything in the world...or so I'm told. You are supposed to be by his side. And seeing that you know that makes me happy."

"I do belong by his side," she agreed. "And finding Caleb has complicated my plans."

"I can only imagine," Ivan looked toward her. "Are you telling me you are quitting anyway?"

"Oh, no." She waved her hands at him, as if trying to push that thought away. "I am totally committed to my career. Well, not totally. I am going to work hard to prove myself to you and learn everything you have to teach me. But I also want to balance it with my life with Caleb. I guess my priorities have shifted a little."

"Listen, Elise." Ivan glanced toward the restaurant. She was wasting his time when he was so busy, but he was patient with her, and she warmed to the dragon shifter. "You're my brother's mate. And that means I am willing to give you some leeway here that I wouldn't give anyone else."

"I understand. And I promise not to take advantage of that."

Ivan chuckled. "I thought you would object."

"I'd be stupid to object. I know how Caleb feels about his family. And the way he speaks about you all makes me believe that you all feel the same way about each other. So, since you want each other to be happy, it's easy to see that you'll be more...accommodating to me because I am your brother's mate."

Ivan pointed at her. "It's a good thing you have his back."

"Just like he has mine." She stepped forward and kissed Ivan on the cheek before backing out of the kitchen. "Thanks, Ivan. I won't forget this."

"Just remember you still owe me a dish of wonderful food," he called after her as she left the kitchen.

"I won't." She entered the reception area and looked around, Caleb and Aiden were gone.

"Through there and down the corridor." Jeremy looked up from the reception desk and aimed her in the right direction.

"Thanks." She hurried down the corridor, suddenly aware that she smelled of woodsmoke and her hair was a mess. When they left the forest, she'd planned on going straight home and showering. Elise sniffed her clothes. She'd definitely have to go change before they left.

When she reached the door leading to Valerie's apartment, she raised her hand, ready to knock.

"Elise." Flora opened the door. "Are you coming, too?"

"Yes, I just had to go tell Ivan. I was worried I might lose my job here but he's okay with it." She pressed her lips together as she looked over Flora's shoulder. "Is there any more information? Aiden just said that their sister thinks she's being followed."

"There's not a lot else. Just a few details. She was driving home last night, and she sensed someone." Flora ran her hand over the back of her neck. "You know, with her shifter senses."

"But she couldn't tell who it was?" Elise followed Flora into the apartment, but they stopped just inside the doorway rather than joining the others.

"No, she said whoever it was, they were too far away. Like outside the range of her senses." Flora fluttered her fingers around her head. "I don't quite get the whole shifter senses thing. It seems some shifters can sense things farther away than others."

"Does she know if it was a shifter watching her? And how does she know it wasn't just some random person?" Elise was certain Zara wouldn't have troubled her brothers if she thought it was nothing. However, Elise grasped at the idea that their sister was an attention seeker.

They'd only just met and maybe the thought of having

two big bear shifters to watch over her had made her dream up this story.

"There was also an incident at her house. She's certain someone had been in there when she got home a couple of nights ago. She'd been to her aunt and uncle's house for dinner and when she got back, one of the windows was open. She was sure it had been shut when she went out."

"A burglar?" Elise asked.

"That's just it, nothing was taken, but a photograph of Aiden and Caleb had been moved. Or just not put back in the exact same place."

"What is she, OCD? Things get moved."

"Zara is doing work on the house. There was a thin layer of dust and the picture frame definitely wasn't in the right place." Flora rested her hand on Elise's arm. "She's a smart woman, Elise. She isn't making this up, even if we hope she is."

Elise brushed her hand through her hair and ducked her head, her cheeks flaming pink with guilt. "I was just hoping...you know?"

Flora slid her arm around Elise's shoulder. "I know exactly what you mean, we don't want our mates to get in danger or get hurt. It's natural to try and explain this away."

Elise hugged her friend. "We'll have their backs."

"Oh, you bet we will." Flora sniffed Elise's shoulder. "So, you spent a night in the wildwood."

"We did." She stepped back. "I was supposed to be going home to cook a recipe for Ivan to prove I'm worthy of my job, but all that's on hold now."

"We'll figure it all out and then you can come back and cook. Ivan and the restaurant aren't going anywhere."

"But Caleb is." She gave a short laugh. "I've dreamed of working in a restaurant with a great chef for so long. But I was willing to throw it all away today for a man I've just met."

"Being the mate of a shifter is a totally new experience, isn't it?" Flora took Elise's hand. "Come and have some coffee. Then we'll figure out a plan and leave."

"Elise, there you are." Valerie handed her a cup of coffee. "There's food, too. Help yourself."

"Thanks." She thumbed toward the door. "Maybe I should head home, though, and get changed and shower. I don't want to hold you up."

"We need to go to the cabin and grab some stuff, too," Aiden said. "I also want to call Oscar Renshaw." Aiden glanced at Valerie and then looked away.

"Why Oscar?" Elise had heard of the detective, but the man was now retired. However, she was certain she was missing something when the other people in the room exchanged glances.

"Oscar gave me a file on our case," Aiden explained. "I want to ask him if he can dig deeper on the man who we believe is responsible for killing our parents."

Elise inhaled sharply. "You think this is connected." That explained their concern for their sister.

If it was, they'd need their mates to be strong for them. She clenched her fists. Emotionally and physically.

Elise took Flora's hand and faced the others. "I told Caleb I was here to protect him as much as he is here to protect me. I'm not afraid. We'll do what we need to do."

Flora nodded. Their mates would never have to stand alone.

20

CALEB

"Now Karros wants to come, too?" Caleb crossed his arms across his chest. "This isn't some vacation to the world beyond. This is serious."

"And I'm serious." Karros came out of the house with a pack slung over his shoulder. "You have no idea what you might be facing. If the person who killed your father is stalking your sister, then you might need all the help you can get."

"Caleb. We should all go." She placed her hand on her heart as she stared into his eyes. Leaning forward, she said, "It feels right. I can't explain it."

Caleb held his mate's gaze. Her eyes shone, reminding him of the stars above their heads last night. "If you feel it's right then okay." He wasn't especially pleased with Karros coming along. But he was a man who trusted and relied on his instincts. If Elise had a feeling that Karros should come, then he wasn't going to argue.

"We'll need to take Aiden's truck since it has six seats. It's going to be a squeeze if we have to bring Zara back with us, but we'll manage."

"Thank you." She kissed his cheek and swung around to face Karros. "Are you ready to go?"

"All packed." Karros held up his pack.

"I just need to get all the food we foraged into the fridge." She sighed as she headed into the house. "I don't know how long we're going to be so it might all be spoiled by the time we get back."

"Then we'll have to go back." Caleb followed behind her and wrapped his arm around her waist, pulling her back toward him. "It was the best night of my life."

Elise ducked her head and blushed. "I bet you say that to all the women in your life."

"I don't recall any other women," he growled and sent shivers down her spine. "For me, there is only you. There will only ever be you."

"I thought we were in a hurry." Karros came into the kitchen and Caleb let Elise go, wishing he'd denied her request for Karros to come.

He's right, Caleb's bear said. We are in a hurry. Everything else can wait.

Caleb passed the food to Elise who packed it into containers before storing it in the fridge. As they worked, Karros grabbed some snacks from the cupboard which he put in a separate pack.

The guy is thinking of his stomach, his bear said. Perhaps we have more in common than we thought.

That depends on whether he intends to share, Caleb answered.

"Okay, I think that's everything." Elise sniffed the mushrooms before she put them in a container. "These shouldn't ferment too much more if I put them in the fridge, but if your bear does eat them, we should proceed with caution."

"You're going to feed the fermented mushrooms to a bear?" Karros asked in shock.

"Not just any bear." Elise placed her hand on Caleb's

shoulder and the familiar jolt of recognition course through him. "Caleb and his bear share a special connection. He's quite house-trained."

House-trained, his bear grumbled, and Caleb laughed.

She doesn't mean it as an insult, she is just trying to explain to her brother that we are not going to rip anyone's head off if we eat a few too many mushrooms, Caleb explained.

"I'll take your word for it," Karros replied. "But a drunk bear just sounds dangerous."

"There's nothing dangerous about Caleb's bear as long as you are on the right side of him," Elise replied. "And you will stay on the right side of him, won't you?"

It was more of a warning than a question and Karros bowed his head. "I am not stupid enough to provoke any bear, whether it's a shifter or not. I like my life and want to keep it."

She went to him and patted his cheek. "You also like your face. And want to keep it."

"Come on," Karros chuckled. "Let's get going. Your sister needs us."

Ah, so that's why he insisted he came, Caleb's bear said. He cares for his sister and knows how much you care for Zara. He is being protective of our sister because he can empathize with us.

And there was I thinking he was coming along because he doesn't think we are strong enough to keep Elise safe. Or because he thought it would give him a chance to prove to Flora she'd chosen the wrong man. As if he thinks we might need his help. Caleb studied Karros for a moment. His bear might be right. Karros was more compassionate than they'd given him credit for.

Ten minutes later, they were driving to the hotel, where they had arranged to meet up with Aiden and Flora. Caleb had decided not to tell his brother that Karros was coming along, too.

"When was the last time you visited the world beyond?" Caleb asked.

"Some time ago. A couple of years, maybe more. I went to a food festival. There were all different flavors of food from around the world. I found it stimulating." Elise inhaled deeply. "I can still taste some of them and the smell..."

"You and food," Karros replied.

"I've never known you to complain about eating the food I've prepared," Elise countered.

"I'm always happy to support you in your career." Karros glanced at Caleb. "You find it funny?"

Caleb's laughter bubbled up inside him, despite the seriousness of the situation. "I can hear my brothers and me in you two. The way you bicker. You don't mean to hurt each other, you just like to have these small disagreements."

"It's part of being siblings," Elise acknowledged. "At least we have plenty of experience when it comes to our own children."

"Ah, so this means you are having children." Karros nodded with approval.

"It does." Elise tucked her arm through her brother's. "We're going to need lots of babysitting help. I want to continue with my career."

He placed his hand on top of hers. "You know I'm there for you no matter what. Whatever you need, I'll do what I can."

"You're a good brother." Caleb stared straight ahead, they were nearly back at the hotel.

"Thanks. It means a lot." Karros paused. "And you're a good mate for my sister. I know how much her career means to her."

"I am here," Elise squeezed his hand. "You're talking as if I am invisible."

"You could never be invisible," Karros told her. "Not when you make so much noise."

"I don't make a lot of noise." She shuffled in her seat and sat up straighter. "What noise do I make?"

Caleb chuckled and then Karros started laughing as Elise poked him in the ribs. "Ouch."

"Don't be so mean." She hugged him as Caleb drove into the parking lot of the hotel and stopped the engine.

"I'm going to tell Aiden that you're coming." He leaned forward and looked at Karros. "If he really hates the idea..."

"I won't come," Karros replied. "If he really hates the idea, I'll wait for you here. As long as you promise to keep in contact with me. And if you need me, I'll come find you."

"Thanks." Caleb bowed his head at Karros and got out of the truck.

"You're trusting Karros to drive your truck back to his house?" Aiden had his head under the hood of his truck as he checked the water and oil.

"No, he's coming with us."

Aiden nearly thumped his head on the raised hood as he jerked his chin up. "What?"

"Karros wants to come, and Elise has a feeling it's a good idea," Caleb explained, even though it sounded lame.

"Seriously? You know that he was engaged to Flora until a couple of days ago. I know it's hard to say no to your mate, but I think it's a terrible idea." He closed the hood and wiped his hand on a rag.

"Is it?" Caleb asked.

"Yes." Aiden stared at his brother as he wiped his hands clean. With a sigh, he shook his head. "But you've obviously thought it through and think it's a good idea."

"Elise reminded me that we have no idea what we're walking into. We have no idea what kind of threat is out there waiting for us. What kind of threat is stalking our sister. What kind of danger we're walking into with our mates."

Aiden glanced over his brother's shoulders, his eyes fixed on Karros who was still seated inside the truck.

He's smart, Caleb's bear said. If he'd gotten out as if this was a done deal no matter what Aiden said, it might have caused problems. Aiden might have felt pressured, but this way our brother gets to make a decision.

Of course he's smart, Caleb joked. He's Elise's brother and he knew to let Flora go when she found her mate. He could have clung on, but he didn't.

So we like him now? His bear chuckled.

We do. And we have to since he is Elise's brother and very important to her. She trusts him so we must trust him, too.

With our lives? Caleb asked.

Yes. With our lives. But let's hope it never comes to that. His bear lowered his head and paced back and forth, the thought of anyone threatening them or their loved ones was almost too much. He wanted to tear into whoever was threatening Zara.

"Elise is right. Ivan offered to come but there's no way he can leave the hotel restaurant. Logan and Dario are busy with the store and with Penny and Helena pregnant, I don't want them to take unnecessary risks."

"And Rift?" Caleb asked. Not that there was room for anyone else in the truck. But if there was an issue with Karros accompanying them then maybe their snow leopard brother could come with them instead.

"Rift is going to finish the job on the roof." Aiden shrugged. "We were supposed to finish it today. We can't leave it for too long, there's rain forecast tomorrow, and we have no idea when we're going to be back."

"Okay, Karros it is." Caleb nodded.

"Karros it is what?" Flora came out of the hotel carrying a

pack and linked arms with Aiden. "What are you two planning? I thought we were focused on going to check up on Zara."

"We are and Karros has offered to come, too." Aiden faced his mate. "Are you okay with that?"

"Am I okay with that?" She leveled her gaze at Aiden. "Shouldn't you be the one answering that question?"

"I already have. I told Caleb I'm okay with it because we might need backup." Aiden's jaw tensed as Flora's eyes narrowed. "So, you're okay with it but not happy about it."

"That just about sums it up." Aiden nodded toward the truck. "All I want to do is protect my family and if Karros can help with that then I appreciate it."

"He'll have your back," Flora told her mate. "No matter what he feels about our relationship, if he says he's there for you then he'll be there for you. He won't go behind your back and he knows for sure that my relationship and our arranged marriage are dead."

"As long as he's not coming along to make sure that I end up dead," Aiden said lightly but his expression was set firm.

"He's not that kind of man. I promise you." She kissed Aiden's cheek. "And you have no reason to be insecure, you know I am yours. If anything happened to you, I would never take another man to my bed nor will I ever wear another man's ring."

"Okay." Caleb put up his hand. "That is far too much information." He chuckled as he walked away, heading back to his truck to tell Karros his offer to accompany them had been accepted.

"So, we're all going." Elise and Karros got out of the truck as he approached.

"Yes, if you're sure that's what you want to do." He lowered his head and looked Karros in the eyes. "This is going to be hard for you."

"I know." Karros nodded and headed around to the back of the truck. "Let's just get the packs and get on the road."

"Will he be okay?" Caleb whispered to Elise.

"He'll be okay. He's got to learn how to act around Flora now that they are no longer engaged. This might be the easiest way. He'll see how happy she is with Aiden and maybe he'll move on. Then when we get back, he can focus on finding the love of his life."

"You make it sound so simple." Caleb slipped his arms around her and pulled her close.

"Okay, I might have one request while we're on this trip," Karros called from the back of the truck.

"And that is?" Elise asked.

"You can tone down the smooching and the kissing. Some of us are single and don't need to be reminded every five minutes that you are in *lurve*."

Elise grabbed Caleb and kissed him, clinging to him as Karros made puking noises.

Siblings, his bear laughed.

21

ELISE

"We survived the trip." Elise climbed out of the truck. Flora had sat in the front with Aiden while Caleb, Elise, and Karros had sat in the back. With no smooching.

She cast a sidelong glance at her brother as he got out of the truck and stretched his arms over his head. He'd been so quiet on the journey, but he looked okay.

"Stop staring." Karros suddenly locked eyes with her.

"I was just checking that you were okay." Elise switched her attention to Caleb who was talking quietly with Aiden. She suspected they were using their shifter senses to search the area around the nearby house.

"I'm fine. But I'd be better if you stopped looking at me." He moved closer to her. "This is a nice place." He inhaled deeply. "The mountain air is so cool and fresh."

"Are you tempted to live here?" she asked.

"Not live but a long visit might be nice." He glanced at Flora.

"It would give you a chance to reset your thoughts and emotions."

"That sounds as if you want to get rid of me," he replied.

"Not get rid of." She linked arms with him. "I just want you to be happy."

"Zara." Caleb raised his hand as a pretty woman, a few years younger than the twins but with similar facial features, opened the door of the nearby house. "Are you okay?"

Elise pulled Karros forward as they hurried toward the young woman who was clinging to the doorframe. Were they too late? Had someone attacked her?

There was no sign of blood and with some effort, Zara pushed herself back to a standing position. "Sorry, I don't know what happened." She threaded her hand through her hair. "I felt faint. I don't know why."

"Shall we go inside and sit down?" Caleb asked as he put his arm around her.

"No." She shook her head. "I don't think I want to go inside. I think I'm right where I'm supposed to be." Her eyes were unfocused as she looked toward Karros.

"Oh." Flora put her hands over her mouth, her cheeks flushed pink as she looked from Zara and then to Karros.

"Oh, what?" Aiden asked as he followed her gaze. "Oh."

"Well, that both simplifies things and makes them a whole lot harder," Caleb said.

"What are you talking about?" Elise asked.

"Zara just met her mate." Aiden's jaw tightened.

"It looks as if we're going to be family in a weird way after all." Flora cracked a smile.

"Oh." Elise shook her head as she looked at Zara, who was now intently focused on Karros as if nothing else in the world existed. "Oh."

"Exactly," Flora said.

"What have I missed?" Karros asked as everyone stared at him.

"Karros, this is our sister, Zara." Caleb put his arm around Zara. "And if I'm not mistaken, you are her mate."

"Mate?" Karros shook his head as his eyes narrowed. "Is this some kind of joke?"

"No, why would it be a joke?" Aiden's voice hardened.

"Because the easiest way to stop me from loving Flora and wanting her as my wife would be for you to find me someone else. A shifter who says she's my mate and we're supposed to be together forever." Karros didn't sound happy at all.

"That's exactly what we are," Zara told him as the color came back to her cheeks.

"This is just..." Karros looked to Elise for help.

"Fate," she told him. "This is just fate."

"You're telling me that fate decided to make me the mate of your mate's sister?" he asked hotly.

"Yes," Zara told him.

"It's too convenient," Karros insisted but he didn't back away from Zara. It was as if his feet were glued to the spot.

"Can't you feel it?" Elise put her hand on his stomach. "Can't you feel it here? There's a connection between you. An unbreakable bond. You must feel it."

Karros looked at his sister for a long moment. Perhaps he didn't feel it. Maybe not every shifter mate did. She hadn't thought about that. Elise had assumed that the connection was strong between all mates.

"Don't you feel it?" Zara stepped forward and placed her hand on Karros's.

It was as if he'd been hit by a bolt of lightning, his body jerked and his skin paled as he stared at Zara. As his eyes widened, there was no doubt in anyone's mind that he felt it. That his life and love were now bound to Zara.

Elise glanced at Flora. How would she react to losing the man who had loved her for all her life? The smile on her friend's face said it all. She was smiling ecstatically, her hands clasped together as she watched.

"I can feel it." Karros's voice trembled as he stared at her. "I don't understand it, but I can feel it."

"You're not supposed to try to understand it," Zara told him. "All you have to do is accept it."

"Accept it." Karros glanced at Flora for a moment. Then he took a big breath and let it out slowly as if he were finally letting go of the woman he had loved. And so graciously lost.

"Yes. You just have to accept what is in your heart," Elise told him. She reached for his hand. "And you have the biggest heart out of everyone I know."

Karros hugged her, his face buried in her shoulder. He might be her older brother but right now, he was vulnerable and exposed, his emotions raw.

"Shall we go inside?" Caleb put his arm around his sister and guided her into the house. "If someone is watching you, the last thing we want to do is let them see what's happening."

Karros lifted his head, his eyes flashed with anger as he turned and looked out into the distance. "Now more than ever I wish I had your shifter senses."

"They won't do you much good," Zara told him. "I can't seem to get a fix on whoever or whatever is out there."

"Do you have any clue?" Aiden asked as they went inside, and he shut the door behind them.

"Not really. The first couple of times I sensed there was someone out there, I went out the next morning and scoured the area, trying to pick up the scent of anything different. But it's impossible, there are so many shifters who pass by." She led them into the kitchen, her cheeks were less flushed, and she seemed to be recovering herself. However, she was constantly looking at Karros as if her eyes were drawn to him of their own accord.

They entered the kitchen area, which was in a bad state of repair, although the tools laid out on the floor suggested she was working on it.

"You've worked hard on the house," Aiden complimented his sister as she made a fresh pot of coffee.

"Since I planned to come and visit you for a couple of days I've been trying to get ahead of schedule. Uncle Peter has been coming around to help in the evenings." She smiled fondly. "Not that I need it, but I think he and Aunt Harriet are keeping a close watch on me."

"Are you sure whoever you sensed wasn't one of your cousins?" Flora sat down at the table. "Maybe one of them comes past when they are out and checks on you."

"I had a similar idea. But I know what my cousins feel like and anyway, their senses are no better than mine. This is too far away, like something brushing against my mind." She put her hand to her temple. "I know it's vague but can't explain it any better than that."

"Vampires?" Karros finally found his voice.

"A what?" Zara's eyes went wide. "Vampires aren't real."

"Yes, they are," Aiden confirmed. "Not only are they real but they also have the ability to glamor people and take away their memories."

"Like the effects of the sycombre but a lot worse," Elise said. "Sorry, you don't know what that is either."

Zara pulled out a chair and sat down heavily. With her elbows on the table, she put her head in her hands. "I'm beginning to realize there's a lot I don't know about."

"This is a shock. We all felt the same way when we found our mates." Caleb glanced over to Elise.

"A real shock and I'm not a shifter. I can't imagine how intense this is for you all." She touched her brother's arm. "But that's the great thing, we know it's true. We feel it in our hearts. There's a connection. It's like I can sense Caleb with a part of me."

"That's exactly how I felt the first time I met Aiden." Flora sidled over to her mate and he slid his arm around her shoulders. "Of course, I tried to push him away at first." She fixed her eyes on Karros. "I was confused because it wasn't part of the plan. I also felt resentful that once again someone or something was deciding my fate. But honestly, things got a lot easier when I just gave in to the inevitable."

"You make it sound so romantic," Aiden teased.

"Hey, I'm being honest. Isn't that what we're supposed to do?" She dug him in the ribs.

"Yes. Be honest with each other about your feelings," Caleb advised. "It's the best way. It's the only way because this isn't going to stop."

"Thanks for the advice." Zara glanced shyly at Karros.

"Yes, thanks for the advice." Karros smiled softly at Zara. "We just take it slow."

"We just take it slow." She wiped a hand across her eyes. "I'll get us that coffee."

"You sit down and take a moment. We can make coffee." Caleb squeezed his sister's shoulder before opening the cupboard next to him. "Cups?"

"Oh, in that cupboard there." Zara pointed to a cupboard to his left and Caleb set to work, with the help of Aiden.

"How are you doing?" Elise asked Karros quietly.

"I'm okay." He ran his hand through his hair. "I feel a little removed from reality if I'm honest, as if this is happening to someone else and I'm an observer."

"It gets easier." Flora joined them. "I'm so happy for you, Karros."

She hesitated for a moment before holding her arms out wide to the man she would have married if Aiden hadn't come into her life. Karros slipped into her arms and hugged her. "Thanks. When you told me you were mates with Aiden, I never understood how you could know he was the one for you. I mean really know."

"But you feel it now." Flora pulled away from Karros and wiped her hand across her eyes. "These are happy tears, by the way."

"Ah, and there I was thinking that you were crying because I've found another woman to love." Karros put his hand over his mouth and his eyes drifted across the room until they locked with Zara's.

"Yes. You have found the love you deserve." Flora blotted her cheeks. "I'm so happy for you."

"I know you are." Karros inhaled deeply and went to the table and pulled out a chair. He sat down awkwardly across the table from Zara. "I'm Karros."

"Zara." She held out her hand to Karros. "Good to meet you."

He chuckled, her cheeks pink as he slid his hand into hers. "Good to meet you." His eyes widened with recognition as their skin touched and Elise recalled the first moment Caleb had touched her. The intense feelings that flooded her body were like an inferno, as if something inside of her were being torn apart and made anew.

The wonder on Karros's face was intense, as if he'd just found the most precious thing in the world. Zara mirrored that expression back at him.

"So that's what we looked like," Flora said to Elise.

"I guess it is." She slipped her hand around Flora's shoulders. "Are you okay?"

Flora wiped more tears from her cheeks. "I'm blubbering like a baby but only because I'm so happy for Karros. After he let me go... His sadness... I wanted him to heal and find the love he deserved. Real love with someone who would reciprocate his feelings. Something I could never do."

"He knows you never loved him, but he was holding onto the hope that if you gave him a chance, you would learn to love him." Elise loved her brother so much, she'd wanted him to find real love, too.

"Now he's with someone who doesn't need to learn to love him. And I know the intensity of that kind of love." She glanced at Aiden who kept looking at Karros and then at Flora. "I couldn't be happier."

"Me neither." Elise inhaled deeply and her breath shuddered through her body as she tried to contain her tears. But they came anyway, happy tears for her brother.

Although even though they were witnessing a small miracle, they could not forget the reason they were here.

Her brother's mate was in danger.

22

CALEB

"So, can you tell us anything else?" Caleb needed to focus on the threat to his sister, but he was so incredibly happy for her and Karros, it was hard. They should be celebrating their good fortune, instead they were stuck in the small kitchen trying to figure out who was lurking in the shadows of Zara's life.

"No." Zara ran her hand through her hair, her cheeks were flushed, and she looked as if she'd been hit by a hurricane. "Even if my head was clearer, I don't think there's anything else I can add. That's why I called you guys. I was planning on coming to visit but I'd feel terrible if I led anyone to Wishing Moon Bay who might cause you problems."

"Is this possibly just connected to finding Wishing Moon Bay?" Flora asked. "You said there was that guy who stalked Helena and Penny because he wanted to get back there. Is it possible he's the one behind this?"

"No." Caleb shook his head. "Silas dealt with him."

"Silas again. He sure does get caught up in a lot of shady

stuff." Flora blew the air out of her cheeks. "Okay, let's brainstorm this."

"I've gone over it from every angle and can't figure out who it is or what they want," Zara said. "So I'd be grateful for any input."

"Okay. Is this possibly related to your parents?" Flora asked.

"Why now?" Zara asked. "After all this time, why come after us? And what is there to gain? Our parents are dead, he can't exactly punish them anymore. He took their lives and they never got to see their kids grow up."

She ducked her head and sobbed, her hands covering her face. Karros reached across the table and grasped one of her hands. Sandwiching it between his two hands, he rubbed her skin as if trying to give her his warmth and strength.

He really does care for her, Caleb's bear said.

Of course he does, Caleb answered. They're mates and we heard what Elise told Flora.

We shouldn't have been listening, his bear chastised.

It's hard not to hear when we're in the same room. It wasn't as if I was trying to eavesdrop, Caleb protested.

It's done, his bear answered sagely. And it's good to know our mate feels the same way about us as we do about her. That she can feel the same connection even if it's not as strong.

We already knew she did. But hearing her talk to Flora about it. To know she's happy. He sighed and forced his attention back to the problem before them.

Who was stalking Zara?

"I'm going to call Oscar Renshaw." Aiden put his coffee cup down on the counter and headed toward the back door leading into the yard behind the house. "I called him earlier to see if he could dig up some information on the guy who is suspected of killing our parents. Let's see if he's figured out a connection."

"Again, after all this time." Zara didn't want to believe it was connected to their parents' deaths and neither did Caleb. That was in the past, they had all moved on. Aiden and Caleb had agreed that taking revenge now would hurt them more than the guy responsible. They didn't want to be consumed with hatred and revenge when they had so much ahead of them.

However, the person responsible might not feel the same way. Or perhaps it was someone else, a family member who had chosen to take revenge.

This is like looking for a needle in a haystack, his bear grumbled.

"I think it's worth making the call," Caleb agreed. "But what doesn't make sense is that this must be a very powerful shifter."

"Or a highly trained one." All eyes turned to Karros. "I heard that some shifters could train their senses to be really powerful. Like an athlete can train their body."

"He might be right," Caleb agreed.

A fae who knows more about shifters than shifters, his bear grumbled.

"So now we think there's a highly trained shifter watching me?" Zara asked.

"Why hasn't he, or she, made a move?" Elise asked.

"Because of Wishing Moon Bay?" Karros suggested. "If Zara was planning on visiting, they might be simply biding their time."

"But how did they connect Zara to town?" Flora turned her laser focus on Zara. "Have you been going around telling people you are visiting Wishing Moon Bay?"

"No," Zara insisted, and Flora earned herself a reproving look from Karros. "The only people who know are my aunt and uncle and my cousins. We agreed not to mention the town to anyone else." She placed her hand over her heart. "Your secret is our secret."

"I'll call Oscar." Aiden closed the door behind him, leaving the other people in the kitchen in silence.

"What if it's the man who took you and Aiden when you were kids?" Flora asked Caleb.

"Then at least we'll finally be able to catch him and bring him to justice." Caleb gripped his coffee cup so tightly, he could have crushed it in his hands, but he flexed his fingers and relaxed. Losing his temper was not going to help.

Of course, we're angry that this person might be back and causing a threat to our sister, his bear said.

But why follow her? Caleb asked. Why not just take her if that's what he wants? I can't see why he'd just follow her.

To lure us back here? His bear's suggestion that they had walked into a trap didn't sit well with him and he pushed his senses out, trying to locate anyone lurking around the house.

There was no one.

I doubt this is about us. He must be crazy if he thinks he can take us and Aiden again, we'd fight him now and he wouldn't stand a chance.

So what is it about? Caleb asked.

That was the question no one could answer.

"I'm going to go take a look outside." Caleb stood up abruptly. Sitting around drinking coffee was not going to help them.

"I'll come with you." Elise shot a look at Flora who also stood up.

"I'll go check on Aiden." She bolted for the door.

"Do you want me to come with you?" Zara asked.

"No. Stay here." Caleb grinned as he caught sight of Elise's expression.

"I don't think we were very subtle, do you?" Elise asked as she closed the front door behind them.

"Not really, but those two are so focused on each other right now they won't even have noticed." Caleb chuckled. "Is that how I looked when we first met?"

"Oh, you looked as if you had eaten bad seafood." She waved her hand around her face. "A little green. Not a good advertisement for the hotel restaurant."

"Funny." He rolled his eyes, but she was right, meeting his mate had knocked the air out of his lungs and left his knees weak. His mind had emptied of all thought except his mate and how to win her heart.

They left the house behind and followed the road for a short distance until a trail cut past between two houses and wound toward the foothills of the mountain. Caleb stopped walking and stretched his senses out to their limit.

"Was Karros right?" Elise asked. "Is there a way to make your senses stronger and more far-reaching?"

"I suppose. I've never thought about it. But I expect you could train them." He shrugged. "My senses have always worked so well that it never occurred to me to test them."

"Are your senses the same as your brother's?" Elise asked.

His brow furrowed. "We never overly compared. Aiden and I have the same senses for sure but that could be because we're twins. Rift has heightened sight, he can't necessarily see farther but he can see more clearly, the details are sharper. Ivan probably has the best senses."

They walked along the trail and Caleb kept his senses stretched to their limit, which was mentally exhausting. As he walked, he tried to push a little farther, to hear more distant sounds, and to sense the presence of any living creature outside his normal limit.

"Of course, it could be that Zara's senses are just not so well developed." Elise's suggestion snapped his attention back to her and he relaxed, allowing himself a moment to recover.

"That's possible." He stopped walking and put his hands on his hips. "Or she might have imagined it."

"Do you think that's possible?" Elise asked. "Zara seems levelheaded. She doesn't seem like the kind of person to see monsters where there are none."

"She's not. At least from what I've learned, she's not, but we don't know her that well. She might be our sister, but we don't know her. Our relationship is new. It takes time to get to know someone. To really know them."

Elise linked her arm with him and rested her head on his shoulder. "Does it?"

"Mates are different, we have that connection, remember? I think it makes it easier to read a person, to know their heart." He turned to face her and threaded his arms around her shoulders. "I feel that I know you. That I know the essence of you."

"The essence of you." Her eyes misted with tears. "I like that." She blinked rapidly. "I'm so grateful for you."

He lowered his head and kissed her lips, tightening his hold on her. This is where he wanted her to be always, in his arms with his lips on hers.

That would make life very awkward, and we'd starve to death, his bear pointed out.

Caleb sighed and broke their kiss. His bear reminded him that they were here to solve the mystery of their sister's stalker. Kissing would have to wait for later.

"Let's keep going on this trail." He pointed upward. "Once we get higher, we should be able to get a view of Zara's house."

"Do you think that's where they would have stood and watched Zara?" Elise asked.

"Yes, it's beyond the limit of my senses when we were back at the house. I expect it's beyond Elise's, too. But someone with binoculars would have been able to watch the house from there."

"Which means we might be back to looking for a non-supernatural being." Elise patted his arm. "Impressive."

"You think so?" He caught hold of her hand when the trail became steep and harder to climb.

"I can manage," she insisted, although she didn't pull her hand away from him.

"I know. But that doesn't mean I don't want to help make your life easier." They walked on until they reached a small outcrop. Anyone standing there had a good view of the houses below, including Zara's house.

"Can you sense them in the house?" Elise asked.

Caleb shook his head. "No, they are out of range."

Elise leaned down and stared at the ground while walking back and forth along the outcrop. "Let's see if we can find any clues."

"You're like a detective," Caleb told her as she brushed her hand across the dirt and uncovered a bottle cap.

"I don't think my skills are going to help us solve this." She examined the bottle cap. "This has been here for a few months at least."

"I can't see anything." He inhaled deeply. "And nothing smells different. Zara is right, there are so many scents here, though, it would be impossible to pick one out."

Caleb straightened up and stared farther up the trail. The foothills stretched up toward the mountain. Someone with a powerful telescope could stand on any part of the mountain and spy on Zara in her house below.

"We're not going to find anything here, are we?" Elise asked.

"No. I hoped we might. About the only thing we have done is expanded our list of suspects to include every non-shifter along with any shifter. Until we figure out why someone might spy on Zara, we're not going to figure out the who."

"Let's go back to the house. I should check up on Karros. He looked as if he'd been hit by a bus." Her expression brightened, a smile chasing away her fears.

"It's a good thing I like the guy," Caleb told her. "If he'd acted like an idiot over us being together, I'd have been forced to go into big-brother mode and warn him he'd better not ever hurt my little sister."

"I get the feeling your little sister can take care of herself. But I don't think you need to worry at all. Karros is the sweetest guy, and he is smitten by Zara. They're going to be just fine."

As long as they could find and neutralize the threat against Zara before whoever was watching her could carry out their plan.

23

ELISE

They headed back to the house, their search for any clues futile. Caleb was right, they needed to figure out why someone might be watching Zara before they could figure out who.

"When we get back, why don't you talk to Zara alone, while I talk to Karros," Elise suggested as they neared the house.

Caleb stopped walking and glanced at her. "I assume there's something specific you want me to ask her. Although, she said she has no other information that would help."

"What if we're blowing this all out of proportion?" Elise lowered her voice, fully aware that Zara was also a shifter with heightened senses. After the discussion on how far a shifter could push their senses, she didn't want to risk this conversation being overheard. The last thing she needed was to offend the woman who was both sister to her mate and mate to her brother. "What if Zara has a..." She ran her hand through her hair and looked around.

"Just say it, Elise. We're floundering here so any ideas are better than no ideas." Caleb brushed her hair back from her face. "You won't offend me. You might look at this from a different perspective."

"A non-shifter perspective." She chewed the inside of her cheek for a moment.

"Please, tell me," Caleb urged.

"Okay. Karros was in love with Flora. I mean really in love with her."

Caleb's eyes narrowed. "But now he has Zara."

"Relax, that's not the point." She placed her hand on his upper arm. "Compare his behavior to Tisserand's."

Caleb's nostrils flared. "Tisserand was a controlling jerk who wanted his own way."

"But if you put the two together." She entwined her fingers.

"I don't understand." Caleb knitted his brows together.

"That's because I'm not explaining it very well." She blew the air out of her cheeks and looked down at her feet. "So I'm just going to say it even though you might..."

"Elise." He looked her straight in the eyes. "Say it."

"Okay. Your sister might have had a boyfriend. And since she's a shifter, the relationship might not have been serious for her...but it might have been for him. He might have fallen in love with Zara and when she didn't reciprocate his feelings, he might not have taken it well." Elise shrugged. "Is that possible?"

"Absolutely." Caleb rubbed his hand over his chin. "We saw firsthand what can happen when things didn't work out your way when we dealt with Tisserand."

"The thing is, Zara might not want to admit it in front of Karros."

"He'd understand. More than most people, he'd understand since it's so similar to his own relationship with Flora." Caleb continued toward the house. "But you're right, let's split them up and I'll ask Zara."

"I wonder if Aiden has any news from Oscar." They were nearly at the house. She couldn't wait to talk to Karros and find out how he was feeling. She was so happy for him. If only his meeting with Zara had come under better circumstances.

A lump of emotion welled in Elise's throat and she blinked back tears. She needed to focus instead of dissolving into a pool of emotion. The sooner they figured this out and dealt with any threat to Zara, the sooner they could all get on with their lives.

"How are you doing?" Caleb's gentle tone nearly pushed her over the edge, but she stifled a sob.

"I'm so happy for him, I can hardly breathe. I just wish we weren't here under these circumstances. Why couldn't they have just met when Zara visited Wishing Moon Bay without this threat hanging over them?"

"We don't get to choose the circumstances when we meet our true love," Caleb replied sagely. "But we should both realize that we've all come together like this at this time for a reason."

"Karros is here because Zara needs him." She nudged him playfully. "And you met me because you needed me."

He smothered a smile. "I have needed you all my life."

"Cute cover-up." She tilted her head to one side and studied him. "You know what I mean."

"I do. When Flora and Aiden met, it was because she needed him. But maybe this time it's the other way around. I need you." He pointed at her. "Although, you did need me to get you a job with Ivan."

"I concede that point." She bowed her head. "And maybe it's just better if we realize we do need each other. It's not something we have to keep score of."

"Right. Let's go inside and test our acting skills." He kissed her cheek, inhaling deeply as her hair brushed his face. There was something incredibly sexy about having a man love every part of you.

And she loved every part of him.

He pushed the door open and went inside. After a moment she followed, trying to compose her thoughts and emotions which had been all over the place since she'd met Caleb. Her once calm life was gone, it was as if she'd been cast out onto a tumultuous ocean in a rickety boat. Yet she knew while there was breath in Caleb's body, she would never fall overboard or lose her way.

"Okay. Are you ready?" Caleb asked and she practically bumped into him as he stopped suddenly.

"Yes." She nodded but didn't meet his eyes.

"Are you sure?" He moved closer, until there wasn't room for air between their bodies. "If there's anything else you want to talk about. If you have any other ideas."

"No." She placed her hand on his chest and took comfort from the steady thump of his heart.

"Okay then." He inhaled and inched away from her, but she caught hold of him and pulled him back.

"I just want you to know that I love you." She patted his chest. "I mean really love you. It's like it's there, inside of me. I don't know where it came from or when it started, it's just there."

He smiled shyly. "Are you sure you don't have shifter blood somewhere in your ancestry?"

She snorted and covered her mouth. "My Grandma Sylvie would go crazy if she heard you say that." Her brows knitted together. "Although, my Grandma Hannah who lives by the wildwood would get a kick out of it."

"You're back." Aiden appeared behind them, making her jump and pull away from Caleb as if they'd been caught misbehaving.

"We went to check out the surrounding area," Caleb

replied. "There's an outcrop in the foothills. I wondered if someone had been spying on the house from up there. It's far enough away that my senses wouldn't have picked up on them but close enough that someone with a powerful telescope would have been able to see."

"Did you find anything?" Aiden asked.

"No."

"I've already scoured the mountainside," Zara called from the kitchen. "I had the same idea."

"And nothing?" Caleb went to the kitchen and Elise followed. She needed to get Karros outside. Perhaps into the back yard.

"No." Zara shook her head. "Plus, it's not just here that I sensed someone. I went for a run from my aunt's house and sensed it there, too."

"Could someone have followed you from here to there?" Aiden asked.

"Not easily. Not without me knowing. The roads are so quiet, I'd have seen the headlights." She shrugged. "Unless they guessed that was where I was going."

"You look as if you need some fresh air, Karros." Elise went to her brother and tucked her hand under his arm. "Come on, let's go outside."

Karros looked up at her as if he had no idea who she was then he blinked and nodded. "Fresh air might help."

"I think so." She glanced sideways at Caleb who winked.

"I feel numb," Karros admitted as they walked to the end of the yard and sat down on a wooden bench that looked as if it might fall apart at any moment.

"This is a shock." She leaned forward and rested her elbow on her knee. "Are you okay about it?"

"About having a shifter as a mate?" He stared at her for a long moment before he blinked. "Our parents are going to go crazy."

She took hold of his hand and threaded her fingers through his. "At least we're in this completely and utterly together. They'll have to disinherit both of us."

"I don't care so much about that," Karros confessed. "I just know how happy they were when Flora agreed to marry me. I ruined their dreams once."

"We should tell them soon," Elise agreed. "Because knowing Grandma, she's probably already busy arranging marriage number two."

"I told them not to." Karros rubbed his hand over his eyes. "When I broke the news about Flora, after their initial shock and anger, Dad said they would figure something else out. That he'd call Grandma Sylvie and get her to find me another wife."

"I had no idea." Elise squeezed his hand. "You never said."

"I wasn't marrying Flora for any other reason than I loved her." His eyes sparkled with tears. "I never just wanted to marry for the sake of getting married, I wanted to get married for love."

"And now you have found the truest of love." She sat up and wrapped her arms around him. "We're incredibly lucky."

He raked a hand through his hair and chuckled. "It's starting to sink in."

"Zara seems nice. Did you get a chance to talk to her while we were out?" Elise stared at the house. Had Caleb asked Zara about any potential stalker ex-boyfriends?

"A little. Mostly we just sat and held hands and stared into each other's eyes. It's like we didn't need words." He covered his face with his hands. "Is this even real?"

"It's very real." She leaned back and inhaled, the air was warm and carried the scent of pine. "So incredibly real."

"The weirdest thing was that when we left Wishing Moon Bay as we were driving here, I knew I was still in love with Flora. It was like a burning pain in the pit of my stomach. I was worried I would never get over her and find a way to be happy."

"And now?"

"Now..." He hesitated. "It's going to sound shallow, but it's gone. The intense love I had for Flora has changed, it's muted, like the love for a best friend."

"That's how it's supposed to be." She turned her face to the sun. "I wish we were here for a vacation rather than because your mate is in danger."

Karros clenched his hands into fists. "I'm not a violent man but right now, if I could get my hands on whoever is stalking her, I would tear them apart."

"Caleb's right, we must have shifter blood in our family."

"He said that?" Karros asked.

"Yeah. Although, I think it's probably simply the connection we have with our mates. We are connected and that connection links us on a deeper level."

"So, we'll become more shifter-like, and they'll become more fae-like." He grinned. "I like that idea."

"Me, too." She jerked upright as the kitchen door opened and Caleb appeared. "What's wrong?"

"Oscar called Aiden with an update." Caleb beckoned to them and she got up from the bench and turned to offer her hand to Karros.

"Wait." Karros stood up and pulled her toward him. "In case things get a little crazy, I want you to know that I'm happy we're in this together."

"You mean that we're both going to disappoint our family?"

"No, that we can share this experience together. You and me." He wrapped his arms around her and hugged her close.

"I couldn't ask for a better brother, Karros. I want you to know that." She hugged him back. "And we're all here for you and Zara. Anything you need, either now or in the future, we're here for you."

"Back at you." He let her go and stood up straight. "Let's go in. I hope we have a lead because I'm going to explode if I don't figure this out."

"If we don't figure this out," Elise reminded him.

"Go, team." Karros fist-bumped the air.

"We are a team. And we're going to be the winning team. I promise you." She linked arms with him, and they went inside together.

24

CALEB

"The guy Oscar suspects, Reginald Barnes, was behind our parents' murder was released from prison three months ago." Aiden glanced at Caleb and then at Zara.

"Which means he could be the person who is stalking Zara?" Karros tensed his jaw and made his hands into fists.

He has the protective nature of a shifter, Caleb's bear said.

He does. Let's hope he never has to fight to protect her.

"It's possible. At least it's possible that he is paying someone to stalk Zara. He's not in good physical shape from what Oscar heard from one of his old colleagues. Certainly not healthy enough to walk all over these mountains." Aiden sighed. "Which means we either stay here and try to flush him out or we take Zara back to Wishing Moon Bay and see what other information Oscar can come up with."

"You want me to run away?" Zara asked. "What about our aunt and uncle? They might not be safe. If I leave, whoever is watching me might hurt them to get back at me if I run."

"True." Caleb shook his head. "There's no right answer here."

"Oscar has also started working on our case." He pointed to Caleb. "Since we went there with Flora, he's been trying to figure out who took us."

"He has?" Caleb asked. "I thought he gave you all the information he had in the file."

"He has managed to get hold of the original file." Aiden poured himself a cup of coffee and sat down at the table. "He's gone through it thoroughly."

"And?" Caleb sensed his brother was holding something back.

"He is chasing a lead now. But he's not overly optimistic." Aiden inhaled deeply. "However, there is some evidence he's trying to get hold of. Something that we might be able to use for a location spell."

"A location spell?" Zara asked.

"Yes, if we have something that belongs to a person, it's possible to locate them," Karros explained.

"Just like that." Zara snapped her fingers.

"Not exactly. It takes magic." Elise looked down at her hands. "The fae can do them but our magic is not as powerful as that of the witches."

"Does Oscar have any evidence that our kidnapping and the murder of our parents are related?" Caleb asked. "I don't want us getting off track and following a lead that is worthless."

"He has never found a connection. That doesn't mean one doesn't exist." Aiden raked his hands through his hair. "If only we could remember what happened." He tapped the side of his head in frustration. "We were there. We were old enough to remember so why don't we?"

"Vampire?" Elise offered as an explanation.

"No." Caleb shook his head. "We think we just blocked it all out. We even forgot we had a sister."

"Well, there is one thing we could try." Elise glanced

nervously at Karros who stared at her, his brows knitted together.

Whatever it is, Karros doesn't seem very happy about it, Caleb's bear said.

"I don't know if that's a good idea." Karros crossed his arms over his body as he leaned against the doorframe. "There might be a good reason you buried your memories."

"Whatever it is, we'd like to hear it. Then we can decide." Aiden closed in on Karros.

"I agree." Caleb slipped his arm around Elise who looked down at her feet for several moments.

She's trying to decide whether to tell us or not, his bear said.

"Please, Elise. We'd like to hear your idea. Give us the chance to decide whether we act on what you have to say or not." He pulled her toward him.

"Okay, our Grandma Hannah is a wise woman of the wildwood, she lives and breathes that place." Elise swallowed hard. "She believes that everything is connected. Like a web." She paused. "She believes that if you can link to that web then you can access any memory. All you have to do is enter the right state of mind, it's like a dream walk."

"Any memory?" Caleb asked.

"Any memory in here." Elise cupped his face in her hands. "You never forget anything, you just store it away. The things that we don't need to remember, like what you had for breakfast when you were five, are stored there in the same way that traumatic experiences that we have chosen to forget are stored there, too. But it's possible to access those memories when you dream walk. A skilled practitioner like my grandma can direct you to where you need to go."

"So, we need to access this web through dream walking and if we do, we'll remember what happened to us?" Caleb's voice shook as he spoke.

"But there might be a good reason why you chose to forget," Karros added.

"You mean something traumatic might have happened and we both chose to forget." Caleb nodded. "We've both thought of this before. It's a thing that constantly comes back to you. Like a question that needs answering."

"It's like when we found out that our parents were dead. It was hard and painful, but it gave us closure." Aiden glanced at his mate. "I think it's something we need to do."

"I'd rather suffer the memories and deal with the threat to Zara." Caleb had made up his mind and Aiden nodded in agreement. "If it's too bad, we can always get Silas to take the memories away again."

"Silas, the vampire?" Zara asked. "Just to be sure I'm keeping up with all of this."

"Yes. Silas the vampire." Aiden went to Zara and placed his hand on her shoulder. "You can stay here, or you can come with us. It's up to you."

"I can't risk anyone else getting hurt. You should go. If you are absolutely certain it's what you want to do. I don't want you to suffer because of me. I don't want you to relive memories you chose to bury because someone is stalking me. We can deal with it differently." She chewed her bottom lip before saying, "We could set a trap. You and Caleb could hang around out there and..."

"If this is a powerful shifter, they might sense us and bide their time, never showing themselves," Flora said gently. "We could think the threat has gone and then as soon as we leave, they could come back. As much as I hate the idea of Aiden or Caleb reliving a part of their lives they chose to forget, I do think this is the best way."

"I'll stay here with Zara," Karros said firmly.

"Good idea," Elise replied before anyone could object.

Not that anyone would object. If Zara was staying, then Karros's place was by her side.

"We should leave now." Elise stepped forward. "If we keep driving, we can be at my grandmother's house before dark."

"Does that mean we can dream walk tonight?" Caleb needed this over with as soon as possible. The thought of reliving those days was scary but if it helped their sister, the sooner they did it the better.

"You can dream walk whenever you want. It doesn't have to be nighttime," Elise explained. "My grandmother will mix a special blend of herbs and once you drink it, you'll sleep, your mind will relax, and she can guide you to where you need to go."

"So only one person has to do it?" Zara asked.

"We'll both do it." Aiden knew Caleb would feel the same way and he nodded in agreement.

"We do this together. We remember together and we heal together." Caleb went to Aiden and hugged him. "This is our shared past."

"And we're always stronger together. We always have been, and I don't think that's going to change anytime soon." Aiden held his brother in his arms.

"I feel bad to have dragged you all this way and then for you to turn around and go straight back home," Zara said.

"Don't be sorry. I think things have turned out just right. Karros, we're relying on you to protect Zara," Caleb warned.

"Zara is a shifter, she'll probably end up protecting him," Aiden laughed and earned himself a reproving look from his sister. "Sorry. We're really happy you're here for her."

"Come on. Let's go." Flora tugged on Aiden's jacket. "Are you okay to drive or do you want one of us to take the wheel?"

"I'm fine. We just need to stop somewhere for some fuel.

For us and the truck." Aiden hugged his sister and shook Karros's hand before they left the house.

"Good to meet you, Zara. Karros, take care." Flora didn't hug either of them. There was still an awkwardness that only time could heal.

"Bye, big brother," Elise hugged Karros.

"Goodbye, little sister." Caleb held Zara in his arms. "If you need anything, just call."

"You're going to be out of reach once you enter your dream walk," she reminded him.

"Elise or Flora will have our phones. If you need anything, call. I'll ask Ivan to be on standby."

"You're going to send a dragon." She pressed her lips together and nodded. "I like that idea."

"He can get here fast." Caleb let her go and stepped toward the door.

"But it's risky for him to be out of Wishing Moon Bay. Especially since the nights are clear and the moon is nearly full." Zara glanced at her mate who was talking quietly with Elise. "We'll be okay."

"If you need him, call," Caleb insisted.

"Don't worry, if we need him, I'll make sure to call," Karros assured them.

"Maybe I do like the idea of you being my sister's mate," Caleb said.

"Does that mean you didn't like the idea?" Karros asked warily.

"He's joking. We are all happy you two are meant for each other. Now, we're going to leave. Take care and I will call you later. And then tomorrow morning." Elise hugged Zara briefly. "Look after him."

"I will," Zara replied.

"Hey, what happened to *me* taking care of Zara?" Karros asked.

"If it makes you feel better, we can pretend you can take care of me," Zara replied.

"But when you see her shift into a bear, you'll realize she'll definitely be the one to protect you. At least physically." Elise glanced at Caleb. "But caring for and protecting someone you love is not just about who is physically stronger."

"Elise is a wise woman," Zara said. "Sometimes the cuts that can hurt the most are deep inside." She stepped forward and flung her arms around Caleb. "Take care. I hate that you are doing this because of me."

"I'd do anything for you, Zara. You're my sister." He hugged her tightly before he stepped back. "We need to go."

"Call us," Zara said.

Elise smothered a smile as she caught Caleb's eye. Zara and Karros were already an *us*. The bond between them was undeniable.

Things will work out, his bear said as they left the house and went to the truck where Aiden and Flora were waiting.

I know, Caleb answered. I just hope dream walking helps so we can put all of this behind us.

He glanced up at the mountains surrounding them and pushed his senses to their limit, and then a little farther. Karros was right, with practice and training he could probably extend them much farther.

It was a skill he would master in case he was ever called on to protect his family again.

25

ELISE

"How much farther?" Aiden stifled a yawn as he drove through the wildwood. They'd been on the road for hours and the light was fading as they neared their destination.

"Another couple of miles." Elise rested her head on Caleb's shoulder, and he looked down at her and smiled. Was it only yesterday that they had camped out in the same forest and made love under the stars?

It was as if a lifetime had passed. Certainly, life had changed in the last twenty-four hours. Especially for her brother.

She put her hand in her pocket and drew out her phone, checking for any messages from Karros, but they were too deep inside the forest to get a good signal. This was one of the reasons her grandmother loved living here, she was cut off from modern life.

As a wise woman of the wildwood, she liked a simple life, one where she was in tune with the natural world around her.

Although, she did like to watch her favorite shows on TV

and surfing the internet to increase her knowledge was acceptable. Elise had also once caught her watching cat videos and chuckling at memes.

"You're smiling," Caleb told her.

"I'm thinking of my grandmother. She's such a complex woman, but her heart is pure. Even though she lives by the old ways and traditions, she is the most open-minded person in our family." Elise placed her hand over his. "You'll like her."

"But will she like me?" he asked.

"Does it matter either way?" Elise turned to look at him. "I love you. We're going to share our lives together no matter what. Does it matter to you what my family says or think?"

"Yes." He slid his hand around her shoulder and cradled her head. "It matters to me because I want you to be happy and even though you'll tell me it doesn't matter to you what they think, I know that it'll hurt all the same."

"She'll like you," Elise assured him. "It's my other grandma you need to worry about."

"Okay, well, I'll take it slow, one at a time." Caleb tightened his hold on her. "I'll do whatever it takes."

"Don't tell my grandmother that. She'd have enormous fun making you live up to those words." Elise chuckled.

"I think I'm going to like your grandma." Caleb took a deep breath and puffed out his chest. "I'm ready for the challenge."

"Good, because we're here." She sat up straight and pulled away from him as she pointed to the left. "Take the next left up here."

"I don't see where to turn." Aiden leaned forward, staring into the twilight.

"There, just after the big rowan tree." She kept pointing to the left as a rowan tree covered in bright berries appeared in the gloom.

"I still can't..." Aiden turned onto what looked like a game trail, but it was just wide enough for the truck. As they drove off the road it, became clear they were on a rough trail, although there was no sign of Elise's grandma's house.

"It's hidden away," Flora said. "I remember coming here when we were children. I always used to think the house was like the one out of the fairy tale."

"Which fairy tale?" Elise asked.

"The one where the children get lost and wind up at the witch's house made of gingerbread."

"Hansel and Gretel." Caleb ducked his head and stared out of the window. "I'm starting to get that vibe."

"Well, firstly, my grandma's house is definitely not made of gingerbread and secondly, she's not a witch. One way to upset her is to call her a witch. She's a fae." Elise glanced at Caleb. "You have been warned."

Flora chuckled. "I expect she could still turn you into a toad, though."

"Please, don't put ideas into her head. Once she knows you are shifters, she might decide your other side needs a makeover and instead of turning into a fierce bear, you might end up being a fluffy bunny rabbit." She put her hands up as if they were paws and showed her bunny teeth.

"No one can change what we are," Aiden insisted, although he didn't sound too sure.

"No, she can't actually change you into something you're not but that doesn't mean she can't make you think that you are." Elise chuckled. "I can just see two bears hopping around like bunnies."

"I'm going to pretend that you are joking and be really careful about what I say around your grandmother," Caleb told her.

"Oh." Flora leaned forward as the truck headlights illuminated a car parked outside of a log cabin. The trees around it seemed to crowd in protectively.

Caleb shivered and placed his hand on her thigh. "Why do I get the feeling that if your grandma was ever under threat, the trees would reach out their spiny branches and grab hold of me and drag me off into the trees, never to be seen again?"

"You're scared of the big bad trees?" Elise teased.

"Not unless they come alive. Your wildwood does have a reputation." He tensed as she leaned forward and stared at the car parked in front of the house.

"What is it?" Elise sat back in the seat and took hold of his hand. "As if things can't get more complicated..."

"Is that your Grandma Sylvie's car?" Flora half-turned in her seat, her eyes wide as she caught Elise's eye.

"Yep." Elise nodded and squeezed Caleb's hand.

"I'm assuming it's not the nice, accepting grandma we need to help us dream walk." Caleb sighed and wriggled in his seat as Aiden parked the truck next to the car. "It seems we're going to need to be at our most charming."

"You look worried," Caleb whispered to Elise.

"Not worried. Anxious, I guess." She touched his cheek. "This could be a problem. Not just for us and our relationship but also for Zara."

"You mean we might not be able to dream walk?" Caleb raked a hand through his hair as he exhaled slowly. "We don't have time to waste."

"Why don't I go inside with Flora and see if my grandmother is leaving anytime soon?" Elise suggested. "She might not be staying overnight in which case we could wait until she leaves and then you and Aiden could come inside."

"And if she doesn't leave?" Caleb asked gently.

"Then we're screwed." Elise chewed her bottom lip.

"We should all go inside together," Caleb responded. "I know you're worried but if your grandmother thinks that we're hiding, that we're scared of her, then it's going to be harder to win her round."

"I think Caleb is right," Aiden agreed.

"You haven't met Elise's Grandma Sylvie," Flora told her mate.

"Is she really that bad?" Caleb asked. "Surely she wants you to be happy."

"She does." Elise turned around to face the front of the car. "And normally she probably wouldn't be too upset. But..." She glanced at Aiden.

"Oh, of course, I keep forgetting that Aiden is the reason Karros won't be fae royalty." Caleb groaned. "Fate is messing with us."

"I don't think you have to worry about fate messing with us. Not when you have Elise's grandmother in there." Flora covered her face with her hands. "I haven't spoken to her since I left this realm for Wishing Moon Bay."

"Yeah, from what Karros said she's pissed with you, too, Flora." Elise reached for the door handle. "Come on, we're in this together, let's face it together."

"Is this one of those times where you're going to protect me?" Caleb asked as he got out of the truck.

"It might just be." She walked toward the cabin but then stopped and waited for Flora and Aiden to get out of the truck too.

"I was trying to convince Aiden to make a run for it." Flora hooked her arm through her mate's. "But he said he couldn't leave his twin here alone."

"All joking aside," Caleb began, "we're here because Zara needs us. We're here because we need your grandmother to help us dream walk so we can remember what happened to us."

"And hopefully, that will lead us to the person who is

stalking her." Aiden nodded firmly. "No one can get in the way of this. We do what we have to do."

"My grandmother might see that as a challenge." Elise sighed and rolled her shoulders as they approached the house. "Why don't you let me do the talking?"

"Okay, and should we not eat anything? Or drink anything?" Caleb asked.

"You think she'll try to poison you?" Elise rolled her eyes.

"No, but we were there when Flora gave a piece of fruit to Sapphire and she instantly forgot fae existed," Aiden reminded them.

"Oh, yeah." Caleb shook his head. "I don't want to forget you and I don't want you to forget me."

"The sycombre fruit won't work on shifters like that," Flora told them. "If it did, my father would have forced us to eat it."

"The fruit is okay if it's a memory that's not anchored in deep emotions. Plus, I'd just told Sapphire, so the thought hadn't had time to spread through her brain. Sycombre fruit works best on short-term memory." She tapped her head. "Although, there's some skill to using it. And Elise's grandmother is the most skilled wise woman in any of the fae realms."

"I don't think they needed to hear that." Flora clapped her hands together lightly. "We're safe, nothing will happen to us. Nothing physical at least, but I've known Elise's grandmothers my whole life and they are..." She sighed. "Let's just get this over with."

Elise went to the door and knocked. The two shifters and Flora hung back a little way as if ready to make a run for it. She half-turned to look at them. "Try to relax."

"Okay." Caleb rolled his shoulders, but the tension didn't leave his body.

"Nonthreatening," she whispered and pointed to his clenched fists.

He held his hands up, his fingers splayed wide. "Nonthreatening."

"Better." Then she snapped to attention as the door opened and an old woman with hair as white as snow faced them. "Grandma Hannah."

"I wondered when you would get around to knocking. All that whispering." The old woman glanced at Elise and then tilted her head sideways to look at the others. "Flora. Boys."

Elise ducked her head and smothered a smile, wondering if the boys were going to insist they were men. They chose to simply nod and say hello.

"Grandma Hannah." Elise held out her arms and leaned forward to embrace her grandmother, only hesitating for a moment when she noticed the old woman's raised eyebrow.

"It's good to see you, Elise. Even if you have brought two shifters to my door." She hugged her granddaughter and then fixed Flora with a sharp look. "And the woman who broke your brother's heart."

"Can we come in?" Elise asked quickly.

Her grandmother inched her head back and studied Elise's face. "You bring trouble with you."

"Not exactly." Elise's eyes misted with tears. "But we do need your help."

"Then you'd better come inside. All of you." With a quick, disapproving look, Elise's grandmother turned around and headed into the cabin.

Elise glanced over her shoulder, inclined her head toward the interior of the house, and then followed.

26

CALEB

"Why does this feel worse than when we entered the dragon's lair?" Aiden whispered.

"Because Elise's Grandma Sylvie is probably fiercer than Fiona." Flora put her hands to her mouth and wiggled her fingers. "Only without the teeth and claws."

"Great." Caleb straightened his back and followed his mate into the house. If they were going to face the two fae grandmothers, then he wanted to be by her side.

And keep quiet, his bear reminded him. *We should be very careful what we say.*

I agree, but that doesn't mean I'm going to let them treat Elise, or any of us, badly. We have done nothing wrong.

Aiden was responsible for Karros breaking off his engagement with Flora. He did ruin their plans.

They can't blame Aiden, that was due to fate, Caleb answered.

Do the fae believe in fate? His bear frowned. *I mean it's kind of in their name.*

Caleb shook his head. *One letter missing can make all the difference.*

Well, if they don't believe in fate yet, by the time we leave, we'll make sure they do and that they accept the decisions of both their grandchildren.

Caleb nodded and accepted the challenge. If they were going to find true happiness, Elise's family had to accept that two shifters were about to join their family.

"Elise is here," her grandma said.

"Elise?" another older woman answered. "I thought she'd gone to Wishing Moon Bay."

"I did, Grandma Sylvie." Elise glanced over her shoulder as the others entered the living area. "But I need Grandma Hannah's help."

"Oh, you need Grandma Hannah's help." There was a hint of disapproval in her tone as she got up from the sofa where she'd been drinking coffee and eating cake. Caleb's stomach rumbled at the thought of food. After leaving Zara's house, they had stopped briefly for fuel and grabbed some sandwiches from the local grocery store in Bear Creek. Then they had driven straight here without stopping.

It was way past dinnertime and Caleb's empty stomach didn't help his mood. He certainly didn't want to waste time listening to an argument as to who was the better grandma.

That's not a good start, Caleb's bear agreed.

I suppose rivalries between grandmas are as much a thing as rivalries between brothers. Caleb moved in front of his brother and Flora, moving to stand beside Elise.

"Oh, and Elise has brought some friends." Grandma Hannah's tone was lighter, laced with amusement.

Perhaps we have at least one grandma on our side already, Caleb said hopefully.

Or maybe she's just interested to see how this is going to play out. She can probably afford to sit back and watch Grandma Sylvie savage us with her tongue. His bear ground his teeth together.

"Shifters." Grandma Sylvie moved around the side of the sofa and saw Caleb and Aiden for the first time. "And Flora."

"This is Caleb." Elise ignored her grandma's hostile expression. "And this is Aiden."

"Twins. Identical twins." Grandma Hannah came closer and stared at them. "Very identical. Extraordinary."

"So this is the man you left Karros for?" Grandma Sylvie didn't seem in the least interested in them being identical twins.

"I didn't leave Karros for Aiden. I am Aiden's mate and Karros realized that my heart would never belong to him," Flora said firmly. "He did the right thing for the right reasons."

"Ah, and now you think Hannah will do the right thing for the right reasons." Sylvie nodded. "What happened, did your bear lose his chew toy?"

"Sylvie." Hannah's warning tone pierced Sylvie's hostile teasing. "Why don't we give the young people a chance to talk? I think we both know they would not be here, given the current circumstances, if this wasn't important."

"We were also having an important discussion," Sylvie insisted. "Remember?"

"I recall our discussion," Hannah answered.

"We were trying to decide on who Karros should marry," Sylvie said. "Since he's in the market for a new wife. I came to tell Hannah that I have been in discussion with a very prominent family." She fixed Flora with a hard stare.

Does she think she'll make Flora jealous? His bear shook his head. She doesn't get the whole shifter mate thing, does she?

I don't think she truly understands it. No. Caleb groaned inwardly. She's going to be really pissed when she finds out that Karros is not interested in marrying anyone other than Zara.

"I think you should let Karros decide who he's going to marry," Elise said firmly.

"How is he supposed to do that when he's still in love

with Flora?" Sylvie kept her eyes fixed on Flora. "By the time he gets over his broken heart, he'll be too old to settle down and have children."

"He isn't in love with me anymore," Flora stated.

"I expect that's what he says to make you feel better. He always did care more for your feelings than his own." Sylvie crossed her arms over her body.

"What exactly do you need, Elise?" Hannah asked.

Elise let out a long breath. "I need..." She glanced at Caleb and Aiden. "*We* need you to help Caleb and Aiden to dream walk."

Hannah's eyes widened and she swayed back and forth before she regained her composure. "Dream walking."

"Yes. They need to remember something that happened to them when they were younger," Elise explained, ignoring Sylvie who tutted loudly.

"What kind of something?" Hannah moved around the room until she stood before Caleb, her eyes narrow as she studied him.

"When we were children..." Caleb's mouth became suddenly dry. He coughed and cleared his throat. "When we were children, our parents were killed, and we were put in foster care."

"Until Valerie adopted you," Sylvie said. "And that's when you came to Wishing Moon Bay."

"You've been busy," Elise commented. "Did you pay someone to investigate them?" Her cheeks flushed pink, and her eyes glittered like diamonds as she stared at Sylvie.

"Yes." Sylvie jutted her chin out. "I wanted to know if there was anything we could use as leverage to get Aiden to break off his relationship with Flora."

"You did what?" Flora asked.

"I did what any self-respecting, caring family member

would do for her grandchild. He was destined to be your husband." Sylvie was unrepentant as she stared at Flora.

"That doesn't matter." Aiden reached for Flora's hand and rubbed his thumb over the back of her hand to comfort her. "Will you please help us?"

"What do you need to remember?" Hannah asked. "And why?"

"Before we were adopted by Valerie, we were in foster care. But someone stole us from our foster parents. We were found by the police inside an apartment, but they never found who took us." Caleb held his hands out to Hannah. "It's important that we remember."

"Why do you need to remember something that happened so long ago?" Hannah stepped sideways and stared at Aiden as if he were a specimen in a jar. Then her eyes widened. "Someone is in danger."

"Our sister. Someone is stalking her, and we think it might be connected to what happened to us. Our father was responsible for putting a bad man behind bars. This man, we believe, murdered our parents. Then we were taken from the foster home."

"Why? When your parents were already dead, why were you taken?" Hannah asked.

"Because we're shifters. There was a trafficking ring back then and we believe we would have been sold," Caleb admitted.

Elise stepped closer to him and reached for his hand. He entwined his fingers with hers and looked down at her face, drawing comfort from her.

"No!" Sylvie put her hands over her mouth. "Not you, too."

"You make it sound as if I caught a disease or something." Elise shook her head. "I love you. Both of you, but you must respect my decisions and my decision to be with Caleb is one of the best ones I have ever made. One that makes me happy. Isn't that what you should be interested in?" She aimed her comment at Sylvie.

"I suppose if you have chosen a shifter then there's little we can do about it. Does Karros support this decision?" Sylvie asked. "I doubt it since he isn't here. And he gave up his life here for you. So that he could help you with your career. I suppose you're going to give that up and spawn a brood of shifters."

Elise glanced at Caleb. He shook his head slightly. This wasn't the time to argue with her grandmother or to break the news that Karros had also found a mate and would be breeding his own shifter children.

She inclined her head and inhaled deeply. "Karros is supportive of my decision and no, I'm not giving up my dream of becoming a chef and one day running my own restaurant. Caleb's brother is the reason I went to Wishing Moon Bay. He's one of the best chefs."

"And who is going to raise your babies?" Sylvie asked.

"I have a very supportive family," Caleb replied. He was tired of Sylvie being so hard on Elise and shifters in general. "They will help us. Isn't that what families are supposed to do?"

"It is." Hannah averted her gaze and ignored Sylvie's hard stare.

"And that's why we're here." She moved toward Grandma Hannah and reached out for her hand. "Caleb and Aiden need to unlock their memories so they can help their sister."

"You always did have an open heart and an open mind." Hannah tilted her head to one side as she studied her granddaughter. "I can't fault you for following your heart."

"Will you help us, please?" Caleb asked.

"If Caleb wasn't my mate, if he was my friend or just someone who came to you for help, you would help him."

Elise squeezed Hannah's hand. "Just because you don't approve of me having a mate, and you don't agree with Karros letting Flora go so she could be with Aiden... Will that stop you from helping them help their sister?"

"I have loved you since you were in your mother's womb," Hannah replied. "I remember putting my hand on her stomach and feeling you kick." She smiled wistfully.

"Grandma," Elise began, "I never set out to disappoint you or hurt you. Neither did Karros. You know that."

"You've never disappointed me." Hannah wrapped her arms around her granddaughter's shoulders. "You are so brave."

Sylvie snorted. "The brave thing would have been to think of your own family."

"You don't really mean that, Sylvie," Hannah replied. "You're only upset about Karros breaking up with Flora because you know how much he loved her."

Sylvie's eyes misted with tears as she jutted out her chin like a petulant child. "I can't understand why Flora would hurt him like that. He was so happy when he came home and told us that Flora had agreed to marry him. He was willing to accept that you didn't love him because he thought he could make you happy."

"I know that but after I met Aiden, there was no way I could go through with marrying Karros. It wouldn't have been fair to him. It wouldn't have been fair to any of us. And he understands that," Flora said.

"He tells you he understands it. But does he?" Sylvie asked.

"Yes. He does." Caleb couldn't hold back any longer.

Elise still held onto Hannah's hand as she reached for Sylvie's hand, too. "Karros understands exactly how Flora felt when she met her mate."

Sylvie's mouth opened and closed like a goldfish as her eyes went wide. "No."

"Yes. Karros met Zara, Caleb and Aiden's sister, today. They are mates." She waited for the news to sink in. "Which is why we really need for you to help us."

"You are both mated to shifters?" Sylvie didn't sound impressed as she looked up at the ceiling. "Is this some kind of a cosmic joke?"

"Love is never a joke, Sylvie," Hannah said quietly.

"No, it's not." Elise placed her hand on her heart. "I never thought I could feel this way. I had grown to believe that love had passed me by. When I saw how much Karros loved Flora, I always wished that I could experience that same love. Until he lost her to Aiden and then I was grateful I'd never had my heart ripped in two like that."

Caleb moved to stand behind her and she leaned back, nestling against him. "I will never hurt Elise. I will never break her heart."

"And Karros has found true happiness with a woman who will love him as intensely as he loves her." Elise swallowed down her tears. "We need your help to make that happen. If not, then he might lose another love. This time in the most tragic of circumstances."

"Well then. We'd better begin." Hannah hugged her granddaughter briefly before letting her go. "I'll get the ingredients we need to help you dream walk. Elise, you can help me. I'd like to pass some of my knowledge on to you. It's a pity you don't like making potions as much as you like making food."

Caleb's shoulders sagged forward as relief flooded him. He couldn't bear the thought of losing the sister he'd only just found. Not when he and Caleb had lost so much already.

27

ELISE

"So, he's the one?" Hannah scanned the wooden shelves before her, picking up ingredients for the dream walking potion.

"He is." Elise held the ingredients her grandmother passed to her. "Are you disappointed?"

"You've found love. Why would I ever be disappointed in that?" Hannah pointed to a higher shelf. "Can you reach the namjil juice?"

"Sure." Elise placed the items down on the table behind her before standing on her tiptoes and reaching for the purple namjil juice. "Here."

"You didn't answer my question." Hannah grabbed a couple of vials off a lower shelf and placed them on the table. "Do you think I'm disappointed?"

"I don't know," Elise answered honestly, her Grandma Hannah had a way of figuring out if you were telling the truth with her laser-sharp stare.

"Elise, I have always been proud of you. I love your passion for cooking even though I would love for that passion to have been directed to the fae arts. My own mother didn't want me to learn the arts. She wanted nothing more than for me to become the wife of a man with a good status in the court." Hannah popped the top off one of the vials.

"I didn't know that." Elise fetched a mortar and pestle and ground up some talica seeds.

"She used to make me go to court and parade me around as if I were a pig at the market."

Elise giggled. "I think I'd describe you more of a beautiful bird, maybe a Jabavel."

"Thank you." Her grandma bowed her head. "My point is that I have been where you and Karros are now. The knowledge I wish to give you, what I learned from those days, is that our families often act out of love and kindness. Not malice. My mother came from a poor family. When she was a child, the other children used to look down on her because she never had the right clothes or shoes."

"She was trying to protect you."

"Me and my children. She'd seen her own mother's heartbreak at not being able to provide for her daughters. My grandfather died when she was still young." Hannah added the ground talica seeds. "She wanted to cushion me from that."

"But you didn't go along with your mother's wishes." Elise handed Hannah another vial.

"I married well. But I married for love, too. For me, love was the most important thing. I couldn't have lived with a man I didn't love. I couldn't marry a man who wouldn't support me and my thirst for knowledge of the fae traditions." Hannah raised her eyes and stared at Elise. "Do you think Karros would have been happy with Flora?"

"Yes."

"Really?" Hannah's eyes bore into Elise.

"Yes. I do think he would have been happy. Not in the way he deserved but he could have found a way to make it work." She smiled shyly. "At least that's what I believed until he met Zara."

"And you met Caleb." Hannah's eyes twinkled. "The way you look at him makes my heart swell. You are a lucky woman. He adores you."

"I never thought I would ever feel this way about a man. I had given up on having a family. All I wanted was to pursue my career. Then I met Caleb and it all changed in an instant. Which was scary." Elise leaned on the table watching Hannah put the finishing touches to the potion.

"Love is supposed to be scary. It's supposed to consume you like flames but also comfort you like a warm blanket on a stormy night." Hannah placed her hand on Elise's cheek. "You're glowing. Sylvie can see it, too."

"Does that mean Karros and I are not going to be banished or disinherited?" Elise asked.

"Not by me, and I suspect Sylvie will come around. She just needs to make you and Karros work for her forgiveness first. As for your parents, I'll talk to them." She tilted her head to one side. "I am the wise woman of the wildwood after all."

Elise slid her arms around Hannah's neck. "The wisest woman of the wildwood."

"Okay. I have to add the secret ingredient to the dream walking potion." She closed her eyes and placed her hands over the small ceramic pot into which she'd placed all the ingredients. Elise watched and listened as Hannah infused the potion with her magical essence. For a moment the potion glowed, the contents swirling around as if they were being stirred.

"Is it done?" Elise asked as Hannah opened her eyes and fetched two small silver goblets from the shelf behind them.

"It's done. Although I can't guarantee it will work. Dream walking is not something that can be forced. I can guide them back to where they need to be but remembering is up to them. If they think it's too painful, their minds will keep the memories locked away."

"They'll face their pain and their fears for their sister." Elise inhaled deeply and let the breath out slowly as she steadied her nerves.

"You're scared for them." Hannah placed her hand on Elise's shoulder. "Whatever they remember, they'll cope with it because they have you and Flora to comfort them. And protect them."

"We should go and get this over with. I'm worried for Karros, he stayed at Zara's side. If anything happens to her, he'd never forgive himself but he's no match for a shifter if that's who is after Zara." Elise picked up the two silver goblets.

"Your brother has a fierce heart, I've seen how he watched over you. He's also incredibly resourceful. He'll keep Zara safe." Hannah followed Elise out of her workroom and back into the living area of the cabin where the atmosphere was still frosty.

"We have the potion ready." Elise paused before she passed one cup to Aiden and then the other to Caleb who was standing by the window, staring out into the darkness. "Are you both sure about this?"

"Yes." Caleb's fingers brushed hers as she handed him the cup. "We'll be okay."

"I'll be right here if you need me." She leaned forward and kissed his cheek.

"That's why I know we'll be okay," he replied.

"What do we do?" Aiden asked from the sofa where he was sitting next to Flora who clung to his arm, as if she were scared to let him go.

"Grandma Hannah will guide you." Elise turned to face

Hannah as she entered the room. "She'll be there with you and can pull you back if it gets too scary."

"Flora, if you move to the chair, Caleb, you sit next to your brother. I can direct you back to the time you need to remember. I just need a few brief details from you." Hannah beckoned to Elise and together they moved a low padded footstool toward the sofa.

Once she was satisfied with the position of the footstool and had asked Aiden to shuffle closer toward Caleb, Hannah sat down. Flexing her fingers, she placed one hand on each knee and leaned forward slightly, her focus switching from one brother to the other.

Elise held her breath as Hannah spoke quietly to the twins, who guided her back in time to where they needed to go. To a time they couldn't remember. Her heart ached for the two young boys who had lost their parents.

"They forgot they had a sister?" Grandma Sylvie's voice made her jump. How had she gotten so close without Elise realizing it?

"Yes. I think they were so traumatized over what happened, they pushed the pain away as a coping mechanism." Elise wiped her hand across her eyes. "It scares me. The thought of them opening themselves up to that pain is unbearable."

"I can only imagine." Sylvie's brows knitted together. "And they think whoever was behind their parents' deaths was behind their kidnapping from the foster home?"

"Yes. But no one knows for sure, which is why they need to remember." She covered her mouth with her hand as Hannah told them to drink the potion and close their eyes.

In a calm voice, Hannah guided the twins back in time, probing their minds until they were right where they needed to be.

"Now, I want you to open the door and let yourself

remember. It's all in the past. No one can hurt you." Hannah sat in silence while the twins unlocked their memories.

The room was deathly quiet. It was as if they were all afraid one sound might break the spell and ruin Caleb and Aiden's chance of unlocking the secrets in their heads.

Then Caleb's shoulders jerked forward, and he grasped the edge of the sofa cushion with his hands. He sucked in a deep breath as if he were struggling to breathe and Elise darted forward, only to be restrained by Sylvie.

Elise swung her head around to look at her grandma, ready to pull away and go to her mate. But Sylvie shook her head, her eyes misted with tears as she wrapped her arms around her granddaughter and held her close.

Tears rolled down Elise's cheeks as she clasped her hands around Sylvie's arms and held onto her. Her grandma was right, she needed to let this happen. She had to set her own feelings aside in the same way the twins were setting their feelings aside for the sake of their sister.

"How much longer?" Elise whispered as the clock on the wall ticked on endlessly.

"You know better than to ask that question," Sylvie whispered in reply.

Grandma Hannah stared at the twins, her hands on theirs as their eyes moved beneath their lids as if they were experiencing REM sleep. Could she sense if they were okay? Would she wake them if the twins became too stressed?

Caleb opened his mouth and sucked in air as if he'd been drowning. Hannah grabbed his hand and pulled him forward, whispering in his ear. His eyes opened and he sagged back against the sofa, a sheen of sweat on his forehead.

Grandma Hannah got up and leaned forward, whispering in Aiden's ear. With a shudder Aiden's eyes opened and he blinked as he focused on the room around him.

"The dream has ended," Grandma Hannah told them. "You will remember what you saw. Your dream walk is now part of your memory."

Grandma Sylvie let go of Elise and got up. "I'll fix us all a drink. I think we need it."

She went to the kitchen area and grabbed some glasses and a bottle of whiskey Grandma Hannah kept for medicinal purposes. The glasses clattered together as she carried them in on a tray which she set down on a side table.

"Elise, there are some freshly made cookies in a container on the counter. Why don't you fetch those, too?" Grandma Hannah instructed as she got up from her footstool and placed her hand on her lower back.

"I'll get them." Elise darted out of her seat, grabbed the cookies and returned to the living room. "Here." She pulled the lid off the container and thrust the cookies under Caleb's nose.

"Thanks." He put his hand to his temple and yawned as he took a cookie.

"Aiden." She offered him a cookie as Flora knelt by his feet, her face a mask of concern for her mate.

"You should eat something," Flora told him. "It'll help ground you."

"I don't feel much like eating." Aiden reached for a cookie, his face pale as he took a bite.

"Drink, too, and then you can go rest," Grandma Hannah told them.

"We have to get back to Wishing Moon Bay," Caleb replied wearily.

"You should rest," Elise urged.

"No, we need to go visit Oscar." Caleb ate his cookie and sipped his liquor, the color slowly coming back to his cheeks.

"So, you remember?" Elise's throat constricted as she

swallowed down her emotions. Of course they must remember, they both looked as if they were in shock.

"I remember everything," Caleb replied hoarsely.

"Everything?" Aiden asked.

"Yes. Do you?" Caleb half turned to look at his brother.

"I remember our family." Aiden's eyes glistened with tears. "I remember Mom and Dad and Zara. I remember being sad after they died and living with our aunt and uncle." He stopped talking and rested his head in his hands.

"Don't force yourself to remember if it's too painful." Flora wrapped her arms around her mate.

"It's painful, but it's also…" Aiden placed his hand over his heart. "It fills me with such happiness. It's like I have them back in some small way."

"And do you remember who took us?" Caleb whispered.

"No. I got lost in the rest of it." Aiden coughed and cleared his throat. "I'm sorry."

"There's nothing to be sorry for." Caleb reached for his brother and hugged him. "I'm just grateful we got to remember Mom and Dad and baby Zara."

"Will you tell us what you remember?" Elise asked quietly.

Caleb let go of his brother and reached for Elise's hand, squeezing it tightly. "I will."

Elise leaned forward and kissed the back of his hand, needing her mate to know she was there for him. Whatever he remembered, she would be by his side as he dealt with it.

Even if he planned to track down the person who hurt them and bring him to justice.

28

CALEB

"Caleb." Elise's soft voice pulled him out of the past and back to the present.

"I drifted off." He blinked, trying to clear his head as he tried to make sense of what he'd seen when dream walking.

"You did." She brushed her fingertips across his forehead. "Do you want to go lie down? Perhaps if you rest and sleep for a while, you'll feel better."

"No." He shook his head, adamant that rest was the last thing he needed. "I want to go see Oscar."

"That can wait until tomorrow." Grandma Sylvie studied him closely. "You don't have to prove you're a hero or anything."

"That's not what this is about," Caleb replied. "It's about keeping Zara safe."

"Why don't you tell us what you saw? What you remembered?" Grandma Hannah prompted as she set down a tray of hot tea on the footstool. "Here, drink this. It's an herbal mix that'll help clear your head. But I agree, you should stay here for the night."

Caleb shook his head once more. "The sooner we speak

to Oscar, the sooner we can deal with whoever is stalking Zara."

"And you have the information we need to do that?" Aiden's eyes were red-rimmed as if he'd been crying as he entered the room. He'd gone outside for some fresh air with Flora after getting shakily to his feet.

"I do." He closed his eyes. "I can remember his face. I remember the apartment where we were found." He tilted his head to one side as he plucked the memory out and examined it closely. "I can see the inside. I can remember a phone call the guy had."

"And how does this help?" Elise asked. "You know where you were found. The police have that information. As for the face and the phone call, it only helps if the police can match it to someone in their database."

"The phone call is key. But there's something else." Caleb turned to Aiden. "We went through the file together. There was an item of evidence mentioned. A small toy they found that didn't belong to either of us."

"Yes. The police assumed it belonged to another child that might have been taken before us."

"It wasn't. At least I don't think it was." Caleb inhaled deeply. "I think it belonged to Murray's daughter."

"Murray? Who is Murray?" Aiden slumped down on the sofa next to Caleb.

"I… The name just came to me." He tapped the side of his head. "Just like that."

"That is a side effect of dream walking," Grandma Hannah told them. "New memories might slip in. As you go over the events, you'll suddenly recall a small detail that wasn't there before. Our minds are miraculous things."

"So, Murray. He had a child?" Elise prompted.

"He did. And the toy belonged to her." Caleb frowned. "He had a conversation with someone on the phone. About the child. Someone was angry with him. He'd promised to do something…" He groaned. "I don't remember."

"Don't worry." Aiden reached for his brother and pulled him close, patting him on the back. "This might be enough."

"Do the police have the toy?" Flora asked. "If so, we can do a location spell."

"That's what I was thinking." Caleb reached for a cup of tea from the tray. "That's why I want to go straight to Oscar's house now."

"Wait." Elise put her hands up. "Why not just call Oscar? If he hasn't already got the evidence, there's no point in you going over there right now. It's late and he won't be able to do anything about it tonight."

"But he might be able to figure out who this Murray is. If he's connected to the guy he thinks murdered our parents then it should be easy to track him." Aiden drank some of the tea, too.

"And none of this can be done by phone?" Flora stood in front of the twins with her hands on her hips. "Seriously. Think about it."

"You can call Oscar, get a good night's sleep, and then we can go home tomorrow. You'll be much more useful if you're well-rested." Elise chewed the inside of her cheek as she stared up at Caleb. "Please."

She placed her hand on his knee, her eyes imploring him to be sensible, to do as she asked.

We should rest, his bear said. This has been a great shock. There's so much to process. Not just about Murray, but our parents, too. And Zara. We can remember her as a baby. You and Aiden sat on the edge of the bed cradling her when she was born. Our mom and dad, they were so proud of us all.

I need to do this now, Caleb insisted. I need to do it before I give in to the memories of our family. Because those are the memories I want to dwell on. Those are the memories I want to relive over and over again. Instead, I keep going over the other memories on repeat because we need to figure this out, so he doesn't tear our family apart again.

His bear bowed his head. *Then we should go.*

"I have to do this now," he said quietly as he set his teacup down on the tray. "Until we figure this out, Zara and Karros could be in danger."

"I agree." Aiden drained his cup and pushed himself to his feet. "Even if we don't go see Oscar, we should get back to Zara."

"Bear shifters sure are hardheaded." Grandma Sylvie stood before the two bear shifters. Despite her short stature compared to the bears, she wasn't daunted as she wagged her finger at them. "Now, since you are insisting on leaving, I want Flora or Elise to drive. You two need to rest. You'll be no good protecting those you love if you're tired."

"I'll drive," Flora volunteered.

"Okay," Elise agreed. "Grandma Hannah, can I grab the ingredients we need for a location spell, please?"

"Of course, I have what you need in my workroom. I'll also pack some of the herbal tea. I suggest you drink some when you get home, or wherever it is you're going." Grandma Hannah bustled off to fetch the ingredients while Elise poured the twins another cup of tea.

"Here. Drink this. Once we're on the road, you can call Oscar and tell him what you remembered. I'll call Karros and check in on them." She pressed a teacup into Caleb's hand. "Drink."

He nodded and leaned forward, pressing his lips to her cheek as he accepted the cup. "Thank you."

"For what?" She cocked her head to one side.

"Everything. For being you. For bringing us here. For persuading your grandma to help us." He straightened up, although he looked a little unsteady on his feet.

"We're partners. Remember." She slipped into his arms and he held her close, his chin resting on the top of her head.

As she nestled closer to him, his eyes locked with Grandma Sylvie who smiled sadly before she turned around and wiped a hand across her eyes.

Those were good tears, weren't they? his bear asked.

I think they were, Caleb replied. It seems miracles do happen.

Their journey here had been successful in more ways than one. Caleb only hoped that the details he'd remembered would be enough to help them track down the person stalking Zara. Unfortunately, just figuring out who it was wouldn't help them if they couldn't actually locate the person.

It's a pity you couldn't figure out if Murray was a shifter, his bear said. If we had some idea what he was, we might be able to track him. All those tracks on the mountain. At least if we knew Murray was a bear or a wolf, we could narrow down our search.

If it's him, Caleb reminded his other side. Just because he was the one who took us, it doesn't mean he's come back. In some ways, it doesn't make sense.

But if it's not him, then who is it? His bear grumbled in concern. They might be no closer to solving the mystery after all.

"Here's everything you need for a location spell." Grandma Hannah came back to the living area with a small cloth bag and handed it to Elise. "And here is the tea." She handed a tin box to Flora. "Drink it every four hours over the next couple of days and you should feel more like your normal selves."

"Thank you." Caleb embraced Grandma Hannah in a bear hug, thankfully she didn't object. "If there's anything you need, just let us know."

"A bear shifter who owes me a favor."

"Two bear shifters." Aiden hugged her as soon as Caleb let her go. "Because we're family."

"I suppose we are." Grandma Hannah wrapped her arms around Aiden. "Look after yourselves and each other. My grandchildren are very special to me."

"We will." Aiden let her go and turned around, ready to leave.

"I'm going, too," Grandma Sylvie announced. "I'm going to go talk to your parents, Elise."

"Oh." Elise groaned and her shoulders slumped forward. "Can't it wait until after we've figured this out? I don't have the time or the energy to deal with their disappointment right now and neither does Karros."

"Which is why I am going to tell them I approve, and they should, too. I can see you're happy. And I suspect Karros is, too. All he ever wanted was to find a woman to settle down with. If that happens to be a shifter then so be it." Grandma Sylvie shoved her arms into her coat sleeves while ignoring the stunned faces staring at her. "Come on, I thought you all had somewhere to be."

She ushered them out of the house, but Elise blocked her path and hugged her tightly. "Thank you. We're going to be just fine, you know."

"I do know," Grandma Sylvie replied gruffly. "I don't think I understood before, but I do now. I know what is important to you. I can see it in your eyes every time you look at Caleb. If that isn't the look of love, then I don't know what is."

"I love you." Elise let her grandma go.

"And we love you, too. I only ever acted from a place of love and caring. I just don't think I was very good at being open about my feelings." She took Elise's hands and stared at her for a moment. "I'm looking forward to being a great-grandma."

"I'll see what I can do." Elise waved goodbye and then ran to catch up with Caleb.

"Things are settled then?" he asked as he helped her into the truck.

"I think they are. At least with my family. Now we just have to figure out who is stalking Zara." She settled back in her seat as Flora started the engine and put the truck in drive.

"At least we have a lead," Caleb stared out into the darkness as they drove back through the wildwood. "It's more than we had a couple of hours ago."

"I'll call Oscar." Aiden dialed the number on his phone. "No signal."

"You'll have to wait until we're on the other side of the trees," Flora told him. "The trees block the signal this deep inside the forest."

Aiden tapped his phone screen again but there was still no signal. Caleb took out his phone and glanced at the screen, but he couldn't call out either.

"I'll call Karros as soon as we get a signal." Elise stared at her phone screen, too.

"Whatever did people do before cell phones?" Aiden asked.

"They were more patient," Flora replied.

"Is that a criticism?" Aiden asked.

"If you want it to be." She eased her foot down on the gas as they reached a straight section of road.

"Now who is impatient?" Aiden asked as he checked her speed.

"I'm going slower than you do," she replied. "It just feels faster because you're not in control."

"Oh, I got a signal." Elise's phone beeped as a message came through. Then it beeped again and again.

"Someone's popular," Caleb said.

"Is it your parents?" Flora asked. "Don't say Grandma Sylvie called them and broke the news?"

"No, it's from Karros." She tapped the screen, her heart rate quickening as she scanned the first text and scrolled down to the next one.

"What's wrong?" Caleb reached for her hand, sensing her growing panic.

"Zara sensed someone was watching her. She went to confront them." Elise glanced up with tears in her eyes. "She hasn't come back."

"How long?" Caleb asked quickly.

"I don't know." She sucked air into her lungs before letting it out slowly. "I can't tell when the texts were sent because of the lack of signal." She turned the phone screen to face Caleb. "I don't know if the time means what time the message was sent or what time I received it."

"Okay, calm down, deep breaths." He took the phone from. "We can call Karros. For all we know, Elise might be back by now."

He quickly scanned the rest of the texts, there were five in total, the first explained that Elise was missing, the last ones asking Elise where she was. Caleb pressed dial and put the phone on speaker.

"He's not picking up. Why isn't he picking up?" Elise whispered.

Flora pressed her foot down on the gas, sending them speeding through the forest. Her grim expression reflected in the rearview mirror and despite his unease at the truck traveling too fast on the winding road, Caleb trusted her to keep them safe.

She has good reflexes, we learned that when we were searching for Imelda, his bear said supportively.

"Karros?" Caleb cursed under his breath as the phone went to voicemail.

"I'll call Ivan." Aiden grabbed his phone and pressed dial.

"Will he go and check that they're all right?" Elise asked.

"No, I'm going to ask him to meet us at the edge of the fae realm. He can fly us to Zara's house. We should be there..." Aiden sucked in a breath as his brother answered. "Ivan. I need a favor."

We also need a large dose of luck, Caleb's bear said as they raced toward the edge of the fae realm.

Caleb closed his eyes, his thoughts haunted by the man whose face he now remembered. The man who had stolen two young shifters.

What was his plan for Zara? Caleb tapped the screen and listened to Karros's phone ring and ring until it once more went to voicemail.

Damn it. What was happening?

On the day he'd finally recalled long-forgotten memories of his parents and his baby sister, Caleb was not ready to lose Zara once again.

29

ELISE

"Where is he?" Elise stared out of the window as Flora drove out of the fae realm and slowed to a stop. They had agreed to rendezvous with Ivan but so far there was no sign of the dragon shifter.

"He'll be here." Caleb reached across and placed his hand on hers.

"Flora, park the truck off the road. We should grab anything we might need and get ready to go as soon as Ivan gets here." Aiden opened the truck door and got out.

"It'll be okay." Caleb glanced down at the phone in his hand, willing it to ring.

"Will it?" Elise sobbed before covering her mouth. "Sorry, crying isn't going to help anyone."

"It's okay to cry." Caleb froze and looked up at the roof of the truck as if it were invisible.

"Is Ivan here?" Elise asked.

"He is." Caleb leaned over, kissed her cheek, and then opened the door. "Come on, let's move. We should be at Zara's house in about a half-hour."

"That soon?" Elise asked.

"Ivan is fast. He doesn't usually fly fast when he's got people on his back, but this is an emergency." Caleb pocketed the tea Grandma Sylvie had given them while Elise shoved the bag containing the ingredients for the location spell inside her pack.

Once Aiden had spoken to Ivan, he'd called Oscar and relayed all the information to the ex-detective. Oscar had promised to do whatever he could to get hold of the toy if it were still with the case evidence. He also said he'd find out who Murray was.

With Zara and Karros potentially missing, they had to trust Oscar to do his job while they flew to Bear Creek.

"Oh, my goodness." Elise covered her face with her hands as the distant thrum of dragon wings grew louder.

"He won't hurt you," Caleb assured her.

"I'm not afraid. I just never thought I'd get to see a dragon so close up." She stared into the sky as the moon reflected off Ivan's scales, which shimmered like the ocean.

"We're going to get more than close." He took her hand and they joined Aiden and Flora.

"I hope I don't fall." Elise shivered as the dragon flew over them and then dropped to the ground to land lightly before them.

In a blink of an eye, the air shimmered and the dragon disappeared to be replaced by Ivan's human form. "Have you made contact with them?" he asked.

"No, there's still no answer from either phone," Aiden replied.

"Okay. Let's go. I know where Bear Creek is, but you'll have to guide me in to land," Ivan called.

"We should land in the mountains. There's a shallow outcrop above Zara's house. If it's all clear, we should land there." Caleb nodded to his brother. "We can't thank you enough for this."

"We're family, right? I'm sure there'll be a day when I need your help." Ivan inhaled deeply and then the air popped and fizzled as he disappeared.

Even though Elise was prepared for the sight of the dragon, he still took her breath away as he appeared as if from nowhere. However, she didn't have time to stare at him, to absorb every feature of his massive body, his shimmering scales, and his noble head. Instead, Caleb pulled her forward and she ran toward the dragon, who crouched down, extending his leg so they could climb on board.

Caleb went first and sat at the front. Leaning down, he held out his hand to Elise, who reached for it and pulled herself onto the back of the dragon. Not exactly as if she were mounting a horse, but she tried to calm her nerves by telling herself that's all she was doing.

Riding a horse. Riding a horse, she repeated to herself over and over again.

Flora sat behind Elise, and then Aiden sat at the back, his arms around Flora. Flora put her arms around Elise's waist, while Elise hung on to Caleb as if her life depended on it. Which it probably did.

When the dragon pushed himself back onto all fours, she let out a small cry, which she swallowed down. She didn't want to draw attention to them.

But as he crouched down and then sprang into the air, she couldn't contain the wail of excitement and pure terror that escaped.

"It's all right, you're safe!" Caleb yelled as the dragon leaped into the air.

As he leveled out and flew toward the edge of town, where tall hills rose up as a barrier between Wishing Moon Bay and the world beyond, her terror was replaced by a sense of elation. This was the most incredible thing she'd ever done.

Ivan was the most incredible creature she'd ever seen.

Mentally, she apologized to Caleb, but she was certain he understood how incredible the dragon was.

Ivan's dragon stretched out his neck, his wings beating a fast tempo as they raced across the land. Straight and true, he flew toward Bear Creek, only diverting a little to skirt around towns.

The land blurred beneath them. If anyone happened to look up at the sky as the dragon flew overhead, they would likely believe the dragon was nothing more than a fast-moving cloud.

In the distance, she saw the high mountain peaks silhouetted against the moonlit sky. They were close. Soon they would land and the search for Karros and Zara would begin.

Would Ivan help them? Were his senses stronger than the bears'?

The wind brought tears to her eyes as they climbed higher, skimming the peaks of the mountains before swooping down the other side. The dragon flew low, skimming the treetops, and she was certain he was enjoying the freedom of flight despite the reason they were here.

Then he suddenly banked right, tucked in his wings, and dropped out of the sky like a stone.

Ivan's four passengers clung to each other as the change in direction and speed nearly unseated them.

Down, down, the dragon headed for a small clearing where he landed with a thud, rocking forward before steadying himself.

"What's wrong?" Aiden scrambled off Ivan's back and helped the others down.

As soon as they were on the ground, Ivan shifted. "There's another dragon." His words came out in a gasp.

"Another dragon?" Elise looked up at the sky. "Here?"

"I can sense another dragon." He stared at the others in the moonlight. "Can't you?"

"No." Caleb stared up at the sky. "I can't see anything, I can't hear a dragon or sense one."

"I can." Ivan took a couple of steps away from them, his expression one of longing.

"Have you ever met another dragon?" Elise went to him and placed her hand on his elbow, turning him to face her.

"No." He shook his head. "At least not one I can remember. I was raised by Valerie. The dragons across the ocean never bothered with me. It was as if I was tainted in some way."

"You never flew across the ocean to the dragon isle? You were never tempted?" Elise asked.

"No." He looked down at the ground. "I always thought they were hostile to outsiders. And I am an outsider. I came from out here." He held out his arms. "I'm from the world beyond. I don't fit in anywhere. Except with my family. With my brothers."

Ivan pulled away from her and stared into the air. "I can feel the dragon." He tilted his head to one side. "Closer now. Can you feel it?"

Aiden and Caleb exchanged worried glances. "We should leave," Caleb said quickly.

"Leave?" Ivan asked. "There's another dragon here."

"Aiden?" Flora asked. "What's wrong?"

"There's a family of dragons that live close by," Aiden explained.

"A family of dragons. You knew and never told me?" Ivan's cutting accusation caused Aiden to flinch.

"We couldn't tell you," Caleb explained.

"Why?" Ivan asked.

"Because they can't know about Wishing Moon Bay." Aiden held out his hands. "I'll explain more when we're safe."

"You go," Elise said. "I need to stay and look for Karros."

"We should all stay," Aiden said. "Except Ivan."

"No." Ivan shook his head.

"Please. You have to leave," Aiden replied. "It's not safe."

"Try calling Karros again," Flora told Elise as the brothers stared each other down.

Elise nodded and pressed dial. The phone rang and rang before going to voicemail. "Damn it!"

"Keep trying." Flora locked eyes with Elise. They were in danger. All of them. But how much danger?

Elise hit dial again.

"I can sense the dragon," Caleb said quietly.

"I want to meet them," Ivan said quietly.

"Valerie told us it was too dangerous," Caleb explained.

"Valerie. She knows about these dragons, too?" Ivan's eyes glowed with pain.

"Yes. When she adopted you, the dragons came to claim you, but she wouldn't let you go. The dragon we met in Bear Creek, Fiona, intervened." He held out his hands, imploring Ivan to keep calm. "Something happened. I don't know what. But Fiona was made to forget. She's never supposed to know about Wishing Moon Bay. She's never supposed to go there."

"Why?" Ivan's eyes widened. "Is she my mother?"

"No. I don't think so. Valerie just said it was safer for all of us if she never remembered. And if she finds you, she'll ask questions." Caleb looked up at the sky. "She's so close."

"Maybe it's one of the other dragons," Flora said. "It might not be Fiona."

"My phone." Elise's hands trembled as she held the phone in both her hands and tapped the screen. "Karros. Are you okay?"

"Yeah. I dropped my phone. I couldn't find it." He sounded breathless.

"Are you both safe? We've been trying to get a hold of you both." Her voice wavered as she spoke.

"We're fine. Zara ran out without her phone. I dropped mine when I ran after her. I managed to track her down and then we were searching for my phone. I heard it ringing when you were calling." He paused. "We're heading back to the house now."

"Did you see whoever was stalking you?" She bit her nail as the hairs on the back of her neck stood on end. The thrum of dragon wings drifted toward them on the breeze.

"No. Neither of us could figure out where they were. It was as if they were just out of reach." He sounded tired.

"Okay, we'll come to the house," Elise said.

"You don't have to. Whoever was out there seems to have gone."

"I'll call you back and let you know if we're coming," Elise said and ended the call.

"I'm staying here." Ivan folded his arms as the thrum of wingbeats filled the air.

"It's too late to run," Aiden conceded.

"I think whoever this is, whoever the dragon is, that's who has been stalking Zara," Elise told them. "The reason Zara couldn't ever track them was because the dragon was in the air." She pointed toward the sky.

"Then it's time we faced them and figured out what is going on." Ivan's jaw tensed yet his eyes were filled with hurt and betrayal.

"You can still leave," Aiden said quietly. "If the dragon shifter is after Zara, this isn't your fight."

Ivan slipped his arm around his brother's shoulders. "We're family. If someone threatens Zara, they threaten us all."

"I'm sorry we didn't tell you," Aiden told him.

Ivan inhaled deeply and let the breath out slowly. "You

did the right thing. Valerie would never have kept this from me unless it was for my own good. And I guess Fiona must have agreed to forget about me."

"Yeah, since dragons are too bullheaded to do anything they don't want to do," Caleb teased.

"Yeah, that, too." Ivan's arms slid from around his brother's shoulders as the beat of the dragon's wings slowed, and dust swirled around them as a mighty dragon appeared above them. "Is that what I look like?" he asked in awe.

"I think you're more impressive," Caleb replied.

"I love you both," Ivan said as he stepped in front of them, preparing to meet another dragon for the first time.

30

CALEB

Why had they asked Ivan to bring them here? Caleb cursed their decision as the dragon landed in front of them.

Because our sister was in trouble, his bear replied.

But she's safe now. She's back at her house with Karros, while we plunged Ivan into trouble. The hairs on the back of Caleb's neck stood on end as the dragon folded its wings and stared at them.

Can you tell if it's Fiona? His bear gnashed his teeth together, wanting to come forth and protect those around him.

No. I can't tell. But this dragon is older than Ivan and much bigger. Caleb inched forward, putting himself firmly between the dragon and his mate.

The dragon is going to shift. His bear lowered his head and growled menacingly inside Caleb's head as the air shimmered around the dragon.

"So, here we are." Fiona put her hands on her hips and stared at the five people in front of her. "I thought I smelled dragon on you when you last came to visit me. But it was so faint I thought I had to be mistaken."

"I've never met another dragon shifter," Ivan told her. "At least, not that I remember."

The statement seemed innocent enough, but Fiona was old and wise and also incredibly distrustful, it seemed. "So where *did* you come from?"

"I...have no idea," Ivan stuttered.

Fiona swiveled her head to look at them each in turn, her eyes lingering on Elise and Flora the longest. "And you. You're not what you seem. When Flora came to the house before, I should have paid more attention."

"We're exactly what we seem," Flora answered sharply.

"Your ears..." Fiona squinted as she studied them then she yanked her head around and stared at Ivan once more. "Wishing Moon Bay."

Ivan side-eyed his brothers but none of them answered.

How are we supposed to talk our way out of this? Caleb's bear asked.

I have no idea, Caleb answered.

"How old are you?" Elise stepped forward.

"A lady never reveals her age. A dragon never reveals anything." She studied Elise for a long moment. "You didn't come with them last time." She glanced at Caleb. "You've only just met. Mates that have only just met."

"We are." Elise nodded. "I'd say you were a few hundred years old at least."

Caleb sucked in a deep breath. Was his mate crazy? Ivan might not be a typical dragon, but he knew not to goad him. And Elise was certainly goading Fiona.

"I'm older than that. Much older."

"And you've lived out here in the world beyond all this time?" Elise asked.

"The world beyond." Her eyes narrowed and she stepped

toward Elise, getting a little too close for Caleb's comfort. "The world beyond what?"

"It can't be easy living in secrecy." Elise jutted out her chin, but Caleb could sense her unease. "But you've managed to all these years."

"Not all of those years," Fiona replied, a sadness in her eyes that wrenched Caleb's heart. She turned away and stared out across the mountains. "Once there were many of us. But not anymore."

"What happened to them?" Ivan whispered.

"We were hunted almost to extinction. It was so long ago that we're a myth now. But a few of us hung on." She turned back to Ivan, her expression softer. "Which is why I had to find you. When I sensed you, I had to track you down. And here you are, an enigma."

"No, I'm a chef," Ivan answered lightly.

Fiona chuckled. "A dragon chef. Why not?"

"Is this why you have been spying on Zara?" Caleb asked.

"No." Fiona's flat answer was unexpected.

"Why were you spying on her?" Flora asked.

"Wishing Moon Bay." Fiona tapped her temple. "There's something in here, locked away. Locked away in Wishing Moon Bay."

Caleb's heart hammered in his chest. *She knows.*

No. She doesn't know. She just knows there is something to know. His bear blinked. That wasn't supposed to sound like a riddle.

And yet a riddle is exactly what this is. Caleb pressed his lips together trying to figure out their next move.

"How did you survive, Fiona?" Elise pushed the dragon shifter for an answer to what seemed like a pointless question.

Perhaps she's stalling for time, Caleb's bear suggested.

She might be, but why? There's no way out of this for us. We need Ivan to shift and for us all to climb on his back if we intend to escape. I don't think Fiona's going to just stand there and let us leave.

Perhaps Elise has something from the wildwood she could use on the dragon shifter. Some of the sycombre fruit. His bear licked his lips, unable to *not* think of the sweet-smelling mushrooms they'd brought back from the wildwood. If they could clear this up, they could be back in Wishing Moon Bay and eating fermented mushrooms within the hour.

"I survived by using my senses. I survived by my own ingenuity. I survived by keeping my head down and never drawing attention to myself." Fiona licked her lips and glanced at Ivan. "Where did you come from?"

"You helped Ivan," Elise announced.

Everyone around her sucked in a startled breath.

Caleb shook his head in disbelief. How could his mate betray them like this?

"I helped Ivan?" Fiona stared at the young dragon shifter. "I've never seen him before in my life."

"You have," Elise told her. "But you chose not to remember."

"I chose not to remember?" Fiona shook her head. "How?"

"*Why* would be the better question, don't you think?" Elise drew closer to Fiona and Caleb reached out, wanting to pull her back toward him, pull her out of striking distance of the dragon shifter.

"Why?" Fiona rubbed her hand across her chin, her eyes unfocused.

"Because you do what you have to do to survive. You always have." Elise's body language softened. "You did what you had to do to protect people you care about."

Fiona tilted her head back and raised her chin. "That's why I don't remember Ivan or Wishing Moon Bay."

"Yes." Elise put her hands up. "You helped him find a

home, a family of his own. A family who loves him. And maybe that's how it's supposed to be. If you knew why, if we knew why, then we might all be in danger. Your family might be in danger."

Fiona looked at them each in turn. "And family is what matters most. We protect those who love us. We protect those who need us." She sighed. "Tell your sister I won't be troubling her anymore. I got caught up in the moment. I heard her talking to you on the phone when I visited the other day. When I heard her say Wishing Moon Bay, it was like there was an itch inside of my head that I just couldn't scratch. It drove me a little crazy."

"That's it, you're going to let it go?" Caleb was stunned. More than stunned. Was this finally over?

"Your mate is right. I have survived millennia. If I agreed to forget, there must have been a good reason. I trust myself to accept that. For now at least." She half-turned to look at Ivan. "It seems you were wrong. You have met a dragon shifter before."

"I wish I remembered," Ivan answered.

Fiona shrugged. "Aiden and Caleb know where we live if you want to spend time among your own kind." Her eyes darted back to Elise. "I won't ask questions. I won't try to find Wishing Moon Bay."

"You promise?" Ivan asked.

"I promise." Her eyes narrowed. "Unless there comes a time you need me to remember. Unless you need my help once more."

"Agreed." Ivan bowed his head.

Fiona nodded, then the air shimmered all around her and she shifted before taking off and disappearing into the night.

"She's gone." Ivan sounded sad somehow as he stared into the night.

"We know where she lives," Aiden told his brother. "And

maybe it's time you visited with other dragons and found out more about yourself."

"I don't know. Do you think Fiona will stick to her word and not try to find Wishing Moon Bay?" Ivan asked.

"I think she'll keep her word." Flora slipped her arms around Elise. "You were amazing. See, shifters do need fae."

"Oh, I don't know about that. I felt more desperate than amazing." Elise ducked her head and blushed.

"No, you were amazing." Caleb went to his mate.

"I wasn't sure it would work. I was afraid that I'd betrayed you all for nothing," Elise admitted.

"You are going to be a wonderful addition to the hotel restaurant staff," Ivan told her.

"I am?" Elise asked warily.

"Yes, because you're a fae and fae think differently than shifters," Ivan told her.

"And that's a good thing?" Elise asked suspiciously.

"A very good thing," Caleb told his mate. "You saved us just then."

"I didn't do anything special," she insisted.

"You did," Flora agreed. "You made Fiona stop and think. You made her realize that she wouldn't have agreed to give up a part of herself unless it was for her own self-preservation."

"And because others would have gotten hurt if she'd pursued it. Fiona helps shifter children find families. She helped Ivan stay with Valerie. She would understand she did what she did for the right reasons."

"She trusted in herself. Just like you trusted in yourself," Caleb told her proudly.

"I don't think I did anything special," Elise insisted.

"You protected me," Caleb told her. "And everyone else."

"I did, didn't I?" She winked at him. "See, you don't need big muscles and sharp claws to keep those you love safe."

"Shall we go join Zara and Karros and tell them the news?" Flora stifled a yawn. "It's been a long day."

"We can't stay long," Ivan said. "I have to get back to town. I have breakfasts to prepare in the morning."

"Maybe in a few weeks, you could let Elise run the kitchen for a day. You could come here and spend some time with the dragons," Caleb suggested.

"Smooth, are you trying to impress your mate?" Ivan asked.

"I don't have to impress her, she loves me already." Caleb laughed.

"What are we going to do about...the other stuff?" Elise hesitated.

"About Murray?" Caleb asked.

"Yes. Are you going to let it go?" Elise asked.

"Aiden?" Caleb asked.

"I think we should leave it up to fate," Aiden answered.

"What does that mean?" Flora linked arms with him and leaned on his shoulder.

"If we find out who he is, then I think it's time we truly faced our past and finally gave ourselves some closure." Aiden sucked in a lungful of air. "But if we hit another dead end, we let it go. Perhaps we were supposed to go on this journey, so we could find out a little bit more about who we are."

"We've been given a gift. The memories were buried. Perhaps that was all we were meant to find." He patted Ivan on the back. "And it led us here. Perhaps that was the point, too. All of this was for you to finally meet your own kind. Dragons."

Ivan gave a short laugh. "Except I already knew my own kind. There are six of us. Six brothers bonded by more than blood. And a mother who loves us all."

"You're okay with Valerie not telling you about Fiona?" Aiden asked.

"Yes. I'm not saying I didn't feel hurt and betrayed, but Mom has always watched out for us all. And if Fiona understands and accepts what happens, who am I to argue with an ancient dragon?" Ivan answered.

"I wouldn't call her ancient to her face," Flora advised. She looked up at the stars above their heads. "She might be out there listening."

"If she's that old, no wonder she has such amazing senses. I'm going to practice pushing mine farther," Caleb said.

Elise slipped her arms around his neck as Ivan moved away from them and shifted into his dragon. "You know, we will finally have the house to ourselves. I suspect Karros will be staying with Zara for a few days even though the threat has gone."

"You're right." He looked down at her as Aiden and Flora climbed onto Ivan's back. "I can't wait to spend some time alone with you. Just you and me. For the rest of our lives."

"And our children." She tilted her head up and he kissed her lips.

"Lots of children," he murmured.

"I rode on the back of a dragon." She chuckled as he made a face. "Sorry, it just hit me."

"Am I going to have to get jealous?" he teased.

"Never. A bear shifter is the man for me." She clasped his hands as they turned to Ivan. "But he is impressive."

"I can show you impressive," Caleb told her as they hurried toward Ivan.

"Yes, please," she teased.

Ivan stamped his foot impatiently and Caleb caught hold of Elise as the ground shook beneath them.

As Caleb helped Elise onto Ivan's back, he smiled to himself, a wave of love sweeping over him as his heart swelled. In one incredible journey, he'd found his mate and finally put the pieces of his past together.

Whatever came next, he'd be okay, because his mate was by his side. Along with his family.

They were truly blessed.

31

ELISE

"Good morning." Caleb stroked her shoulder before pressing his lips to her skin.

She shivered and turned to face him, cupping her hands around his face. "Good morning."

Caleb inched up the bed, his lips seeking hers and she sighed, content to be with him here in this moment. So what if she had all his family coming for a late lunch today?

She swallowed hard and pulled away from him, but he slid his arm around her waist and pulled her close. "There's plenty of time to get everything ready." He brushed her hair back from her face. "Let's just enjoy each other. The rest can wait."

He slipped his hand under the sheet and cupped her breast, his thumb brushing against her nipple created tension in her body. As if she weren't tense enough. Maybe he was right, she could spare some time for the love of her life.

"I guess I can give you five minutes of my time."

He chuckled. "Wow, so generous. You are spoiling me."

"Don't get used to it." She wagged her finger at him.

"I'll temper my expectations," he purred as he nuzzled her

neck, his hands stroking her skin, moving lower, much lower.

"Oh." She closed her eyes as he stroked her mound and then pushed a finger inside her. "Maybe I could make it seven minutes."

He laughed, a deep rumble in his chest she couldn't resist. "A whole seven minutes."

"And the timer already started."

He caught her in his arms and turned her onto her back. "I can see why you are such an amazing chef. Such attention to detail."

"A good chef also knows what tastes good." She kissed his neck as she stroked her fingers over his chest. "Good food is about igniting all the senses. Taste, touch, smell."

"You smell delicious." He nestled his body between her thighs and reached down between their bodies, guiding himself inside her.

"And you feel divine." She tensed around him as he thrust into her.

Caleb lowered his head and captured her mouth with his lips as she wrapped her legs around him, urging him to take her. As her arousal peaked, she forgot all about her busy schedule. If he asked her to, she'd stay here with him for the whole day.

Elise traced the contours of his body, she could never get enough of him, his toned muscles under sun-bronzed skin made her mouth water. She kissed his chest, her tongue curling around his nipple and he inhaled sharply, his breath hissing through his teeth.

She closed her mouth over the taut bud and sucked hard, her teeth grazing his skin and he growled, reminding her of his other side, of his uniqueness.

He thrust into her harder, his breathing ragged as he

moved in and out, his skin grazing her skin as they raced toward their orgasm.

He came first, fisting the pillow as he filled her with his essence, setting off a chain reaction in her body. Now that the threat to Zara had passed, they could think about their future, of their life together.

Even if the specter of Murray still hovered over them.

Elise closed her eyes and pushed thoughts of the man who had once hurt her mate to one side. She wasn't going to let the guy spoil today.

Opening her eyes, she focused on Caleb's face, on the curve of his smile as he looked down on her, his eyes filled with love. To love and be loved, he'd taught her so much in the few days they'd known each other.

And he'd given her so much more. He'd given her a brighter future, a richer future than she could ever have wished for. Even when she threw her wish stone in the ocean.

Caleb had shown her there was so much to life that she'd never allowed herself to hope for. She'd left the fae realm with one thought, to be a great chef, to find fulfillment in her work.

Meeting Caleb had shown her how narrow her dreams had been.

She loved him with all her heart.

"I'll go put some coffee on while you take a shower." He kissed her mouth and slid out of bed, but she caught hold of him and pulled him back toward her.

"Did I ever tell you that I love you?" she asked.

"You did. But I don't mind hearing it again." He dropped a soft kiss on her lips.

"I love you." She smiled up at him shyly.

Caleb brushed her hair back from her face. "And I love

you." He pecked her lips. "Now, go take a shower. Then you can tell me what you need me to do."

"I get to boss you around, I like that idea." She jumped out of bed and hurried to the bathroom with a backward glance over her shoulder just to remind herself he was real.

After a quick shower, Elise went to the kitchen, gulped down a cup of coffee, and then set to work on the menu she'd prepared for today. It was intended to show off her flair for flavors and textures, with an accent on fae flavors. She'd used recipes she was familiar with and added subtle changes to them in the hope of impressing Ivan.

However, over the last couple of days, it had become obvious her job at the restaurant was secure, as long as she didn't blow it. For the first time, Ivan was ready to let go of some of the running of the hotel restaurant and hand responsibility to Elise so that he could spend some time with the dragons at Bear Creek.

Elise wanted to prove to him she was worthy of his trust and was there to support him. He'd lived in isolation from other dragons all his life. It was time he enjoyed some time with others, flying over the mountains with other dragons would be exhilarating.

"Karros and Zara are here." Caleb was washing lettuce as a car approached.

"I can't leave the sauce." Elise glanced down at the sauce in the pan and kept staring.

"They know where to find us," Caleb assured her.

A few minutes later, her brother knocked at the door and then walked in. "We're here."

"I've missed you." Elise turned off the heat and went to Karros, hugging her brother and then Zara before quickly going back to the stove.

"I missed you, too." He inhaled deeply. "I also missed your cooking."

"Hey, I can cook." Zara nudged him in the ribs and then her eyes widened. "But not as good as Elise. It all smells wonderful."

"Thanks. I hope it tastes good, too." She stirred the sauce, allowing it to thicken without burning.

"Do you need a hand with anything?" Karros asked. "If not, we're going to look at the yard. We're going to spend the next week working on it before we go back to Bear Creek and finish Zara's house."

"And then we're going to come and live here in Wishing Moon Bay," Zara blurted out excitedly.

"That's incredible news." Caleb dried his hands and came to hug his sister.

"We're going to start a business together. We've talked it over with Aunt Harriet and Uncle Peter. I don't want them to think I'm abandoning them after they've done so much for me. But they think it's a great idea." Zara reached for Karros's hand. They looked so happy together and Elise turned her attention to the sauce, so no one saw her tears. Her heart ached with happiness.

"Wishing Moon Bay will be a fresh start for us both." Karros inched toward the door. "Do you need us?"

"No, you go enjoy the fresh air." Elise wiped her hand across her eyes then turned around. "Oh! You could set up the chairs and table if you want to help."

"We can do that." Karros and Zara left the kitchen as quickly as they arrived.

"Are you okay?" Caleb came up behind her and wrapped his arms around her waist. Elise leaned back on his shoulder and nodded.

"A little overwhelmed, that's all. Only a few days ago, Karros was broken-hearted, now look at him." She tilted her head back and looked up at her mate. "Now look at us."

He kissed her cheek. "I couldn't be happier."

And yet there was a flicker of doubt in his eyes. Since he'd dream walked, she'd caught a glimpse of unease in his eyes. He tried to hide it, but his memories of Murray haunted him.

Despite his words, she suspected he needed closure. He needed to know what happened to the man who kidnapped the twins. Even though Murray had no connection to Zara being stalked, Elise suspected there was a lingering fear in Caleb that he might be out there watching them.

"Everyone else is arriving." Caleb kissed her cheek and went back to washing the lettuce.

"Okay, the sauce is done. Everything else is ready." She sighed as she mentally went over the dishes she'd prepared.

"It'll be fine," Caleb assured her.

"I know. And if it's not, I'll just feed everyone some sycombre fruit and they'll forget all about it." She fetched plates and set them down on the counter.

"My bear could also eat fermented mushrooms and make a fool of himself. That might leave a more lasting impression," he offered.

"I'll bear that in mind, but I think the food is okay."

"More than okay by the smell of it." Flora came into the kitchen with a couple of bottles of wine. "The smells remind me of home."

"I have focused on fae flavors," Elise said.

"*Fae Flavors*," Ivan repeated. "Why don't we add that to the menu? You can come up with some recipes we could serve at the hotel."

"Really?" Elise's cheeks flushed pink with pride.

"Really." Ivan picked up the plates. "Shall I take these outside?"

"What else do you need?" Flora offered.

Caleb's family helped carry the food outside and they were soon seated around the table in the fresh air, eating Elise's food while enjoying views of the distant mountains.

This was her life now. She only hoped one day her family might join them at the table. Grandma Sylvie had lived up to her promise and her parents were okay with Elise and Karros's choice of life partners. Not happy, but okay. It was a start.

"You did it." Caleb leaned across and kissed her cheek.

"We did it." She cupped his face in her hands.

"Partners." He held out his hand and she entwined her fingers with his.

"Partners for life." She shuffled her chair towards his and leaned on his shoulder, sipping wine and watching the happy faces of the people around her.

She was living the dream. A dream bigger than she could ever have wished for.

EPILOGUE

"Okay. This is it." Rift pointed to a small house with paint peeling off the doors and windows and moss on the roof. Only the yard looked as if it had received any TLC in recent weeks.

"That's where the location spell points to?" Caleb ducked his head and looked out of the window.

Oscar had found the box of evidence containing the toy and they had taken the chance and used a location spell in the hope of finding the owner, who in turn might know the whereabouts of Murray.

The location spell had led them here to a rundown part of town a couple of hundred miles away from Wishing Moon Bay. Caleb could only hope today would give them all closure. That he might finally be able to lay to rest the ghost of the man who stole them as children. A ghost who had haunted him for the last couple of weeks.

"Yeah. This is the place." Rift brushed his hand across his forehead. "Is it me or is it hot in here?"

"No hotter than it's been for the whole journey." Elise's concerned glance made him uneasy.

"You look pale," Caleb told him bluntly. "Are you feeling all right? You don't normally get travel sick."

Rift shook his head. "I'm not sick."

"I'll go knock on the door." Aiden switched off the engine and was about to open the door, but Rift placed his hand on his brother's shoulder and pulled him back.

"No. I'm going to go knock on the front door. You are all going to stay here. That was the whole point of me coming with you. I'll go talk to the owner of the toy. I'll get you some answers." Rift sucked in a deep breath and got out of the truck, forcing himself to stand on unsteady legs.

"He does not look good," Flora whispered as Rift took a faltering step forward.

"Maybe we should go with him," Caleb suggested, already inching toward the door.

"Or maybe we should just let Rift handle it," Elise replied.

Caleb leaned back in his seat, but his hand rested on the door handle, ready to scramble out of Rift got into trouble.

"I feel like a child," Aiden rumbled. "We should just go in there."

"You're too wound up about all this," Flora told him. "Rift is calm and..." She stopped talking as Rift rested his hand on the short gate post that marked the boundary of the property. The post wobbled, in danger of falling over and Rift stumbled forward.

"Someone is coming out of the house." A young child appeared. Dressed in jeans and a T-shirt with a ball tucked under his arm, he stared at Rift.

"Mom!" The child's shrill voice was like a shot in the arm to Rift and he jerked his head up.

"Jack!" A woman shot out of the house, grabbed the boy by the shoulder, and pulled him back. Positioning herself between the child and Rift, she placed her feet hip-width apart, her chin jutted out defiantly. "I don't know who you are, or what you want, but you're too late."

"Too late for what?" Caleb hissed.

"I'm looking for..." Rift put his hand in his pocket and pulled out the small toy. "I'm looking for the owner of this toy."

"What?" the woman asked as if Rift was crazy. And he certainly looked crazy. Or drunk.

"Well, I'm not looking for...the owner. I'm looking for information the owner might be able to give me." Rift ran his hand through his hair.

"I'd like you to leave. If Reggie owed you money, I'm sorry but you're too late."

"Reggie." Rift paused for a moment. "I was looking for Murray."

"I can save you some time there, too. My father died years ago."

"She's Murray's kid. She's the one the toy belongs to," Aiden said.

"You know what she also is?" Caleb asked as he processed the news that the man who kidnapped them was gone.

"No!" Elise covered her mouth with her hand.

"Okay, what am I missing here?" Flora asked.

"Murray's daughter is Rift's mate." Aiden gripped the steering wheel, the whites of his knuckles showing as his jaw tensed.

"I'm so sorry," Flora stroked Aiden's back.

"It's okay," Aiden replied. "Just because her father was a bad man, it doesn't mean she's like him."

Caleb nodded in agreement. They might finally find out the truth about what happened all those years ago.

And Rift might also get the family he always wanted, Caleb's bear said as another child emerged from the house and held hands with the woman who stood defiant and protective in the face of the man who would love her forever. No matter what.

Let's just hope this doesn't tear our family apart, Caleb said as he opened the door and got out of the truck. "Come on, I think our brother might need backup."

Aiden nodded. "Yeah, before he makes a complete fool of himself."

"Or she shoots him as an intruder," Elise said. "Because she has 'don't mess with me or my family' written all over her face."

Rift rolled his shoulders and stood up straight. He was a man who needed to prove himself to his mate. But from her expression, that might be hard, if not impossible.

THANKS FOR READING!

I hope you enjoyed my book!

The next book in this series is 'The Snow Leopard's Love', which you can find on my website: harmonyraines.com/all-books/bond-of-brothers-series

If you'd like to keep up with my new releases, and any offers, you can follow me on Facebook at:

facebook.com/harmonyrainesauthor

Or you can head over to my website and sign up to my newsletter for notifications about releases and exclusive deals.

Feel free to message me on Facebook, or send an email to harmony@harmonyraines.com.

Harmony.

THE SNOW LEOPARD'S LOVE

THE BOND OF BROTHERS - BOOK FIVE

Get it here:
US: amazon.com/dp/B097KGPT19
UK: amazon.co.uk/dp/B097KGPT19

BELLE

"I'd like you all to get back in your truck and drive away." Belle's even voice didn't betray her fear as she faced down the group of strangers who had arrived at her dead uncle's house. Reggie had caused trouble all his life, any hope that had ended with his death was fading fast.

They should have gotten someone else to come and empty the house. However, Belle's mom, Katrina, had hoped that emptying the rented house of her brother's possessions might give them some kind of closure.

Belle suspected her mom also hoped to find some evidence that Reggie cared for his family, or at least thought of them in some small way. So far there had been no evidence of that. Not one single photo of his family.

She gnawed her bottom lip. She shouldn't have brought the children with her. Jack and Rosie should have been shielded from any connection with Reggie, who had never done a good deed in his whole life. At least according to Katrina.

But Belle had brought them.

Smart move, Belle told herself as she faced the five

strangers in front of her. She'd put her children in danger. Something she swore she would never do.

"We aren't looking for trouble." The first guy out of the truck had gotten as far as the gate before whatever drug he was on took a hold of him. Now he stood, half-leaning on the broken gate post to stop himself from falling flat on his face.

"Then turn around and leave." Belle glanced down at her daughter, Rosie, as the small child yanked on her hand.

"What's wrong, Mommy?" Rosie cupped her hand to her mouth and whispered loudly.

"Nothing, honey," Belle lied as she fought the urge to scoop them both up in her arms, run to the car and drive away from here and never look back. Yet there was something she couldn't explain that compelled her to stay.

"Who are they, Mom?" Her son, Jack, moved to stand next to Rosie.

"I don't know." Belle crouched down to speak to her son. "Jack, I need you to take your sister inside. Go find Grandma and tell her to take the car and leave." She slipped her car keys out of her pocket and pressed them into her son's hand.

"I'm not leaving," Jack insisted. "Grandma says I'm the man of the house and I'm supposed to protect you and Rosie."

Belle closed her eyes for a moment before inhaling deeply and opening them again. She would have a word with her mom as soon as they got out of this mess.

If they got out of it. The words hit her like a hammer on the side of the head. She was no match for the strangers in front of her. Three tall, broad-chested men and a couple of women who looked as if they knew how to handle themselves.

"Whoa!" The guy at the gate straightened and held up his hands. "No one needs to protect anyone. We're not here to cause trouble."

Belle stood up and nodded to her son. "Go find Grandma."

"Mom..." Jack's protest was cut short with a firm look from Belle and he tugged on his sister's hand, pulling her back toward the house.

"Wait. Please." The guy turned toward the others as they approached. "We just wanted information."

"Why don't you let me handle this, Rift?" One of the women hurried forward, brushing past Rift who still looked wild-eyed and half crazy. "I'm Elise."

"I don't care who you are, I want you to get back in your truck and drive away," Belle replied.

"I know you do and we're sorry to bother you, honestly." She held out her hands as she approached.

Belle kept her attention fixed on the woman while also monitoring the actions of the others who had now joined Rift at the gate. "But you *are* bothering me and even though I've asked you to leave, you are still here, *bothering* me."

She reached for her cell phone. Maybe she should call the local sheriff's office. But she didn't want to draw attention. After today, she'd hoped the specter of her uncle would disappear from their lives forever.

She'd deal with this alone.

At least she hoped she was alone. She glanced toward the house. Would her mom do as she asked and take the kids and run for safety?

"We've driven a long way to find the owner of the toy." Elise pointed to the small plush toy Rift held in his hand. "And now that we're here, we could do with your help."

"I don't know anything about the toy. It doesn't belong to either of my kids, I've never seen it before in my life." Belle jumped at a noise from inside the house.

"I've seen it before," her mom called from the window to Belle's left.

"Damn it, Mom! You were supposed to take the kids and get out of here." Belle gave her mom a reproachful look before turning back to the strangers before her.

"The toy belongs to you, Belle. It was called Jonjo or Jojo, something like that." Movement in the window told Belle her mom was coming toward the door.

Stepping to her left, Belle put herself between the door and the people in the yard. "Stay inside, Mom."

"I want to know where they got the toy from." Her mom stepped outside. "And how they knew it was yours since... I haven't seen it since your father..."

Belle swallowed hard as her mom took a deep shaking breath. "Okay, it looks as if we all need answers. So, as an act of good faith and since you are trespassing, you can go first." She waited for the strangers to answer. "Tell us where you got the toy and how you know it's mine."

Elise half-turned to look at the others. Rift sucked in a breath of the cool afternoon air and with a nod to the others, he took a faltering step forward, his chin raised as he regained his balance, and, it seemed, his wits.

"The toy has been in the possession of the police for the last forty years or so. It was among the evidence in a case of two boys who were taken from a foster home. They were found in an apartment, alone. This toy didn't belong to them, but we thought that whoever the toy did belong to might be able to give us some answers." He held out his hands. "And so here we are."

"Wait a minute." Belle put her hand up to stop him from getting any closer. "You're expecting me to believe that you managed to track me down to my dead uncle's house because of a toy that has been in police evidence for over forty years?" She gave a short laugh and shook her head. "You really should have come up with a more plausible story."

"Belle."

She closed her eyes. Belle knew that tone. "You're telling me you believe them?" she asked her mom.

Her mom stepped out of the house, an arm around Jack who still held on tightly to Rosie's hand. "I'm telling you that toy is yours." She stared at the small toy in Rift's hand. How could it be hers? None of this made sense. But she trusted her mom. "And..."

Her mom brushed her hand across her eyes and sniffed loudly. Her mom, who never cried. Her mom, who was the strongest woman, no, person, Belle had ever met.

"Mom, what is this all about?" Belle whispered.

"Your father... He..."

"He what, Mom?" Belle knew her dad wasn't one of the good guys, she'd known it since forever. Her mom refused to hide who Belle's father really was. But looking in her Mom's face now, she had hidden something. "Mom?"

"He..." She sniffed loudly and wiped the back of her hand across her nose. "I need you to know I had no idea that he... That he..."

"Your father was the man who kidnapped the two children." Rift half-turned to point at the other two men. "These are the two children." He winced. "I mean, they *were* the two children."

"I get it," Belle whispered. Only she didn't get it. Her mom told her that her dad, Murray, was a small-time petty thief who crossed the wrong people years ago and wound up dead in the street like the piece of garbage he was.

"Oh, no." Her mom covered her mouth with her hand and tightened her grip on the children.

"What do you want?" Belle stepped backward, closing the distance between her and her kids. Were they here for revenge, did they plan to take her children to get back at a man who had been dead for nearly forty years?

"We wanted to know the truth. We wanted to know if

Murray was alive." Rift nodded toward the house. "And we wanted to know about Reginald and how he fits into this."

"I'll tell you anything you want to know," Katrina replied. "But first you let my daughter and her children get in their car and drive away. You need to promise me that you won't try to follow them and that when I've answered your questions, you won't ever bother us again."

Rift's shoulders slumped forward, and the others all turned to look at him, their expressions unreadable. Yet it was a simple request. If they got their information, they'd leave and forget all about where it came from.

"My daughter wasn't out of diapers when her father died. This has nothing to do with her." Her mom stepped forward. "Take the kids, Belle." She pressed the car keys into her daughter's hand. "You go and I'll call you to come to pick me up later."

"I'm not leaving you, Mom."

"You wanted me to leave you and get the children to safety. I'm asking you to do the same thing." Her mom took a shuddering breath. "I shouldn't have asked you to come with me today. I had a sense this was going to be all messed up." Her mom put her hand to her temple. "I should have listened to myself."

"Mom." Belle held her arm around her children as she hugged her mom. "It's okay. None of this is your fault. Whatever Dad did, whatever Uncle Reggie did, none of that is on you."

"Please." Somehow Rift had made it right up to the house without them noticing. "We're not here to hurt anyone. We only want answers."

As Belle spun around and faced Rift, their eyes locked together. As she stared at the man before her, there was an undeniable attraction.

Belle sucked in a sharp breath. Katrina always said her

relationship with Murray was a mistake. Belle hadn't exactly done much better with the father of her kids who had walked out on them a couple of months ago. Was she about to make another mistake and put her trust in a man who didn't deserve it?

"Belle," her mom said gently. "It's time you knew the truth."

"The truth about what?" Belle asked.

"Your father. Your uncle." Her mom brushed her hands across her eyes and looked away, staring into the distance.

"What truth?" Belle asked. "You've always told me they weren't good people. You've never hidden the truth from me. I knew why Uncle Reggie was in prison for so long."

"I never hid the truth from you," her mom agreed. "But I never told you the whole truth. I always figured there was no need." She turned and looked at Rift, her eyes lingering on him for a long while before she added, "But I think it's time you heard it all."

"It all?" Belle placed her arms around Jack and Rosie and pulled them close, wishing they were anywhere other than here.

"There's so much you didn't know." She smiled sadly. "So much even I don't know. So much I didn't want to know."

"You're scaring me, Mom," she whispered.

When her mom finally met Belle's gaze, her breath caught in her throat.

She was right to be scared.

RIFT

Isn't there anything we can do to prove to our mate that we don't mean to hurt her? Rift's snow leopard asked.

I don't know if there is, Rift answered. We're strangers to her and we've brought trouble to her door.

I don't think that is her door, his snow leopard answered.

You know what I mean. She doesn't want us here. And I don't think she wants to hear what her mom has to say. Rift stepped forward and his mate instantly tensed and shot him a warning look.

"No closer." She didn't move, her arms wrapped tightly, protectively, around her children, tensed.

"Maybe we can talk while the children play?" he suggested. She looked down at them but didn't relinquish her hold. "I promise, I mean you no harm." He turned to look at the others. "None of us mean any harm."

"You might not mean me harm, but that doesn't mean you won't cause harm," she countered.

Rift bowed his head. "You're right. And I'm sorry for that."

Belle turned to look at her mom. "Does what you have to say involve these people?"

Her mom nodded. "I think it does. I also think they might be able to fill in some of the gaps for us."

Belle closed her eyes and relaxed her shoulders. "Okay, kids. Why don't you go play in the backyard for a while? But stay close to the house."

"Mom..." Jack began.

Belle hunkered down next to him and took hold of his hand. "Jack, sweetheart, I need you to watch over your sister for me. Please."

Jack stared at his mom for a long moment and then nodded briefly. "Come on, Rosie. Shall we go see if we can find the frog you saw earlier?"

"Sure." Rosie skipped away, pulling her brother after her.

"Not too far," Belle warned and looked around, scanning the area for threats.

"They're safe while we're here," Rift assured her.

"You would say that, wouldn't you?" she accused.

A small smile flickered across his lips. "I promise you, I will never hurt you. Or your children."

"He's telling the truth," her mom replied.

"And how do you know?" Belle asked. "Because as much as you trust your intuition, it's not always been great where men are concerned, has it?"

"No." Her mom's face crumpled, and she covered her mouth with her hand.

Belle rushed toward her and wrapped her arms around her, cradling her mom as she stroked her back. "I'm sorry, I didn't mean it."

"But that doesn't mean you aren't right, does it?" her mom sobbed.

Belle didn't answer. She simply held her mom in her arms. "Okay. What do you want to know?"

Caleb and Aiden approached the house with Elise and Flora by their sides. "We'd like to know about your father.

We'd like to know why he kidnapped us when we were children."

"And we also want to know if Reginald killed our parents," Aiden said and received a warning glance from Rift.

Our mate is not the enemy here. His snow leopard's tail swished from side to side as he sharpened his claws.

We need to stay calm, Rift replied. *Everyone is on edge, the situation is too emotionally charged for anyone to think straight.*

"Killed your parents?" Belle's face paled.

"Yes," Aiden answered tersely.

"Do you know anything about this, Mom?" Belle pulled back from her mom and held her upper arms as she studied her face. "Mom?"

"I don't know much about Reggie except what came out at the court case. We became estranged for a couple of years or more before he was arrested and sent to prison. I don't know if he killed your parents. I swear. All I know is… I would not be surprised." Katrina's mouth turned down at the corners as she fought back tears.

"And Murray?" Caleb prompted.

"I knew Murray was mixed up with some bad people. It's the main reason I took Belle and moved away." She wiped her hands across her face. "He never could hold down a decent job for more than a week. He wasn't the kind of man who would work hard eight hours a day, five days a week for an honest wage. So he earned money through dishonest means."

"He kidnapped *children*?" Belle whispered, her eyes drawn to her children as they prowled around the garden searching for wildlife.

"He... I never knew about that. Not kidnapping. I never thought him capable of that." She blew the air out of her cheeks. "Once, when he was drunk, he murmured something about children. Children who could turn into animals."

"Children who turned into animals. Did you believe him? You said he was drunk. Or was he on drugs, too?" Belle asked.

I think Belle's mom knows about shifters. But Belle doesn't. She doesn't know about shifters and so she has no idea that we are fated mates, Rift's snow leopard said.

We'll tell her when she's ready. I don't think that time is right now, Rift answered.

"No, not drugs. He was just drunk. Not even that drunk. It was during one of his ramblings. He'd sit and drink a beer while watching TV, then another beer. He used to like me to sit with him. Then he'd start to talk. He'd build himself up and tell me of all the things he was going to do to make our lives easier." Her mom gnawed on her bottom lip as she stared at Rift.

"And during one of these times, he spoke about shifters?" Caleb asked.

"Shifters?" Belle asked. "What is a shifter?"

"A shifter is a person who can change into something *else*. An animal." Her mom's eyes bored into Rift. "The police had a drawing of a man they suspected of murdering Murray. From an eyewitness. But they never found the man. I thought it was a cover-up and that he'd been killed by one of these shifters because he'd…I don't know…robbed one, assaulted one... So I searched for information on them."

"And did you find anything out? Was he killed by one of these shifters?" Belle shook her head and rolled her eyes. "Of course he wasn't because they *aren't* real."

"They're real, aren't they, Rift?" Belle's mom's eyes narrowed as she stared at him.

Katrina knows we're a shifter, his snow leopard said. I suspect she also knows about mates. And that we're Belle's mate.

That would explain why she is looking at us like that. Rift lowered his gaze and glanced at his brothers. Aiden reached out and placed his hand on Rift's shoulder and nodded, while Caleb pressed his lips together and inclined his head slightly toward Belle and a small smile of understanding crossed his brother's lips.

They know, too, his snow leopard said.

They probably knew as soon as I stumbled around like a clown and had to grab hold of the gate post to stop myself from falling flat on my face. Talk about a bad first impression.

"Rift?" Belle's anxious tone brought him back to the present.

"Shifters are real," he acknowledged. "I'm one."

"And so are we," Caleb answered, pointing at himself and Aiden.

"But not you two?" Belle asked Flora and Elise.

"No, we're fae," Flora said bluntly.

"Fae." Belle cupped her face in her hands and shook her head. "Did I make a wrong turn and end up in crazy town?"

"No, this is all true." Elise lifted her hair and revealed her pointed ears.

"You could have had plastic surgery," Belle said.

"Okay, Rift, I guess you're up." Flora clapped her hands and stepped back. "Show Belle your stuff."

"My stuff!" Rift shot Flora a confused look. "Wait, you want me to shift here? And now?"

"That would clear up this part of the discussion," Flora replied.

"You're serious?" Belle asked.

"Absolutely," Flora replied. "We've come a long way and Aiden and Caleb have waited a long time to figure out the truth about their past, and that starts with you."

"I don't have any information on what my father or Reggie had to do with you or your parents." Belle leaned to the right and fixed her gaze on Aiden and Caleb, who stood a little away from them.

"We know. But you can tell us about them. And that might lead to us uncovering the truth." Rift stepped forward. His mate stepped back.

"And proving that you are one of these shifters will help?" Belle swallowed hard as she stared at him, eyes wide.

"I don't know. But perhaps it'll help you see that you can trust me. Us." Rift met Belle's gaze, his eyes soft as he etched her face on his brain. He never wanted to forget any single thing about her. From her pale blue-gray eyes to her auburn hair, streaked with copper and tied up in a messy bun.

"You're going to show me a magic trick and that's going to make me trust you?" Belle shook her head. "I'm done with this. We have more stuff to pack up in the house. And then I'm going to take my kids home."

"Wait!" Her mom grabbed her arm and then let it go as Belle yanked it out of her grip. "Sorry. I didn't mean to grab you so hard."

"What is it, Mom? Why are you so quick to believe in all this?" Belle's eyes leveled with her mom's for a moment and they stood as if frozen in time. "You really do believe this is true."

"I don't just *believe it*," she answered. "I *know it*." She placed her hand on her heart. "I've seen shifters before." She tore her eyes from her daughter's.

"What?" Belle reached for her mom's hand and held it tight as she coaxed her to speak. "There's more. Something you're not telling me."

"Nathan is a shifter. A wolf." Her mom swallowed hard as she met her daughter's shocked expression.

"Nathan." Belle's forehead furrowed. "Nathan. *Scumbag* Nathan?"

"You shouldn't call him that. When your father died, he was very supportive."

"Was he?" Belle crossed her arms over her body. "Because

all I remember is him stealing the rent money from your purse and disappearing into the night."

"I guess he saw it as payment." There was a hard edge to Katrina's voice.

"Anyway..." Flora cut into the conversation. "Rift will shift. You'll see shifters are real and we can cut through all this pointless conversation."

I thought Flora might have grown more tactful after being around Aiden, Rift's snow leopard remarked.

She is. Most of the time. But this means a lot to her because it means a lot to her mate. Rift put his hand on Flora's shoulder as she drew closer to Belle. *We need to calm the situation.*

Then we'll shift, his snow leopard replied. *Belle will see shifters are real and we can...cut to the chase.*

Or freak her out completely and lose her forever. Rift didn't like the sound of that at all. But it was a possibility. Belle was on the defensive and seeing a man change into a snow leopard might appear like a serious threat to her children.

"This conversation might be pointless to you," Belle replied, "but this all concerns my family. My children."

Flora stared at Belle for a long moment before she replied, "*Point* taken. But you have to see that if we prove shifters are real, and your mom already knows that they are, then we can move on and not have a debate about it."

Belle closed her eyes briefly before nodding. "Go ahead. Shift." She leveled her gaze at Rift and then crossed her arms in front of her body.

"Okay." Rift sighed, this wasn't how he'd pictured his first meeting with his mate going. But he'd work with what he had. "I'll..." He looked around, pushing his senses out to check there was no one close by who might see him shift. He usually avoided shifting outside of Wishing Moon Bay and if he did shift in the world beyond, he usually waited until the cover of darkness.

"You'll what?" Belle's impatience kicked up a notch.

"I'll move around the side of the house, so the children don't see me. I don't want to scare them." He glanced at the children who were hunting around in the undergrowth. They reminded him of Penny's son, Milo. Filled with wonder and enthusiasm, they were digging in the backyard, talking quietly as if searching for something.

"Belle." Her mom touched her arm briefly. "Keep an open mind."

Belle's mouth turned down at the corners. "Mom, this isn't real."

Rift let his mind unfocus and let go of the world. He needed to get this over with and show his mate the other side of him. There was no point trying to explain anymore. Perhaps he should have told her he would never hurt her and not to scream, but he sensed Belle wasn't the screaming type.

The world faded away and his human form slipped from the world, to be replaced a few seconds later by his snow leopard, who twitched his tail as he set eyes on their mate for the first time.

Silence. No one spoke as Belle stared at the creature who had appeared as if by magic. All eyes were on her as her eyes widened and she covered her mouth with her hand. Rift didn't approach her. He sensed she needed to take the first step forward herself. He didn't want to pressure her, even though it took all his resolve to stand just out of her reach.

"Belle." Her mom touched her arm as if trying to wake her from a trance.

Belle blinked several times but didn't take her eyes off the snow leopard. "It can't be real."

"It is. Touch him." Belle's mom took her hand and led her forward. "I know it's a shock. The first time I saw Nathan shift, I thought it was an illusion, that he was playing tricks on me. But once I touched him, once I looked him in the eye, I knew he was real."

"But how?" Belle asked. "It's impossible."

"Clearly not," Flora said.

Belle turned to look at Flora, then she reached out her hand as she stepped toward the snow leopard. "You are incredible."

Rift lowered his head and closed his eyes in bliss as she ran her fingers over his head and threaded them into the soft fur along his back. He rubbed his head against her thigh and purred softly.

"Now do you believe in shifters?" her mom asked.

"It's hard to believe." Belle looked over her shoulder at her mom. "But how can I *not* believe when he's right in front of me? When I can see him and touch him?"

"I can't imagine how hard it must be to accept something that you thought impossible," Flora said gently as she approached. "When you've known about something your whole life and take it for granted, it's hard to put yourself in someone else's shoes."

Belle stroked Rift's back and then crouched down in front of him and cupped his large head in her hands. "You are the most beautiful creature I've ever seen."

Rift's snow leopard stared into her eyes and she stared right back, the connection between them flooding him with warmth. The shock of recognition on Belle's face told him she felt it, too. Would this make it easier for her to also accept that they were mates, and he was meant to be by her side for the rest of their lives?

"Okay." Flora placed her hand on Belle's shoulder and glanced toward the sound of the children who were coming closer. "It's time Rift shifted back to his human form. It's risky for him to be this exposed in your world. And we need to talk."

"In my world?" Belle twisted around to look at Flora.

"Yeah, that's something else you'll have to learn about. But maybe we should go inside?" Flora backed away, leaving Belle to stare at Rift for a few seconds longer before she let him go and rose to her feet.

Rift's snow leopard rubbed his head against her thigh once more and she tickled his head before he turned away. The air fizzed and popped as the two sides of Rift swapped places once more.

Both of them were sworn to cherish and protect their mate and her family. No matter what it took.

Printed in Great Britain
by Amazon

62227331R00170